Elmore Leonard
Up in Honey's Room

"[A] tightly woven, high-speed plot. . . . A stylishly noir
and bitingly satirical exploration into World War II
America. And the irrepressible free spirit that is Honey
Deal ('Sieg Heil, y'all.') is a character readers won't
soon forget."
                                            —*Chicago Tribune*

"Reading *Up in Honey's Room* is like dancing with the
stars, and [Leonard's] the star. . . . You just get to be lost
in the dance with him as he gives unimaginable depth
and dimension to the phrase 'easily and effortlessly.'
He leads; you follow. . . . These are healing moments
caught between book covers. Minor and major mira-
cles. The works of a genuine star."
                                            —*Washington Post Book World*

"When you read Mr. Leonard, you enter Mr. Leonard's
world. A trip like that is its own kind of vacation."
                                            —*New York Times*

"Bullets fly, but, as with most Leonard novels, things really move when the dialogue gets going. . . . Grade: A."
                                            —*Christian Science Monitor*

"[Leonard] is at the pinnacle of his game. Don't miss
Up in Honey's Room."
                                            —*Seattle Times*

"Read the book. . . . Elmore Leonard may be moseying toward his eighty-second birthday, but . . . the old boy is still at the top of his game. . . . *Up in Honey's Room* is a perfect example of a master storyteller spinning a tall one. . . . Where else but in Elmore Leonard's America would one German POW yearn to be a rodeo rider and the other—the SS officer, no less—fall in love at first sight with a beautiful Jewish con girl? . . . Leonard has a keener eye for the absurd than any French existentialist has ever had. To wit: He never, ever fails to see the humor in it."

—*Philadelphia Inquirer*

"A national treasure . . . Leonard springs eternal. His new novel, *Up in Honey's Room,* is both enterprising and lively. . . . There is also plenty of Leonard's trademark wit and trademark benevolence. . . . *Up in Honey's Room* is a picture I would go see . . . a worldly send-up of noir, written and directed by a man who was there, but who has been to a lot of other places since."

—Jane Smiley, *Los Angeles Times Book Review*

"Elmore Leonard has written more than forty novels, and I have read every one of them. Without a doubt, he is my favorite author. . . . Leonard's ear for the spoken word has never been better. . . . Here, Leonard excels, as only he can."

—*Toledo Blade*

"The cast of characters . . . makes readers keep turning the pages. . . . His colorful, pulp-fiction characters linger. . . . Deal and Webster make especially enjoyable reading companions."

—*Richmond Times Dispatch*

"It's always cause for celebration when Leonard pops out another novel. They are always good reads, with sly observation and fine wit."
—*San Jose Mercury News*

"Quirky characters and bizarre personalities . . . [rendered] in his trademark sharp and funny style. . . . Leonard clearly loves these characters, and makes their interactions believable and a blast to read. With Dashiell Hammett-type wit . . . he has once again created characters who live far beyond their story lines. . . . [There are] good times to be had *Up in Honey's Room*."

—*Boston Globe*

"Elmore Leonard excels at creating smart, sexy, confident female characters and the heroine in *Up in Honey's Room* may be the best of them since *Rum Punch*. . . . Leonard tells his story in his flawlessly colloquial prose style, with pitch-perfect dialogue. . . . The humor is back, emerging as usual from Leonard's acute portrayals of human nature."

—*Albany Times Union*

"He's always been a master at making his characters speak, roll over, and play dead, but now, in his forty-first novel, he's figured out how to successfully combine a Western, a World War II spy story, and a light sex comedy. It's a neat trick for an eighty-one-year-old who can still write circles around the young pups. . . . Leonard's dialogue is so sharp and jazzy that it's a pleasure listening to his people zing each other into submission. . . . [His] writing has lost none of its sizzle and freshness. He's at home on the range, in the past, in Detroit and anywhere else his imagination takes him."

—*Portland Sunday Oregonian*

Also by Elmore Leonard

FICTION

NONFICTION

ELMORE LEONARD

UP IN HONEY'S ROOM

wm

WILLIAM MORROW
An Imprint of HarperCollins*Publishers*

UP IN HONEY'S ROOM. Copyright © 2007 by Elmore Leonard, Inc. All rights reserved. Printed in the United States of America. No part of this book may be used or reproduced in any manner whatsoever without written permission except in the case of brief quotations embodied in critical articles and reviews. For information address HarperCollins Publishers, 10 East 53rd Street, New York, NY 10022.

HarperCollins books may be purchased for educational, business, or sales promotional use. For information please write: Special Markets Department, HarperCollins Publishers, 10 East 53rd Street, New York, NY 10022.

FIRST WILLIAM MORROW HARDCOVER PUBLISHED 2007.
FIRST HARPER PAPERBACK PUBLISHED 2008.
FIRST WILLIAM MORROW PAPERBACK PUBLISHED 2013.

Library of Congress Cataloging-in-Publication Data has been applied for.

ISBN 978-0-06-226728-3

13 14 15 16 17   OV/RRD   10 9 8 7 6 5 4 3 2 1

For my boys, Pete, Chris and Bill

UP IN HONEY'S ROOM

One

Honey phoned her sister-in-law Muriel, still living in Harlan County, Kentucky, to tell her she'd left Walter Schoen, calling him Valter, and was on her way to being Honey Deal again. She said to Muriel, "I honestly thought I could turn him around, but the man still acts like a Nazi. I couldn't budge him."

"You walked out," Muriel said, "just like that?"

"I valked out," Honey said. "I'm free as a bird. You know what else? I won't have to do my roots every two weeks. Dumb me, I spent a whole year wanting him to think I'm a natural blonde."

"He couldn't tell other ways you aren't?"

"Anytime Walter wanted some, he'd turn out the light before taking off his pajamas. He was self-conscious about being skinny, his ribs showing, so it was always pitch-dark when we did it. He said American food, all it did was give him gas. I had to learn to cook German, big heavy dinners, sauerbraten with red cabbage, bratwurst. For the first

time in my life I had to watch my weight. Walter
didn't gain at all. He still passed gas, only now it
was okay, it was German gas. He'd cut one, aiming
his finger at me like it's a gun? I'd have to pretend
I was shot."

"And fall down?"

"If I was near the sofa. Or stumble around holding where I was shot. The first time, I did it on my
own, acting goofy? But then every time he cut one
and I heard it, I had to pretend I was shot."

"You and hubby having fun."

"Except he never laughed or even smiled. I'd see
him aiming at me . . . " Honey let a moment of
silence go by. "Tell me how my brother's doing. Is
he working?"

"He's back in jail. Darcy got in a fight he swears
he didn't start. Broke his foreman's jaw and it vio-
lated his parole. Darcy has to finish the sentence he
got for making moonshine and do time for assault.
He's working in the kitchen as a butcher making
five cents an hour while I'm trying to live on tips."
Muriel's voice turned pouty saying, "'What do I
have to do, get you boys to have another round?'
Here're these hotshots with coal dust in their pores
saying things like 'How about showing us your
goodies?' I roll my eyes and act cute, it's worth
about a buck and a half. But hey, I want to hear
about your situation. Walter hit you and it woke
you up or what? You were only married to him
about a year."

"One year to the day I walked out," Honey
said, "November the ninth. I brought him a plate
of Limburger and crackers, he won't eat Ameri-

can cheese. Walter's sitting by the radio, the volume turned up. I said, 'You happen to know what anniversary today is?' He's listening to the news, the German Army going through Poland like rhubarb through a tall woman. France is next and England's getting ready. I asked him again, 'Walter, you happen to recall what anniversary falls on November the ninth?' It was like I lit his fuse. He yells at me, '*Blutzeuge*, the Nazi Day of Blood, idiot.' He's talking about the day Hitler started his takeover in 1923 that didn't work and he ended up in prison. But that date, the ninth of November, became a Nazi holy day. It's why he picked it for our wedding. 'The Day of Blood.' Only Walter called it 'the Night of Blood' as we're going to bed together for the first time. I let him think I was still a virgin, twenty-five years old. He climbed on top, and it was like a one-minute blitzkrieg start to finish. He never asked if I was okay or checked the sheet, he was through. Anyway, I said to Walter, standing by the radio with his cheese and crackers, 'Dumb me, I thought you'd remember the ninth as our wedding anniversary.' He didn't bother to look up, he waved his hand at me to get away, stop bothering him. I took that as my cue and walked out."

Muriel said, "You didn't hit him over the head with the cheese plate?"

"I thought about it but went upstairs and took twelve hundred dollars, half the money he kept stuck away in the bedroom closet. He didn't think I knew about it."

"Is he on the lookout for you?"

"Why, 'cause he misses me? We had so much fun together?"

She told Muriel, now that she wasn't keeping house for the Kaiser she had an apartment in Highland Park and was back at J.L. Hudson's doing what she called "tit work," fitting brassieres on big foreign women who'd come here to work. "Some of 'em, you have to hold your breath or their B.O.'ll knock you unconscious." She told Muriel she ought to come to Detroit and stay with her, get a real job while Darcy's doing his time. Next, she had to ask about her mom. "How's she doing at the home?"

"I doubt she knows where she is," Muriel said. "I walk in and kiss her, she gives me a blank look. It's pitiful, your mom not being that old."

"You sure she isn't faking, playing 'poor me'? Remember I came here I asked her to live with me? She says oh, it's too cold up north. Afraid she'll slip and fall on the ice and break her hip."

"The other night," Muriel said, "they showed an Errol Flynn movie and your mom got excited, she thought Errol Flynn was Darcy." Muriel put on a slow tone of voice and was Honey's mom, wanting to know, "'What's Darcy doing in this movin' pitcher? When'd he grow a mus-tache?' But anytime Darcy came to visit, her only living son, your mom didn't have a clue who he was. I told Darcy how she got him confused with Errol Flynn, Darcy says, 'Yeah . . . ?' Like, what else is new? He thinks he's a dead ringer for Errol Flynn except for the mus-tache. You want to bet he isn't growing one this minute, sitting in his prison cell?"

She said, "You see a resemblance, Darcy and Errol Flynn?"

"Maybe a little," Honey said, remembering Walter Schoen asking the same question, who she thought he resembled, that day they first met. Now Muriel was saying she had to get ready for work, tease her hair and pad her bra. Honey said, "Talk to you soon."

This was in November 1939.

She hung up the phone still thinking of Walter a year ago, in front of Blessed Sacrament Cathedral, waiting for her. Honey coming out of eleven o'clock Mass. Walter buying *Social Justice* from a boy who carried the tabloid in a sack hanging from his shoulder. Walter seeing her as he turned, waiting among the people walking past him, Walter moving now to head her off and she stopped in front of him. He stared at her, finally taking off his hat.

"Your name is Honey Deal, yes?"

She said, "Yeah . . . ?" with no idea what he was up to.

He took her hand and introduced himself, Valter Schoen, with his accent and the hint of a bow and, Honey believed, clicking his heels, though she wasn't positive.

"Last Sunday," Walter said, "I observed you talking to a woman I know is herself from Germany and asked her your name. She told me Honey Deal. I said to her what kind of name is Honey? She could be Nordic, her blond hair."

"I'm German," Honey said, "but born and raised in Harlan County, Kentucky."

They stood looking at each other, Walter Schoen wearing little round pince-nez glasses pinched on the bridge of his nose, his hair shaved high on the sides and combed flat on top. Honey saw it as German military, judging from pictures in *Life* of Adolf Hitler and his crowd. Walter even looked like one of them. He replaced his hat, touching the brim with the palms of his hands, making sure the brim took a slight turn up on one side and down on the other. Honey could see him staring into a mirror to get just the right look: Walter Schoen in a four-button slim-cut suit that had to be tailor-made, a black suit buttoned up on his bony frame; Walter staring like he was making up his mind about her, the paper he'd bought from the kid, *Social Justice*, folded under his arm.

"I must confess to you," Walter said, "for weeks now, every Sunday I spend the entire Mass staring at your golden hair." Walter serious, nodding his head, and she wanted to say, "*My hair?*" But now he was telling her you don't see blond hair so much, "Naturally blond hair except in Nordic countries and of course Germany." Honey touched the pillbox sitting on top of her head, still there covering her blond hair's dark roots, Walter telling her, "I knew a family by the name of Diehl in Munich."

"*D-I-E-H-L?*" Honey said. "That's how my granddaddy spelled our name, but the Immigration people on Ellis Island changed it to *D-E-A-L* and we're stuck with it."

"That's too bad," Walter said. "But it remains German because you are. I was a lad of fourteen when my father brought us here on the eve of the Great War. He opened a meat market and made me learn the business." He turned to Woodward Avenue and looked south toward downtown Detroit, four miles in the distance. "The market I still have is only a few blocks from here."

"So you're a butcher," Honey said. He sure didn't look like one. She thought he was cute in kind of a mysterious foreign way, like a professor with his accent and little round glasses. "How much is your ground beef?"

"We have a special on chuck this week, three pounds for a dollar. While I still operate the market," Walter said, "I am looking to buy a meat-packing plant in the vicinity of the Eastern Market, where farmers bring their goods to sell." He told Honey his mother and father were both buried in Holy Sepulchre and his older sister was an IHM nun, Sister Ludmilla, who taught fourth grade at Blessed Sacrament, the school on Belmont behind the cathedral.

"She is my only relative now in America," Walter said, and began asking about Honey's family, the Deals. "Your ancestors are all German?"

"Oh, yes, definitely," Honey said, leaving out her dad's grandmother from somewhere in Hungary, the woman a Gypsy who had stored money away and left her dad enough to buy a coal mine and go broke. Honey said, you bet, her people were all of pure German stock, because it was what Walter wanted to hear, and because it didn't matter to Honey if Walter was a butcher. So was her brother Darcy, in prison. She liked Walter's air of mystery, a lot different from how the good ole boys in Harlan County acted. Detroit had a lot of hotdog southern boys, too, working in plants. If Walter was fourteen on the eve of the Great War, he would have been thirty-eight the day they met.

He said when his father brought the family here, only months before the beginning of the World War, he was furious. In only three years he would have been a grenadier in the German Army.

Honey said, "You were anxious to fight Americans?"

"I didn't think of who was the enemy, I wanted to serve the Fatherland."

"You wanted to wear a uniform," Honey said, "with a spike on top the helmet. But you might've been one of the twenty million killed or wounded in that war."

He paused but kept looking at her. "How do you know that?"

"I read," Honey said. "I read *Life* and all kinds of magazines. I read novels, some of 'em about war like *Over the Top* by Arthur Guy Empey, and my dad told me what it was like over there. He was gassed on the Western Front when it wasn't all quiet. My dad talked funny, real hoarse. He was funny anyway." She said after a moment, "The shaft he was working flooded and my dad drowned."

Walter said, "Did you know another twenty million died the year following the war?"

"From the Spanish flu," Honey said. "It took both my sisters and my baby brother. My older brother's still home. He's worked mines, but prefers other pursuits." She didn't mention Darcy was in prison.

"So there are good ways to die," Walter said, "and far less desirable ways. Die as a hero or suffocate in a hospital bed."

Honey looked past him toward the cathedral, cleared of churchgoers now. Walter asked if he could drive her home. Honey said she lived only a few blocks north, in Highland Park, and liked to walk. She could tell he wanted to keep talking to her, saying what an advantage it was to be born in the year 1900.

"You know exactly how old you were when important historical events took place. I know I was twenty-three when Adolf Hitler first came into prominence. You say you read, you must know about the famous Beer Hall Putsch in Munich. I was twenty-five when *Mein Kampf* was published and I read it, a little later, from cover to cover."

Honey said, "Did you like it?"

It stopped him. "Did I *like* it . . . ?"

"All these important historical events you remember happened in Germany?"

"I was thirty-two when Roosevelt was first elected your president."

"Isn't he your president too?"

Honey believed she could have fun with Walter. She liked to argue, especially with people who were serious about weird ideas they swore were true. Like the ones who read *Social Justice*, written by a priest she'd heard on the radio, Father Charles Coughlin, with a voice like syrup, but talked about a conspiracy of Jews being international bankers or atheistic Communists, either way out to get us.

"Yes, unfortunately he is the president," Walter said, sounding like he was about to start in on Roosevelt, Honey's choice in the '36 election to beat that boring Republican Alf Landon. She looked at her watch.

"I'm sorry, Walter, but I have to scoot. I'm going downtown to the show with a friend of mine." Her favorite place to get into discussions was in a bar over a rye and ginger and smoking cigarettes, not standing in front of a church.

Walter said, "Wait, please," putting his hand on her bare arm. "I have to ask you, is there someone who comes to mind you think I resemble?"

Like the guy was reading her mind.

"The way you look at me," Walter said, "I wonder if you're trying to remember his name."

"I was, as a matter of fact," Honey said. "He's a high-up Nazi officer, I think one of the main guys under Hitler. I saw a picture of him in *Life* magazine during the past couple of weeks."

Walter said, "Yes . . . ?"

"In his uniform and boots, all-black. Wearing glasses just like yours pinched on his nose. This is the first time I've ever seen a pair this close. Do they hurt?"

"Certainly not," Walter said.

"He was inspecting a bunch of guys lined up standing at attention, wearing what looked like swimming trunks."

Walter nodded, starting to put on a smile. He must've seen the picture she was talking about.

"The guys are sucking in their stomachs," Honey said, "trying to look like they're in shape."

"They are in *top* shape, the peak of fitness." Walter's voice cold now. "Do you know his name or not?"

Yes, she knew it, but couldn't come up with the name, Walter staring at her, very serious about this. She thought, Heinrich—

And said, "Himmler."

Walter's expression eased.

"If I may agree with you, yes," Walter said, "he is the one to whom I hold a striking resemblance, Heinrich Himmler, *Reichsführer,* the highest rank in the SS."

He did, he looked an awful lot like Himmler, the wispy mustache, the same straight nose and the tiny glasses pinched to the bridge. Honey said, "Walter, I swear you look enough like Himmler to be his twin brother."

"You flatter me," Walter said.

He seemed to smile—no, something was going on in his head. Honey watched his eyes shift away and come back to linger on her, his voice hushed to keep what he said between them.

"Heinrich Himmler was born the seventh of October, 1900. Which is the same day I was born."

"Really?"

"In the same hospital in Munich."

This time she said, "Wow," impressed, and said, "You think there's a chance you really are Himmler's twin?"

"The same hospital, the same day, the same time of birth and, as you see, the same likeness. The question I ask myself," Walter said, "if Heinrich and I are of the same blood, from the loins of the same woman, why were we separated?"

Two

Honey's intercom buzzed while she was getting ready to go to work. The male voice said hi, he was Kevin Dean, a special agent with the Federal Bureau of Investigation; he'd like to talk to her about Walter Schoen. Honey said, "You all are just getting around to Walter? I haven't seen him in five years."

Kevin Dean said he knew that, he still would like to talk to her. Honey said, "He didn't do anything subversive then that I know of and I doubt he has now. Walter isn't the real thing, he pretends he's a Nazi."

She buzzed open the door downstairs and put her flannel bathrobe on over her bra and panties, her hose and garter belt. Then paused and said, "Hmmmm." Took off her bra and the bathrobe and slipped on an orange-colored kimono with red and ochre trim to be more comfortable.

It was a morning in late October 1944, America at war nearly three years. In the Philippines again since yesterday.

Honey was a buyer now in Better Dresses at Hudson's, moving up in her world from a flat in Highland Park to a one-bedroom apartment on Covington Drive, a block from Palmer Park where she'd learned to ice-skate in the winter and play tennis in the summer. At night she would hear the streetcars on Woodward Avenue turn around at the fairgrounds and head back six miles to downtown and the Detroit River.

She had returned home only once since leaving Walter, late last year taking a bus to Harlan County for her mother's funeral, dead of respiratory failure, Honey with a twinge of guilt standing by the casket, the daughter who'd left home for the big city to live her own life, meet all kinds of people instead of coal miners and guys who cooked moonshine. She did ask her sister-in-law to come to Detroit, stay as long as she wanted, and Muriel said as she always did she'd think about it.

Well, since Honey was in Kentucky anyway, she might as well hop a bus over to Eddyville and see how her brother Darcy was doing in prison. My Lord, he actually seemed quieter and listened for a change. Or was it seeing Darcy sober for the first time in years? He had taken prison courses to finish high school at age thirty-two and no longer acted bored or like he knew everything. He'd grown a mustache and actually did resemble Errol Flynn a little. She told him, "You *do*," and Darcy said, "Oh, you think so?" He'd have his release pretty soon but wasn't going back to digging coal. "You'll be drafted," Honey said, "if they take ex-cons." He grinned at her the way the old Darcy used to grin, sure of himself, saying he had learned meat cutting and planned to get in the meat-processing business, make some money and stay out of the army. Honey thinking, Maybe he hasn't changed after all.

Then this past August she got a phone call out of the blue, Muriel wanting to know if she'd seen Darcy.

Honey said, "He's here in Detroit?"

"Somewhere around there. I gave him your number."

"Well, he hasn't called. What's he doing up here, working in a plant?"

"How would I know," Muriel said, "I'm only his wife."

Honey said, "Jesus Christ, quit feeling sorry for yourself. Get off your butt and come up here if you want to find him."

Muriel hung up on her.

That was a couple of months ago.

Kevin Dean came in showing his ID, quite a nice-looking young guy who seemed about her age, Honey thirty now. He said he appreciated her seeing him, with the trace of a down-home sound Honey placed not far west of where she grew up. She watched him gather the morning paper from the sofa and stand reading the headline story about the invasion of Leyte, his raincoat hanging open looking too small for him. She saw Kevin as a healthy young guy with good color, not too tall but seemed to have a sturdy build.

"I have to fix my hair, get dressed, and leave for work," Honey said, "in ten minutes."

He had his nose in the paper, not paying any attention to her.

"If Walter's all we're gonna talk about," Honey said, "let's get to it, all right?"

He still didn't look up, but now he said, "We're back in the Philippines—you read it? Third and Seventh Amphibious Forces of the Sixth Army went ashore on Leyte, near Tacloban."

"That's how you pronounce it," Honey said, "*Tac*loban?"

It got him to look at her, Honey now sitting erect in a club chair done in beige. She said, "I read about it this morning with my coffee. I thought it was pronounced Tac*lo*ban. I could be wrong but I like the sound of it better than *Tac*loban. Like I think Tar*a*wa sounds a lot better than *Tar*awa, the way you hear commentators say it, but what do I know."

She had his attention.

"You'll come to the part, General MacArthur wades ashore a few hours later and says over the radio to the Filipinos, 'I have returned,' because he told them three years ago when he left, 'I shall return,' and here he was, true to his word. But when he waded ashore, don't you think he should've said, '*We* have returned'? Since his entire army, a hundred thousand combat veterans, waded ashore ahead of him?"

Kevin Dean was nodding, agreeing with her. He said, "You're right," and took a notebook out of his raincoat and flipped through pages saying, "Walter was quite a bit older than you, wasn't he?"

Honey watched him sink into her velvety beige sofa.

"Your raincoat isn't wet, is it?"

"No, it's nice out for a change."

"Have you talked to Walter?"

"We look in on him every now and then."

"You're wondering why I married him, aren't you?"

"It crossed my mind, yeah."

"Being fourteen years older," Honey said, "doesn't mean he wasn't fun. Walter would show me a political cartoon in his Nazi magazine, the *Illustrierter Beobachter,* sent from Munich he got a month later. He'd tell me in English what the cartoon was about and we'd have a good laugh over it."

She waited while Kevin Dean decided how to take what she said.

"So you got along with him."

"Walter Schoen was the most boring man I've ever met in my life," Honey said. "You're gonna have to pick up on when I'm kidding. You know Walter and I weren't married in the Church. A Wayne County judge performed the ceremony in his chambers. On a Wednesday. Have you ever heard of anyone getting married on Wednesday? I'm saving the church wedding for the real thing."

"You're engaged?"

"Not yet."

"But you're seeing someone."

"I thought you wanted to talk about Walter. What if I asked if you're married?"

Having fun with him. She could tell he knew what she was doing and said no, he wasn't married or planning to anytime soon. Honey wanted to call him by his first name but pictured a guy named Kevin as a blond-haired kid with a big grin. Kevin Dean had a crop of wild brown hair Honey believed he combed in the morning and forgot about the rest of the day. She knew he packed a gun but couldn't tell where he wore it. She wondered if she should call him Dean, and heard lines in her memory, *It was Din! Din! Din! You 'eathen, where the mischief 'ave you been?* Left there from a ninth-grade elocution contest. And saw Dean in the sofa waiting for her to say something.

An easygoing type. He might not be her idea of a Kevin, but that's what he was. She said, "Kevin, how long have you been a G-man?"

See if she could find out how old he was.

"I finished my training this past summer. Before that I was in the service."

"Where're you from?" Honey said. "I hear someplace faintly down-home the way you speak."

"I didn't think I had an accent."

She said, "It isn't East Texas, but around there."

He told her Tulsa, Oklahoma. He went to school there, the University of Tulsa, graduated midyear right after Pearl and joined the cavalry.

Making him no more than twenty-five, Honey at least five years older than this good-looking boy from Oklahoma. She said, "The cavalry?"

"I went to language school to learn Japanese, then spent the next year with the First Cavalry Division in Louisiana, Australia, and New Guinea, training for jungle combat, the kind they had on Guadalcanal. I made second lieutenant and was assigned to the Fifth Cavalry Regiment, the one J. E. B. Stuart commanded before the Civil War. He was always a hero of mine, the reason I joined the First Cav, not knowing we'd be dismounted in the Pacific theater. You know the Stuart I'm talking about?"

"You told me, Jeb Stuart."

"Shot through the lungs at Yellow Tavern, the war almost over. Do you have a hero?"

"Jane Austen," Honey said. "Where were you in the Pacific with the cavalry?"

"Los Negros in the Admiralties, two hundred miles north of New Guinea, two degrees south of the equator. Destroyers dropped us off and we went ashore twenty-nine February of this year, to draw fire and locate enemy positions. I was with a recon unit so we were the first wave. We wanted an airstrip on Momote plantation, thirteen hundred yards from the beach, sitting in there among rows and rows of palm trees, coconuts all over the ground."

Honey said, "Were you scared to death?" at ease with him, able to say something like that.

"You bet I was scared, but you're with all these serious guys sharpening their trench knives. On the destroyer taking us to the drop-off that's what you did, sharpened your knife. Some of the guys had brand-new tattoos that said DEATH BEFORE DISHONOR and you start to think, Wait a minute, what am I doing here? What you don't want to do is throw up or wet your pants. Right before you go in is a tricky time."

"Well, you made it."

"I made it with metal frags in my back. The evening of the second day a Jap threw a grenade I saw coming and it took me out of the war. I never did get to ride with the cavalry. But I got a Purple Heart out of it, an honorable discharge and a visit from the Bureau. They came to the VA hospital and got around to asking if I'd like to be an FBI agent, since I'd finished college, had taken accounting and spoke Japanese, sort of."

"So they send you after German spies," Honey said. "Tell me, does Walter still live in that house on Kenilworth? He's rigid about his appearance, but he sure let the house run down, never put any money in it. He was saving up for something."

"He turned the floor above the market into a small apartment."

"He isn't married, is he?"

"Not since you left him. There is a woman who might be his girlfriend, Countess Vera Mezwa Radzykewycz." Kevin looked at his notebook. "Born in Odessa, in the Ukraine. She claims she was married to a Polish count, killed leading a cavalry charge against German panzers."

"You and the count," Honey said, "a couple of cavalrymen."

He saw her smile and looked at his notes again. "Vera came here in 1943 and leased a home on Boston Boulevard. She has a young guy, Bohdan Kravchenko, also Ukrainian, cooks and keeps house for her."

"If Vera lives on Boston Boulevard she's got money. Walter's interested in her?"

"They see each other."

"The countess climbs the stairs to his apartment over a meat market?"

"Most of the time it's at her place."

"Why do you think she's a spy, because she's keeping company with Walter?"

"I'm not telling you everything we have on her."

"But she was married to a Polish count, a war hero?"

"There's no record of the count as an officer in the Polish Army. That's the cover they made up for Vera. We believe she was trained by the Gestapo, was given money and credentials and came on a ship to Canada as a highly respected Ukrainian refugee. Vera moved to Detroit and gives lectures to women's groups, tells them how awful it is to live under the Nazis, no shampoo, no cold cream. We've got her down as a possible enemy alien."

"Doing what?"

"Gathering information about war production."

"The Germans don't know we're making bombers?"

"Now you're acting smart."

"What I'm asking," Honey said, "is if you think what Vera sends the Germans does them any good."

"It doesn't matter. If she's working as a German agent, the U.S. attorney will bring her up on the charge and put her away. It doesn't matter if her information helps the enemy or not."

"What about Walter?"

"He's been a U.S. citizen since he was fourteen. If he's involved in anything subversive it's an act of treason. He could hang."

Kevin looked at his notebook and turned a page, then a few more and stopped. "How about Joseph John Aubrey?"

Honey shook her head.

"Lives in Griffin, Georgia."

"Oh, Joe Aubrey, yeah," Honey said, "owns restaurants. He was big in the German-American Bund at that time. Walter met him at the rally they had in New York."

"Madison Square Garden," Kevin said, "1939."

"Walter brought me along thinking I'd be impressed by all the fans Fritz Kuhn had, the American Hitler."

"Over twenty thousand," Kevin said, "they filled the Garden. You met Joseph J. Aubrey, talked to him?"

"You don't talk to Joe Aubrey, you listen to his rant or walk away. Joe was an active member of the Bund and a Grand Dragon of the Klan. Bund get-togethers he'd say, 'Heah's some more of the dirty tricks international Jewery is doin' to spread Commonism.' That's what he called it, 'Commonism.' At Klan rallies he'd say, 'We gonna have integration, nigger kids and our white children goin' to the same school—'"

"Over his dead body," Kevin said.

"You're close. Joe said, 'When they pry my hands from my empty rifle and lay me to rest in the cold ground.' Joe Aubrey never shuts up. He got rich in the restaurant business promoting finger-lickin' barbecue."

"He has a plane, a Cessna?"

"Yeah, he'd fly up and spend a few days at the Book Cadillac. He always stayed at the Book. One time he was there, Joe said he was at the desk registering, he looked up and could not believe his eyes. He said, 'You know that dude nigger Count Basil? Wears that kind of skipper cap so you think he has a yacht? He's walkin' around the hotel lobby bold as brass. What was he doin' there? He couldn't of been stayin' at the ho-tel.'"

Kevin said, "Who's Count Basil?"

"He meant Count Basie. Joe doesn't know the 'One O'Clock Jump' from 'Turkey in the Straw.'"

Kevin looked at the notebook page he held open.

"Did you know a Dr. Michael George Taylor?"

"I don't think so."

"He might've come later," Kevin said, looked at his book again and said, "No, he was at the rally in New York. Though I bet Walter knew him from before."

"That rally," Honey said, "a sports arena full of all these boobs *sieg heil*ing everything Fritz Kuhn said, this thug in a uniform standing in front of a giant portrait of George Washington. He led the crowd in reciting the Pledge of Allegiance and then talked forever, saying President Roosevelt was part of the international Jewish banking conspiracy. I remember Joe Aubrey calling FDR Frank D.

Rosenfeld and the New Deal the Jew Deal. That's what the whole thing was about, blame the Jews for whatever was wrong with the world."

Kevin said, "But you don't remember a Dr. Michael George Taylor. An obstetrician, he has quite a large practice here, a lot of German-American women."

Honey shook her head. "I don't think so."

"He studied in Germany a few years," Kevin said, looking at his notebook. "He thinks the Nazis have the right idea about the Jewish problem. He says their methods are extreme, yes, but they do the job."

"How did you learn that?"

Kevin was still looking at his notes. He said, "Dr. Taylor is a friend of Vera Mezwa and a frequent visitor. On one occasion he told her he would be willing to do anything, whatever he could, to further the cause of National Socialism, even if it meant incarceration or even his death. He said, quote, 'The world would be a far better place for my children to live'"—Kevin looking at Honey now—"'under the guidance of the firm Nazi philosophy.'"

"He sounds like a bigger idiot than Joe Aubrey."

"They're his words, what he believes."

"You tapped the phone?"

Kevin shook his head. "We didn't get it that way. I'll tell you something else. Dr. Taylor supplied Vera with amedo pyrine. You know what it is? One of the ingredients you use to make invisible ink."

"The German officer," Honey said, "unfolds

the blank sheet of paper, looks at it and says, 'Our Vera has a beautiful hand, no?'"

"I'm serious," Kevin said, "these people work for the German Reich."

"How'd you find out about the invisible ink?" Honey waited, watching him. "I won't tell anybody, Kevin, I swear."

He said, "We've got somebody on the inside. And that's all I'm saying."

"If I guess who it is, how about, just nod your head."

"Come on—I'm not playing with you."

"Is it Vera's housekeeper? What's his name . . . ?"

"Bohdan Kravchenko. He's a lightweight, but there's something shifty about him."

"What's he look like?"

"Blond hair like Buster Brown's, we think is dyed."

"He's queer?"

"Possibly."

"You turned him around," Honey said, "didn't you? Brought him in for questioning and used a sap on him, got him to talk. Does he give you good stuff?"

"We don't hit people," Kevin said, "when we're asking them questions. What I'd like to know, was Walter close to Fritz Kuhn."

"Walter would talk about Fritz and his eyes would shine. We got home from the rally in New York, I was ready to leave him. But once he found out Fritz had swung with about fifteen thousand from the rally proceeds, Walter changed his tune.

He was quiet for a while, I think confused."

"Did Walter know Max Stephan?"

Honey said, "Jesus, Max Stephan. That whole time he was in the paper—it seemed like every day for months—I wondered if Walter knew about the German flier. What was his name, Krug?"

"Hans Peter Krug," Kevin said, "twenty-two, a bomber pilot." He opened his notebook. "Shot down over the Thames estuary. Sent to a POW camp in Canada, Bowmanville, Ontario. Escaped and reached Detroit eighteen April 1942. Found a skiff and paddled across the Detroit River with a board."

"Walter's name was never in the paper," Honey said. "So I assumed he wasn't involved. You understand this was three years after I'd left Walter."

"But you knew Max Stephan?"

"He was a jerk, as pompous and stuck on himself as Walter, and crude. But this was before Max was charged with treason."

She knew the details: how Krug dropped in on Johanna Bertlemann, a Nazi sympathizer who used the German Red Cross to send canned goods, cakes, clothing, to the POWs at Bowmanville. Krug had copied her address in Detroit off a package she'd sent to the camp. Johanna introduced him to Max and Max took him around to German bars and clubs before sending him off to Chicago. Someone snitched. Krug was picked up in San Antonio on his way to Mexico and Max was arrested.

Kevin said, "He told the agents who arrested him he thought Americans were 'frightfully stupid.' He said he visited some of our major cities,

Chicago, New York, and was rarely questioned or asked to show his papers."

"Part of everyday life in Germany," Honey said.

"But to convict Max Stephan of treason," Kevin said, "they'd need two eyeball witnesses. Or, get Krug to tell how Max helped him. But why would he? All he's obliged to do is identify himself."

"But he did tell on Max, didn't he?"

"The U.S. attorney sneaked up on him with questions that put Krug at ease and made him look good. How did he escape from Bowmanville. Why did he come to Detroit. Krug said his purpose was to get back to his squadron. He was talking now. He said yes, he knew Max Stephan. He told the whole story, how he said no when Max offered to get him a prostitute. He described everything they did during a period of twenty-five hours—before he realized he'd given Max up. And he said *we* were stupid. Max was found guilty and sentenced to hang, the date, Friday, November thirteenth, 1942. But FDR commuted the sentence to life. His home is now the federal pen at Atlanta."

"What happened to the pilot, Krug?"

"The Mounties came and got him. He's back in Bowmanville."

"I read about German POWs escaping," Honey said, "but most of them turn out to be funny stories."

"They're picked up in a couple of days," Kevin said, "walking around with *PW* painted on their work clothes. Or they get hungry, miss three squares a day at the camp, and give themselves up."

"So it's not a problem."

Kevin said, "Except I've got a guy calling me, a U.S. marshal—" and stopped.

Honey watched him bring out a pack of Chesterfields and hold it out to offer her one. The good-looking special agent seemed right at home on her sofa. Honey took a cigarette and leaned over him for a light, saying, "You look so comfortable, I hope you don't fall asleep." Close to him, Kevin trying to keep his nose out of Honey's orange, red, and ochre kimono. She sat on the sofa now, the middle cushion between them.

"You've got a federal marshal calling you?"

"From the Tulsa office, yeah. He asks for me by name since I'm the one spoke to him the first time he called."

"He knew you from home?"

"Actually," Kevin said, "I'm originally from Bixby, across the river from Tulsa. I don't know this marshal but I'd heard of him and I find out he's famous. Law enforcement people respect him, so you listen to what he has to say. He makes remarks the way you do, with a straight face. Anyway, he had the Bureau office in Tulsa send us additional information about the two escaped POWs. They're from a camp near Okmulgee, Afrika Korps officers, one of them a major in the SS. With the information was a statement from the Tulsa marshal saying he knows one of them from lengthy conversations and observing him for a time."

"Which one," Honey said, "the SS guy?"

"The other one." Kevin checked his notebook

and Honey laid her arm along the sofa's backrest. Kevin looked up saying, "The marshal claims he knows the guy, and knows—doesn't just have reason to believe—he *knows* they came here when they escaped."

"To Detroit."

Kevin looked at his notebook again. "The SS major is Otto Penzler. The other one is Jurgen Schrenk, a young guy, twenty-six, a tank commander with Rommel."

Honey said in her way, "Don't tell me Jurgen lived in Detroit before the war. What did his father do?"

She let Kevin stare as she drew on her Chesterfield, raised her face, and blew a thin stream of smoke before saying, "Why else would he come here from a prison camp? He must have friends."

Kevin said, "You're having fun, aren't you? Jurgen's dad was a production engineer with Ford of Germany. He brought his wife and the boy along when he came here as an adviser on speeding up Ford assembly lines. Henry thought Hitler was doing a fine job getting Germany on its feet again. Jurgen's family made their home at the Abington Apartment Hotel on Seward. I think they were here two years, Ford Motor paying expenses."

Honey said, "How old was Jurgen?"

"By the time they left"—Kevin looking at his notebook again—"he would've been—"

"About fourteen?"

"Fourteen," Kevin said and looked up.

"You talk to Walter about the escaped prisoners?"

"In the past week we've talked to most all of the names on our watch list of Nazi sympathizers, including Walter. He said he's never heard of Jurgen Schrenk. How'd you know he was fourteen?"

"I guessed. 'Cause Walter was fourteen when he came here," Honey said. "Or the way he used to tell it, when he was brought here against his will. We're at the Dakota Inn one time having a few, Walter said he attended a going-away party in this bar a few years ago. To honor a family going home to Germany after living here awhile. I don't remember how long exactly or the family's name, or if Walter said anything about the dad being with Ford. Walter was hung up on the kid. He said, 'Fourteen years old, the boy goes home to a new Germany, at the most glorious time of its history. I was fourteen, I was brought here and taught to cut meat.'"

"That's how he said it?"

"Pretty much word for word."

"This was before the war."

"I think he met the boy about 1935."

"If Walter missed Germany so much, what was stopping him from going back?"

"You know how many times I asked him that? He'd say it was his destiny to be here, so he shouldn't complain."

"What's that mean exactly, his fate? There's nothing he can do about it?"

"It means there must be something important he's destined to get involved in. I said to him, 'You don't want to go down in history as a meat cutter?'"

"You picked on him like that, didn't you, and he always thought you were serious."

"Tell me who you think he looks like," Honey said. "I don't mean a movie star."

Kevin said, "The first time I opened Walter's file and looked at his picture? I thought, Is this Walter Schoen or Heinrich Himmler?"

"Tell him he looks like Himmler," Honey said, "Walter nods, lowers his head and says, 'Thank you.' Did you know they're both born the same year, 1900, on the same day, October seventh, in the same hospital in Munich?"

Kevin stared, not saying a word.

"Walter believes he's Himmler's twin brother and they were separated at birth."

"He tell you why?"

"Walter says he and Himmler each have their own destiny, their mission in life. We know what Himmler's is, don't we? Kill all the Jews he can find. But Walter—I don't know—five years ago, still hadn't found out what he's supposed to do."

"He isn't stupid, is he?"

"He knows how to run a business. His butcher shop always made money. But that was before rationing. I don't know how he's doing now."

"Last summer," Kevin said, "he bought a farm at auction, a hundred and twenty acres up for back taxes, a house, a barn, and an apple orchard. He said he's thinking about going into the home-kill business, have a small slaughterhouse and sell as a wholesaler."

"He got rid of his butcher shop?"

"He still has it. But why would he get into meat-packing? It seems like every day you read about a meatpacker going out of business. The problem, shortages and price controls, the armed forces taking a third of what meat's available."

"Ask him," Honey said, "if he's a traitor to his country, or he's selling meat on the black market and making a pile of money."

She pushed up from the sofa and headed for the bedroom telling the special agent, "I'll be ten minutes, Kev. Drive me to work, I'll tell you why I married Walter."

Kevin walked over to Honey's bookcase and began looking at titles, most of them unknown to him, and saw *Mein Kampf* squeezed between *For Whom the Bell Tolls* and *This Gun for Hire*. He pulled out Adolf Hitler's book and began skipping through pages of dense-looking text full of words. He turned to the short hallway that led to Honey's bedroom.

"Did you read *Mein Kampf*?"

There was a silence.

"I'm sorry—what did you say?"

He crossed to the hallway not wanting to shout and came to her bedroom, the door open, and saw Honey at her vanity.

"I asked if you read *Mein Kampf*."

"I didn't, and you know why?"

She was leaning toward the mirror putting on lipstick, the kimono on Honey in the mirror hanging open and he could see one of her breasts, the nipple, the whole thing.

"Because it's so fucking boring," Honey said. "I tried a few times and gave up."

He saw her looking in the mirror at him, holding the lipstick to her mouth, and saw her move the kimono enough to cover the breast.

She said, "I don't think you'd like it."

"I wouldn't?"

"The book, *Mein Kampf.*"

Three

They drove south down Woodward Avenue from Six Mile Road in a '41 Olds sedan, property of the FBI, Honey looking at shop windows, Kevin waiting. Finally he said, "You and Walter started seeing each other and before you knew it you fell head over heels in love?"

Honey was taking a pack of Luckys from her black leather bag, getting one out, and using a Zippo she flicked once to light the cigarette.

"That's what happened," Honey said, "I fell in love with Walter because he's such a swell guy, kind and considerate, fun to be with." She handed the cigarette to Kevin, a trace of lipstick on the tip.

Now she was lighting another, Kevin glancing at Honey in her trench coat and black beret, pulled low on her blond hair and slightly to one side, the way girls in spy movies wore their berets. Honey was a new experience for him.

She said, "The whole time we talked, you know you didn't once call me by my name? Which one do you have a problem with, Honey or Miss Deal?"

He was aware of it and said, "Well, if I called you 'Honey' it would sound like, you know, we're going together."

"My friends at work call me Honey. I'm not going with any of them. The day I was born my dad picked me up and said, 'Here's my little honey,' and loved me so much I was christened Honey. The priest said, 'You can't call her that. There's no St. Honey in the Catholic Church.' My dad said, 'There is now. Christen her Honey or we're turning Baptist.'" She said, "You want to know something? Walter never asked where I got the name."

"Did you tell him?"

"We're coming to Blessed Sacrament," Honey said, "where Walter and I met. It was after eleven o'clock Mass. Yeah, I told him but he didn't make anything of it. He called me Honig, if he called me anything."

"You took that as a good sign, meeting at church?"

"I think it was the only reason Walter went to Mass, to meet a girl with golden hair. He stopped going once he had me, and I stopped since we were living in sin, not married in the Church."

"You believe that, you were living in sin?"

"Not really. It was more like living a life of penance. I'll tell you though, I did like his looks, the way he dressed, his little glasses pinched on his nose, he was so different. I'd never met anyone in my life like Walter Schoen. I think I might've felt sorry for him too, he seemed so lonely. He was serious about everything and when we argued—we argued all the time—I'd keep at him, whatever we were talking about, and it drove him nuts."

"Determined to change him," Kevin said.

Honey sat up to look past Kevin. She said, "There's his market," and sat back again. "With a sign in the window, but I couldn't read it."

"Announcing no meat today," Kevin said. "I passed it on the way to your place. So, you thought you could change him?"

"I wanted to get him to quit being so serious and have some fun. Maybe even get him to laugh at Adolf Hitler, the way Charlie Chaplin played him in *The Great Dictator*. Chaplin has the little smudge of a mustache, the uniform, he's Adenoid Hynkel, dictator of Tomania. But the movie came out after I left."

"You think he saw it?"

"I couldn't get Walter to listen to Jack Benny. He called him a pompous Jew. I said, 'That's the part he plays, a cheapskate. You don't think he's funny?' No, or even Fred Allen. We were at some German place having drinks, I said, 'Walter, have you ever told a joke? Not a political cartoon, a funny story?' He acted like he didn't know what I was talking about. I said, 'I'll tell you a joke and then you tell it to me. We'll see how you do.'"

Kevin Dean was looking straight ahead grinning. "You were married then?"

"*Ja*, I'm Frau Schoen. I tell him the one, three guys arrive at heaven at the same time. It's been a very busy day, during the war, and Saint Peter says, 'I only have time to admit one of you today. How about whoever has experienced the most unusual death.' Have you heard it?"

"I don't think so."

"The first guy tells how he came home unexpectedly, finds his wife in bed naked and tears through the apartment looking for her lover. He runs out on the balcony and there's the guy hanging from the railing, twenty-five floors above the street. The husband takes off one of his shoes and beats on the guy's hands till the guy lets go and falls. But he doesn't hit the pavement, damn it, he lands in a bushy tree and he's still alive. The husband, furious, grabs the refrigerator, drags it out to the balcony and pushes it over the railing. The fridge lands on the guy in the tree and kills him. But, the exertion is too much for the husband, he has a heart attack and drops dead. Saint Peter says, 'That's not bad,' and turns to the second guy who wants to get into heaven. This one says he was exercising on his balcony, lost his balance and went over the railing. He's a goner for sure, but reaches out and grabs the railing of the balcony below his apartment. Now a guy comes out and the one hanging twenty-five floors above the street says, 'Thank God, I'm saved.' But the guy who comes out takes off his shoe and beats on his hands gripping the rail till he falls. But he lands in the bushy tree, he's still alive, his eyes wide open to see the fridge coming down to blot out his life. Saint Peter says, 'Yeah, I like that one.' Turns to the third guy who wants to get into heaven and says, 'What's your story, amigo?' The guy says, 'I don't know what happened. I was naked, hiding in a refrigerator . . .'"

Honey paused.

Kevin laughed out loud.

"He think it was funny?"

"He didn't smile or say anything right away. He's thinking about it. Finally he asked me which of the three guys did Saint Peter let into heaven, and where did the other two have to wait, in limbo? I said, 'Yeah, limbo, with all the babies that happened to die before they were baptized.'"

"Why didn't he get it?"

"He's managed to stick his head up his ass," Honey said, "and the only thing he sees up there are swastikas."

This sweet girl talking like that. Kevin said, "I'm never sure what you're gonna say next."

"I tried one more joke on Walter," Honey said. "I told him the one, the guy comes home, walks into the kitchen with a sheep in his arms. His wife turns from the sink and he says, 'This is the pig I've been sleeping with when I'm not with you.' His wife says, 'You dummy, that's not a pig, it's a sheep.' And the guy says, 'I wasn't speaking to you.'"

Kevin laughed out loud again and looked at Honey smoking her cigarette. "You like to tell jokes?"

"To Walter, trying to loosen him up."

"Did he laugh?"

"He said, 'The man is not talking to his wife, he's talking to the sheep?' I said yeah, it's his wife he's calling a pig. Walter said, 'But how does a sheep understand what he's saying?' That was it," Honey said. "There was no way in the world I'd ever turn Walter around. It was a dumb idea to begin with, really arrogant of me to think I could change him. But you know, I realized even if he did lighten up the marriage would never last."

"There must've been something about him you liked," Kevin said, "I mean as a person."

"You'd think so, wouldn't you?" said Honey in the black beret nodding her head. "Something more than his accent and his stuck-on glasses, but I can't think of anything it might be. I was young and I was dumb." She smoked her cigarette, quiet for a time before saying, "That year with Walter did have some weird moments I'll never forget. Like when he'd aim his finger at me, pretending it was a gun and cut one."

Kevin said, "You mean he'd pass gas in front of you?"

"In front of me, behind me—"

But now they were coming to Seward and he had to tell her, "Here's the street where Jurgen Schrenk and his mom and dad lived in the thirties. The apartment hotel's in the second block."

"The Abington," Honey said. "I had dinner there a few times—they have a dining room. This guy I knew always stayed there. He said he'd walk five blocks south to the General Motors Building on the Boulevard, and walk back with a signed contract in his briefcase."

"What kind of contract?"

"I don't know, he never told me exactly what he did. He was from Argentina and had something to do with Grand Prix auto racing in Europe before the war. He always called cars motorcars. He'd stay at the Abington in a one-bedroom apartment that had a tiny kitchen. If there were twin beds he'd pull down the Murphy bed in the living room. He was a little guy, very slim, but liked big beds." Honey said, "You know, I remember reading about Jurgen and the SS guy escaping. It was in all the Detroit papers."

It brought Kevin back, his image of Honey and a suave type of guy who looked like a tango dancer gone from his mind.

She said, "Jurgen might be the same boy Walter told me about, or he might not. Walter did write to someone who was in the war. I remember he got a letter postmarked from Poland in 1939, but Walter never said anything about it. By that time we were barely speaking."

"Jurgen Schrenk was in Poland before going to North Africa, according to the marshal in Tulsa. The guy who swears Jurgen's here, hiding out."

"You said he's famous?"

"A book was written about him, all kinds of magazine articles, a long one in *True Detective*. The book, *Carl Webster: The Hot Kid of the Marshals Service*, came out about ten years ago."

"Have you read it?"

"Yeah, I got hold of a copy—it's good. Carl's been in some really tight situations. I've talked to some agents who know him, they all say he's the real thing. He's shot and killed at least a dozen wanted felons, or otherwise known bad guys like Emmett Long and Jack Belmont." Kevin paused. "No, it was his wife Louly who shot Jack Belmont. She shot another bank robber too, but I forget his name."

Honey said, "His wife goes with him, he's after bad guys?"

"They were unusual situations. Louly was related to Pretty Boy Floyd's wife, and for a time everybody thought Louly was Floyd's girlfriend."

"Before she married Carl Webster."

"That's right, and now she's in the Women Marines, teaching recruits how to fire a machine gun
from the backseat of a dive-bomber." Kevin said,
"All the guys Carl Webster shot, he used the same
Colt .38 revolver, the front sight filed off. No, one
he shot with a Winchester at four hundred yards. At
night." Kevin said, "Something I don't understand,
you see his name in the paper or in the book, it's
Carl Webster. But when he calls me he says, 'This
is Carlos Webster.'"

"That's his real name?"

"Carlos Huntington Webster. His dad was in
Cuba with Huntington's Marines at Guantánamo
in '98, during the Spanish-American War. Carl's
mother was Cuban and his dad's mother was part
Northern Cheyenne. But does he go by Carl or
Carlos?"

"How old is he?"

"All he's done, you'd think he'd have some years
on him, but he isn't yet forty years old."

"Have you met him?"

"Not yet. He was ready to come to Detroit on
his own, help us look for Jurgen and the SS guy,
Otto. But Carl's boss, the Tulsa marshal, retired
and they made Carl acting head of the office. He
raised hell saying he'd never had a desk job and
never would. The marshals office in Washington
said okay, they'd look around and find someone to
take his place. He told me, if we don't have Jurgen

by the time his replacement arrives, he's definitely coming." Kevin looked at Honey. He loved looking at her profile. She had a cute nose like the girls in the Jantzen swimming suit ads. She didn't act like she knew she was a knockout, but he would bet she did and knew how to use her looks without letting on too much.

"You want to meet him if he comes?"

"I wouldn't mind," Honey said. "But why would he bother seeing me?"

"Walter," Kevin said. "He wants you along when he talks to him."

Four

Every time Carl approached the Mayo he thought of the guy who tried to shoot him in the back as he entered the hotel. The Black Hand extortion guy ten years ago. With an Italian name Carl couldn't think of. The doorman that day had been holding one of the doors open for Carl. He started in and the glass in the door next to him and in the door swinging closed behind him both shattered, blown apart with the sound of high-caliber gunfire and now tires screaming, the Ford coupe gone by the time Carl came around with his Colt revolver.

Today the same doorman was holding the door open, Marvin, a black guy, Marvin asking Carl as he approached the entrance how he was this spring morning. Now looking past Carl and saying, "Uh-oh," under his breath. "Man has a gun."

Carl stopped. He heard his name called and turned to see a young guy in black holding a big heavy show-off nickel-plate automatic against his leg, the shoulders of his suit wide, zooty, the pants pegged at his light-tan shoes. There he was, a full head of black hair shining in the hotel lights, a young gangster, Italian or Jewish, here to shoot Carl Webster. If the kid was Jewish he'd be a kin of the Tedesco brothers, Tutti and Frankie Bones from the Purple Gang. That time in Okmulgee they came around on him pulling their guns, Carl fired twice and the Tedescos went down.

This one, standing on the sidewalk in front of the hotel, said, "You Carl Webster?"

"Yes, I am. Tell me who you're related to."

"You killed my brother."

The third one to come along with a dead brother. Carl said, "You mean the one use to beat the shit out of you when he felt like it? Which one was he?"

"Luigi Tessa."

Jesus Christ, Lou Tessa the backshooter. Carl shook his head. "You know he ambushed me? Right here as I'm going in the hotel? You could've busted me from behind yourself, but you want to do it face-to-face, uh? There's hope for you, boy. What's your name?"

"Why you want to know?"

"So when I tell what happened here I can give your Christian name. Who you were." Carl freed the button holding his suitcoat closed and said, "Wait a minute. I never killed your brother, he went to prison."

"Where he got the chair," the kid gangster said. "It's the same as you killin' him."

"Listen," Carl said, "you don't want to shoot me." He held his suitcoat open wide with both hands. "You see a gun on my person?" Carl dropped his arms, his right hand sweeping the coat aside to bring out the .38 revolver from his waist, hard against his spine, and put it on Lou Tessa's brother, telling him, "Now you see it. Lay your left hand on that cannon you're holding and eject the loads till the piece is empty. You pause," Carl said, "I'll take it to mean you want to kill me and I'll shoot you through the heart."

Virgil, Carl's dad, said, "I thought you liked a shoulder holster."

"I'm not gonna wear it driving. I get in the car," Carl said, "my gun goes in the glove compartment. I checked out of the office and stopped by the Mayo for a drink. You ought to move to Tulsa. That bar in the basement keeps right up."

"What'd you do with the kid gangster?"

"Turned him over to Tulsa police. They'll look him up, see if his big nickel-plate is dirty or not. Vito Tessa, they can have him. I'm leaving from here in the morning, six-thirty."

"How come you're sure the two Huns are in Detroit?"

Carl and his dad were sitting in wicker chairs this evening—in shirtsleeves but wearing their felt hats—on the front porch of Virgil's big California bungalow, the home situated in the midst of his thousand acres of pecan trees.

"What you want to ask," Carl said, "is how I know they're still in Detroit, five and a half months later."

They were talking about Jurgen Schrenk mostly, a POW from the Afrika Korps, tank captain and one of Rommel's recon officers. Finally, 165 days from the time Jurgen and the other one, Otto Penzler, the SS major, broke out of the Deep Fork prisoner-of-war camp—drove out in a panel truck, the two Krauts wearing suits of clothes made from German uniforms—Carl was free to get after them.

This day he drove the forty miles south, Tulsa to Okmulgee to visit his dad, was the seventh of April, 1945.

Carl and his dad were drinking Mexican beer supplied by the oil company—way better than the three-two local beer. It was part of the deal that let Texas Oil lease a half section of the property, the wells pumping most of forty years while Virgil tended his pecan trees and Carl, when he was still a boy, raised beef he'd take to market in Tulsa. Virgil's home was a few miles from Okmulgee and across the Deep Fork stream from the POW camp.

"He's still in Detroit," Carl said, "'cause he hasn't been caught, or we'd of heard. Jurgen'll get by, he speaks American with barely an accent. You have to know what words to listen for. I told you he lived in Detroit when he was a kid? He can talk like a Yankee or sound like he's from Oklahoma, either way."

"I'd see him," Virgil said, "the times he'd come with a work crew of prisoners. I swear they all looked like foreigners except Jurgen. I asked him one time was he thinking of setting fire to oil wells and storage tanks, see if he could perform acts of sabotage."

"After you told him you were on the *Maine*."

"Yes, I did, a marine aboard the battleship the night the dons blew her up in Havana harbor, 1898, and set us at war with Spain. I told him there wasn't a destructive act he could think of that would compare to blowing up the battleship *Maine*."

Carl said he got a kick out of Jurgen slipping out of camp every couple of months to get laid, spend some time with his girlfriend, Shemane.

"She was a hot number," Virgil said, "worked in a Kansas City cathouse. The next time she's seen she's driving by here in a Lincoln Zephyr."

"Looking for Jurgen," Carl said. "He'd sneak out for a few days and show up at the OK Cafe, *PW* printed on the back of his short pants—always wore those Afrika Korps shorts—and wait there for the MPs to come get him. The last time he broke out we're certain it was Shemane drove Jurgen and Otto to Fort Smith and bought 'em their getaway car, a '41 Studebaker."

Virgil said, "You ever gonna arrest her?"

"Shemane's mom was along for the ride. She raised hell with the agents bringing 'em back from Arkansas. She said they were on their way to Hot Springs to take the waters and had not socialized with any Germans or ever would. I told the agents in Tulsa I'd let Shemane think she's off the hook. Wait for her to leave her mom and go up to Detroit. She does, you got Jurgen. She doesn't, they weren't as nuts about each other as I thought. I said to one of the U.S. attorneys, 'What're you gonna bring her up on, sleeping with the enemy? You want to charge this poor girl, who's gone to bed with some of the most prominent criminal defense lawyers in America?'"

Virgil said, "Is that true?"

"Pretty much. I'm counting on Jurgen sticking by Otto, doing what he can to keep him under wraps. Some of those heavy-duty Nazis, the SS guys, refuse even to learn English. Otto's SS, but he's tricky. I have a hunch he can get by pretty well in English. Jurgen still might have a time getting him to quit clicking his heels in public, get him to slouch and say things like 'how they hangin'?' Unless Otto's got too much of a Kraut accent to take him anywhere. But I think the main reason they're still in Detroit, Jurgen has friends there, people willing to help him out."

"Hiding him," Virgil said.

"Or they got Jurgen a new identity, birth certificate, and 4F card. He might even have something working he thinks is fun, while he's teaching Otto to speak American. Jurgen told me one time the Escape Committee, the hard-ass Nazis that run the camp inside, wanted him to study blowing up an ammunition dump they heard about, out in the country south of McAlester. Jurgen telling me about it shows what he thought of the Committee. He said, 'Even if I could blow it up, this place in the middle of nowhere, who would hear the explosion?' He's saying, What good would it do? Working some kind of sabotage now, this late in the war, makes no sense at all. The Battle of the Bulge was Germany's last full-out assault. They pushed off the sixteenth of December with a thousand tanks and by the twentieth of January they had a hundred thousand casualties and lost eight hundred of the tanks. We lost a lot of good soldiers, but we pushed the Krauts back to where they'd started, pretty much done. It was their last assault but, boy, it cost us."

Virgil said, "If the war over there ends pretty soon, what happens to Jurgen and Otto?"

"I take 'em back to the camp. The Committee's had prisoners killed, ones they saw as weaklings pretending they're faithful Nazis. Had 'em hanged in the washroom to look like they committed suicide. Jurgen said in a statement he left with the camp commander, he and Otto had to get out of there or they'd be the next ones strung up. In the meantime the Committee guys have been sent to Alva in the western part of Oklahoma, the camp where they keep the thugs, the super-Nazis."

"By now," Virgil said, "you must have this Detroit FBI agent in your pocket."

"He's a good guy, Kevin's helping me out. He's still new, doesn't know he's not supposed to talk to strangers, like marshals."

"You tell him there's a book written about you?"

"Kevin says it wasn't in the library so I sent him one."

"You started out, you musta had a hundred copies. How many you got left?"

"I still have some. I call Kevin, 'You find my Krauts yet?' Five months they've been looking, no luck. They're working to get the goods on a Nazi spy ring and have different ones under surveillance. I asked him where the spies got their secret stuff, from the paper? He said I sound like a girl he's been talking to, Honey Deal. She was married to one of the Detroit Nazis for a year, divorced him in '39. Kevin says Honey's single, good-looking and smart, keeps up on the war—that impressed him—without having anybody in it to worry about. Kevin has our sheet on the two guys, so he knows Jurgen lived in Detroit at one time and should have friends that are still around. Kevin said, 'Fourteen years old when he went back to Germany, in '35.' He says Honey Deal thinks there's a good chance her ex-husband knew him. Walter Schoen. Kevin said they asked Walter about him. All he did was shake his head."

"I imagine," Virgil said, "you want to talk to this guy yourself."

"I've been thinking about it, and his ex-wife, Honey. I asked Kevin if he thought Walter Schoen was attractive to women. He said, 'You think Heinrich Himmler is? That's who Walter looks like.' What I wanted to know was why a smart, good-looking girl from East Kentucky would care to marry him? Kevin said, 'Honey thought she could change him, turn him around.' I said, 'Hell, that's what all women try to do.' He said she told him marrying Walter was the biggest mistake of her life, so far. I'll get with her first," Carl said, "then Walter Schoen. Kevin talked to his boss and he talked to the Bureau office in Tulsa, and they vouched for me, so I can do pretty much what I want."

"Since the Hun was a friend of yours."

"He could be, once the war's over. I hope he stays alive."

Five

Narcissa Raincrow, Virgil's common-law wife of thirty-nine years, called out supper was ready and served them fried chicken and rice with gravy at the round table in the back part of the kitchen. Narcissa, fifty-four now, had been living here since she was sixteen, hired to wet-nurse Carl when his mother, Graciaplena, died giving birth to him. This was in 1906. Virgil had married Grace and brought her here from Cuba after the war with Spain. Carl was named for Grace's father, Carlos. Narcissa, unmarried, had delivered a child stillborn and needed to give her milk to a newborn infant. When Carl first brought his wife, Louly, to the house he told her that by the time he'd lost interest in Narcissa's breasts, his dad had acquired an appreciation, first keeping her on as housekeeper and cook, finally as his common-law wife. Virgil thought she looked like Dolores Del Rio only heavier.

Narcissa said to Carl eating his chicken, "I got a letter from Louly you can read if you want. I write her, she always answers my letter."

Carl said he talked to her on the phone every week.

Virgil said, "You tell the FBI agent your wife's a marine?"

"I tell everybody I meet," Carl said, "Louly's a gunnery instructor at a marine air base. Shows recruits how to fire a Browning machine gun from the backseat of a Dauntless dive-bomber without shooting off the tail. Louly's having all the fun."

"He misses the war," Virgil said.

"He would still be in it," Narcissa said, "he wasn't shot that time." She said to Carl, "You lucky, you know it?" And said, "Virgil tell you the FBI man called?"

"I tried him, he was gone for the day," Carl said, busy with his chicken and rice. "I'll see him tomorrow."

"How come he asked for Carlos Webster?"

Carl saw his dad stop eating his supper to watch him.

"I told Kevin I was Carlos. I'm thinking of using it again while I'm in Detroit."

"Nobody's called you that since you were a boy," Virgil said. "Or up to when you joined the marshals and they started calling you Carl. You'd tell 'em you're Carlos and come near having fistfights over it till your boss calmed you down. You recall why you wanted to stick with Carlos?"

Carl said, "'Cause it's my name?"

"Still a smarty-pants," Narcissa said.

"You were wearing it like a chip on your shoulder," Virgil said. "You know why?"

"I know what you're gonna say."

"'Cause a long time ago that moron Emmett Long took your ice cream cone and called you a greaser. I told you he couldn't read nor write or he wouldn't be robbing banks."

"He said I was part greaser on my mama's side," Carl said. "I told him my grammaw's Northern Cheyenne and asked him if having Indian blood made me something else besides a greaser."

Narcissa shook her head saying, "Don't you want to hug him?"

"He told you it would make us breeds," Virgil said, "me more'n you. Six years later with a marshal's star on your person, you shot Emmett Long for insulting your ancestry. That's how I tell it to the soldiers in the bar, the ones from the camp they got the Huns in. Then I say, 'Or did the hot kid of the marshals shoot the wanted bank robber for taking his ice cream cone?'"

"The soldiers buy the three-two and the shots," Narcissa said, holding a cold bottle of Mexican beer in each hand. "He tells one story after another and comes home looped."

Carl said, "First he tells how he was blown off the *Maine* and held in the Morro for being a spy."

Virgil said, "Once that's out of the way I tell how you shot the cow thief off his horse from two hundred yards, with a Winchester."

Carl said, "You remember his name?"

"Wally Tarwater. I got all their names written down."

"I see him moving my cows I yelled at him."

"You were fifteen years old," his dad said. "The marshals were ready to hire you."

"I could see he knew how to work beef without wearing himself out."

"Later on," his dad said, "I asked if you looked at him as he's lying on the ground. You said you got down from that dun you rode and closed his eyes. I asked did you feel any sympathy for him. Remember what you said?"

"That was twenty-five years ago."

"You said you warned him, turn the stock or you'd shoot. I imagine all the cow thief saw was a kid on a horse. You said to me later on, 'Yeah, but if he'd listened he wouldn't of been lying there dead, would he?' I said to myself, My Lord, but this boy's got a hard bark on him."

Narcissa, who had nursed Carl for the first months of his life, placed the Mexican beers on the table and stooped to put her arms around his shoulders. Now she was touching his hair saying, "But he's a sweet boy too, isn't he? Yes he is, he's a sweetie pie."

Finally they let Carl Webster step down as acting marshal of Oklahoma's Eastern District and gave the job to a marshal from Arkansas, an old hand by the name of W. R. "Bill" Hutchinson. He and Carl had tracked felons together and shared jars of shine over the years, each knowing the other would be watching his back. Today in the marshal's office was the first time Carl had seen him without a plug in his jaw, in there behind his lawman's mustache. Bill Hutchinson asked Carl if he was sure he wanted to go to De-troit.

"You know it's still winter up there. I've heard they have snow in May."

Carl stared at the angle of bones in Bill Hutchinson's face, the creases cut into the corners of his eyes. Marshals had told Carl he reminded them some of Bill Hutchinson, that same look, only without the old-time mustache the marshal from Arkansas favored.

"I'm going after the Krauts," Carl told him. "You can send me or I'll take a leave of absence and do it without pay. If you want to send me, let me have the Pontiac and enough gas stamps. It's the car I was using before I spent the past five and a half months sitting here with my feet on the desk."

"What else you want?"

"Expense money."

"You know those officers up north are different'n us, their manner of doing things, the way they dress up."

"The agent I'm seeing is from Bixby, Oklahoma, if you know where Bixby's at. Directly across the river."

"I imagine you'll observe the thirty-five-mile-an-hour speed limit," Bill Hutchinson said. "It shouldn't take you more'n two, three days. Can you tell me where you'll be staying?"

Not till Kevin Dean found him a place.

A thousand miles to Detroit from Tulsa through

St. Louis, Indianapolis, Fort Wayne, head for
Toledo following cars on the two-lane highways
moping along at thirty-five, Carl wearing himself
out looking to pass, not able to bear down until
it was dark and he took the Pontiac up to seventy
through Indiana farmland, a five-gallon can of gas
in the trunk just in case. Carl left Tulsa at 6:40
A.M. hoping to make the trip in twenty-four hours,
but it was eight the next morning before he was
approaching Detroit from the southwest and going
on nine by the time he was downtown looking for
West Lafayette. Carl had a map in his head that
showed him the general layout of Detroit's downtown streets with marks indicating the buildings
where the federal courts were located and a few
hotels, in case Kevin Dean from Bixby hadn't yet
learned his way around. Carl turned onto Lafayette and came to the Federal Building, right where
it was supposed to be, waiting for him.

He let Kevin take him through the FBI office in-
troducing him as the Oklahoma deputy marshal
the Hot Kid book was written about, Carl shaking
his head at Kevin sounding like his press agent. It
surprised Carl these boys all seemed to know who
he was.

They had to wait a few minutes to see John Bugas, special agent in charge; he was being interviewed by a writer from the *Detroit News*. When
he came out, a photographer trailing behind, the
writer walked up to Carl standing in the hall and
offered his hand saying he was Neal Rubin.

"Did you know John Bugas was your biggest fan?"

"You're kidding me," Carl said.

"He's looking forward to meeting you. I asked him if he'd read the book about you and John said, 'Every word.' He asked me if I'd read it. I said, 'John, I reviewed it for the *News* and sent you my copy.' That was ten years ago and he'd forgotten where he got it. I asked him what the Hot Kid was doing in Detroit. He said he thought you were just visiting. But I'm betting you're after some wanted felon or escaped convict, aren't you?"

"I don't want to give anything away," Carl said, "and spook him. Have him take off on me."

"You know what my favorite part was? When you out-gunned that Klansman Nestor Lott, Nestor pulling his pair of .45 automatics. He was an oddball, wasn't he?"

"He was a snake," Carl said.

Neal Rubin looked at his wristwatch.

"I got to get going. I'm meeting Esther Williams for lunch at the Chop House and have to change my shirt." The one he had on looked like it was from Hawaii. He said, "Pick up the *News* tomorrow, I'll have something in my column about you."

Carl wasn't sure that was a good idea, but the writer and the photographer were already heading down the hall.

Kevin told John Bugas Carl had only left Tulsa yesterday in his car and was here first thing this morning. John Bugas didn't seem impressed. He asked

Carl why he thought the two escaped POWs were still in Detroit, assuming they did come here.

Carl gave his stock answer. "'Cause Jurgen Schrenk used to live here and there's no word they've been picked up." He told John Bugas his office had done a good job finding Peter Krug, the escaped Nazi flier, and sending the traitor Max Stephan to Atlanta.

"Nice going," Carl said. "I think someone on your enemy alien list is helping out Jurgen and Otto, but isn't showing him off the way Max paraded the Luftwaffe guy around. I think they've found themselves a home and are waiting out the war."

The writer had said Bugas was looking forward to meeting him, but Carl didn't get that feeling, Bugas standing at his desk since they'd entered the office, like he was waiting for them to hurry up and leave. John Bugas wished Carl luck, shook his hand again, and said if he located the POWs, let this office know and they'd decide how to handle it. "Call Kevin, he's your guy."

Carl thought he was handling it, but didn't say anything.

In the hall walking toward the lobby, Kevin said, "He might not've acted like it, but he was anxious to meet you. Yesterday he told me to get you accommodations at the Statler or the Book. He said, 'We want to show this man our respect.'"

Carl said, "He did?"

"When we started talking on the phone," Kevin said, "I didn't know you were famous. I reserved a room for you at the Book Cadillac on Washington

Boulevard. Across the street and down a couple of blocks you come to Stouffer's, the best cafeteria I've ever been in, even better'n Nelson's Buffeteria in Tulsa."

This boy from Bixby was working out better than Carl could've hoped. Carl said, "But this place doesn't offer chicken-fried steak, does it?" and kept talking. He told Kevin he'd check into the hotel and sleep for a couple of hours. "Call Honey and tell her we're having lunch at her store and would like to have her join us. She won't have to put on a coat."

"What if she can't make it?"

Carl said, "Why not?"

"I mean what if she's busy?"

"Doing what? Tell Honey we're expecting her there."

"What time?"

"Say one-fifteen. Have her tell you where we're gonna meet."

Kevin ducked into an empty office to use the phone.

The *News* photographer was taking pictures of the display case that showed some of the FBI's most wanted fugitives. He stepped aside with his big Speed Graphic as Carl approached the display. Carl nodded to the photographer, an older guy in his fifties.

"You finished here?"

"I got time. Go on and look if you want."

Every one of the mug shots was familiar to Carl;

he knew all the names from the photos. Jurgen and Otto were here, ESCAPED PRISONER OF WAR heading each of their wanted dodgers. A flash of light hit the glass covering the display and Carl turned to the photographer lowering his four-by-five.

"I see my picture in the paper," Carl said, "you're in trouble."

"I got you from behind," the photographer said, "someone looking at the bad guys. There's no way you could be identified."

Carl said, "You through here?"

The photographer said, "I guess so," and walked out toward the elevators.

Kevin came in a few minutes later.

"These are the same shots," Carl said, "on file at the camp. I told Jurgen one time he looked awful, like he was waiting for the end of the world. He said becoming a prisoner of war was dreadful at first. That was the word he used, *dreadful*. He said what you have to do is turn the idle time to some advantage. Learn a language or how to do something constructive. I said, 'How to escape and meet girls?' He could slip out of the camp anytime he wanted. He said what he meant was learn a trade. Learn to work on automobiles, leave the camp and get a job at a garage." Carl said, "I think the reason you haven't been able to find him, that's what he's doing, working somewhere, a veteran back from the war. Who's going to ask him what side he was on? He figures out how to fit in somewhere and nobody notices anything alien about him." Carl continued to stare at Jurgen behind the sheet of glass. "The shots don't do anything for him."

"At the end of the trail," Kevin said. They were typical mug shots, taken at the low end of the subject's appearance. "But he looks like he'd be a nice guy."

"For a Nazi."

"That's how you see him?"

"That's what he is."

Kevin broke a silence. "I got hold of Honey. You ask for Better Dresses on seven. Honey says like she's reading it, 'They're for fashion-conscious Detroit women who shop with a discriminating eye.' I told you, you remind me of her. We're having lunch in the Pine Room on thirteen. She has no problem getting away. She said if we have time we might want to stop by the auditorium on twelve and see the War Souvenir Show."

"What kind of souvenirs," Carl said, "stuff guys brought back?"

"I imagine the usual," Kevin said, "Jap swords, German Lugers. I knew guys where I was who bought Jap teeth off the natives. The fillings in the teeth made of steel."

Carl said, "I never fired a Luger." He said, "Iron Crosses and swastika armbands you could get off of POWs without leaving the country. I never asked you," Carl said, "were you in the war?"

"In the Pacific," Kevin said, "till I tried to duck a Jap grenade. I saw it coming and thought of catching it and throwing it back, only I changed my mind, not knowing how much time there was and dove for a hole."

"Where was this?"

"Not too far north of New Guinea, an island

called Los Negros in the Admiralties. You ever
hear of it?"

It stopped Carl.

"You were with the First Cav?"

Now Kevin showed surprise.

"You read about us?"

"I was *there*," Carl said.

Six

Y ou know what you've become?" Jurgen said to Otto. "A pain in the ass."

"Because I want to be German and speak our language and hear it?"

"You're acting like a child."

Otto spoke only German to Walter, when Walter was here, and to the old couple who kept house and were afraid of him. They answered questions and that was all, they refused to carry on a conversation.

Jurgen and Otto sat at the white porcelain table in the kitchen having their morning coffee.

If he spoke German to Jurgen he got no response.

Jurgen said if they spoke only English and tried to think in English, there would be less chance of their being caught. He said, "You want to go out. So do I. But if you intentionally speak German and pose the way you do, daring people to stare at you—'Look at me, the destroyer of British tanks in the desert'—or whoever you are, they will. And if you attract attention to yourself, it won't be long before you're back in the camp."

Otto said, "You want English? Why don't you fuck yourself?"

"It's 'Go fuck yourself,'" Jurgen said.

Two years in the war prisoner camp and now another kind of confinement, months in a house on a farm owned by Walter Schoen: the house standing for a hundred years among old Norway pines, an apple orchard on the property, a chicken house, a barn turned into an abattoir where cattle entered to be shot in the head by a .22 rifle. Otto wouldn't go near the barn. Jurgen couldn't stay out of it, fascinated by the process, three meat cutters who spoke German among themselves cutting and sharpening, cutting and sharpening, reducing the thousand-pound cow to pieces of meat.

This morning Jurgen waited for Walter to arrive in his 1941 Ford sedan, a gray four-door with a high shine, always, anytime Jurgen saw the car. The Ford came through the trees along the drive that circled to the back of the two-story frame house that at one time, years ago, had been painted white. Walter came out of the car and Jurgen pounced on him.

"Walter, it's of the utmost importance that you drive Otto into the city. He wants to see for himself the destruction made by the Luftwaffe. If you don't, Otto tells me he's going to run away and look for it himself."

Walter frowned. He did it all the time, no matter what you said to him, he frowned.

"But there have been no air raids here."

"In the prison camp," Jurgen said, "Otto listened to the reports on shortwave radio from Berlin. They open the program with *Der Blomberger Badenweiler-Marsch* and then report on the latest bombing forays on American cities, war plants too, by the Luftwaffe."

"It could be true?" Walter said.

"Not unless bombers can cross the Atlantic Ocean and return without stopping to refuel," Jurgen said. "But Otto believes it. You know if he leaves the house by himself he'll be picked up within a matter of hours. He'll tell the police he's SS and demand they treat him with military respect. You realize Otto's not familiar with the independent ways that Americans have. He'll become arrogant and tell them he escaped from a prisoner-of-war camp, bragging about it, saying it was easy, nothing to it. Saying he has German friends here. Walter, he'll give you up the same way the Luftwaffe pilot gave up the man who helped him and was convicted of treason, Max Stephan. Otto could give you up without realizing what he's doing."

Walter Schoen, more dedicated to the Reich than Jurgen would ever be, said, "Your comrade is an SS man, one of Himmler's men of honor with a pedigree, his family pure Aryan going back for centuries. There is not even a remote possibility Major Penzler would ever betray a German soldier. Let me say also, you sound very American when you speak. More so than I, and I have had to live here more than thirty years."

Jurgen said, "Let me explain something to you about Otto. He joined the SS because at the time he felt it was an honor, it gave him position. Not because he wanted to be a guardian of racial purity, or to lead a crusade against the Bolsheviks. That's something he told his SS fellows. But, he has said more than once he never took the political indoctrination seriously. I believed that of him. He managed to hook up with Rommel and quite possibly was the only member of the Waffen-SS in North Africa. During the time in Oklahoma he never posed or put on airs. He commanded panzers and was known as the *Scharfrichter*, the executioner of British tanks. Walter," Jurgen said, "what Otto wants right now is to feel once again a sense of war. It's what he is, a warrior. He wants to relive the excitement of crushing Poland. He wants to see buildings the Luftwaffe destroyed on its raids. You say it hasn't happened, you're still waiting for the bombers. I don't know, maybe he needs to bludgeon some poor wretch and kick him senseless. He might do it because his frustration has brought him to the point of going mad. Then he's arrested, and talks and talks. I'm hoping a drive into Detroit will relieve the tension, expose Otto to the way Americans live and he'll see how much we are alike."

Walter Schoen was squinting again, confused. "You believe that's true?"

Something strange was happening during the past six months: people coming to Walter for his assistance.

First Rudi and Madi, both seventy-five, good Germans but destitute, left with nothing when their home burned to the ground. It was in the Black Bottom, the Negro section of Detroit. Rudi said it was Negroes who set the house afire to make them leave. Madi said it was Rudi smoking cigarettes and drinking whiskey until he passed out. Walter had no choice, they were family, Madi his aunt, one of his father's sisters. He drove them out Grand River to the property he had bought at auction and told them they could live here and provide for themselves, raise chickens, plant a vegetable garden, see if the apples in the orchard were worth selling. Walter said he would see them once he got his home-kill business going and would be here to supervise the butchering.

He was working on the barn, fashioning the interior with chutes and hooks to become an abattoir, paving the floor and putting in drains, when the next one appeared, Honey's brother, my God, coming in Walter's market, extending his hand over the counter and saying he was Darcy Deal.

"I always wanted to meet you, Walter, but that goofy sister of mine cut out on you before I got the chance." Darcy saying, "I know your trade, Walter. As soon as I got my release from prison, where they stuck me for making moonshine and where I learned to cut meat, I got this idea and come directly to you with a moneymaking proposition. You ready? I bring you all the meat you think you can sell and give it to you, no money up front. What are you paying now for beef, around seventeen dollars a hunnert weight? What I deliver won't cost you nothing. I bring you steers stripped of their hides and bled out, packed in ice. All you do is cut steaks and sell 'em and we split the take down the middle."

Walter said, "Where do you come by this meat you deliver free of charge?"

"Out of pastures. I rustle 'em up."

Walter asked Honey's brother if he was aware of the rules and regulations imposed by the government on the sale of meat. How it has to be inspected and approved or they don't put a stamp on it.

Darcy said, "Jesus Christ, don't you see what I'm offering you? Fuck the government, I'll get you all the meat you want to sell at whatever you ask, not what the government says to charge. You sell it without your customers having to use any ration stamps. Don't you have German friends dying to serve a big pot roast every Sunday? Aren't you tired of the government telling you how to run your business? Having days there isn't any meat to sell?"

"You're breaking the law," Walter said.

"No shit."

"You can go to prison."

"I've been there. You want the meat or not?"

"How do you kill the animal?"

"Shoot her between the eyes with a .45. She throws her head, looks at you cockeyed, and falls down."

"Are you serious?"

"Don't the cow have to be dead before you skin her?"

"I could show you a way," Walter said, "that doesn't destroy the brains."

"That mean we have a deal?"

It was tempting. Not only make money, take care of Vera Mezwa and Dr. Taylor. Send a few double sirloins to Joe Aubrey.

Walter said, "But I don't know you."

Darcy said, "The hell you talking about? We was brother-in-laws for Christ sake. I trusted you with my sister, didn't I? You ever hit her I'd of come here and broke your jaw. No, me and you don't have nothing to worry about, we's partners. The only difference, you're a Kraut and I'm American."

Walter said, "Well . . ." and asked Darcy if he'd seen his sister or spoken to her lately, curious, wondering about Honey, what she was doing.

"I ain't seen her yet or called," Darcy said. "I'll drop by sometime and surprise her."

Walter said, "Oh, you know where she lives?"

Now the ones were here who needed his help the most, coming at the worst time. Or, was it the best time, if they were to play a part in his destiny?

The Afrika Korps officers walked in the shop and he knew Jurgen immediately from 1935, still youthful, smiling, the same beautiful boy he had known ten years ago. Walter wanted to put his arms around him—well, take him by the shoulders in a manly way, slip an arm around to pat his back. Ask why he had stopped writing after Poland. Ah, and Otto Penzler, Waffen-SS, of that elite group who chose combat over herding Jews into boxcars.

He said to Otto, "Major, your bearing gives you away. The moment you walked in the door I knew you were *Schutzstaffeln*, ready to dispose of your suit, one I see was crudely made from a uniform."

Walter stopped. He didn't mean to sound critical of the suit, made under duress in a prison camp, and said, "Although I must say the suit did serve you. It brought you here undetected?"

They couldn't stay in the rooms upstairs. No, on that day in October they entered the butcher shop he knew he would drive them to the farm and have to let them stay, of course, until they decided what they would do next.

Unless, fate had sent them here—not for Walter to help *them*. The other way around, for them to help *him*. Why not?

He could explain who he was and what he intended to do without giving the whole thing away. Tell them his mysterious connection to Heinrich Himmler and their roles in the history of the German Reich, their destinies. They knew Himmler's destiny. By now he must have rid Europe of most of its Jews and was the Führer's logical successor. Walter, meanwhile squinting at his destiny, knew he would not be dealing with the Jewish problem. The press here portrayed Himmler as the most hated man in the world. Even people Walter knew who were vocally anti-Semitic said it would give them an incredible sense of relief if the Jews would go someplace else. There was talk about sending them all to live on the island of Madagascar. You don't exterminate an entire race of people. We're Christians, the Jews are a cross we must bear. They're pushy, insolent, think they're smart, they double-park in front of their delicatessens on Twelfth Street—also on Linwood—and what do we do? Nothing. We make fun of them. Someone says, But they do make the movies we go to see. Well, not Walter. The last movie he saw was *Gone With the Wind*. He thought Clark Gable the block-ade runner was good, but the rest of the movie a waste of time. Walter had better things to do, work toward becoming as well known as Himmler, per-haps even a Nazi saint. He had finally decided yes, of course tell Otto and Jurgen what you intend to do. They were Afrika Korps officers, heroes them-selves. Tell them they are the only ones in the world who will know about the event before it happens.

The only ones if he didn't count Joe Aubrey in Georgia, his friend in the restaurant business who owned a string of Mr. Joe's Rib Joints, all very popular down there. Though lately Negro soldiers from the North were "acting uppity," Joe said, coming in and demanding service, and he was thinking of selling his chain. Joe had an airplane, a single-engine Cessna he'd fly to Detroit and take Walter for rides and show him how to work the controls. Walter had come to consider Joe Aubrey his best friend, an American who never stopped being sympathetic to the Nazi cause. He would fly up to Detroit and take Walter for a spin, fly around Detroit, swoop under the Ambassador Bridge and pull out over Canada and Walter would say to his friend Joe Aubrey, "What a shame you aren't in the Luftwaffe, you'd be an ace by now." Joe Au-brey thought he knew what Walter had in mind, but no idea how he'd pull it off. The prospect got him excited.

"Goddamn it, Walter, I can't wait."

What was today? The eighth of April. Twelve days to go.

Seven

They came out the side door from the kitchen, Jurgen saying, "I told him you'll go mad and run away if you aren't let out of the house."

"The confinement is worse than the camp," Otto said, "Walter so afraid someone will recognize us. I don't see how it's possible from the photos in the post office."

"I told him you want to see what our bombers have been doing."

"What I want," Otto said, "desperately, is to leave this place and find something to do until the war ends. And I would like to speak German, which you refuse to do, you have become so American."

"You talk to Madi and Rudi."

"Yes, about chickens."

"Ride in front with Walter, he loves to speak German."

"Walter doesn't converse, he makes speeches. He says the greatest all-out attack in the history of modern warfare, the Ardennes Offensive, was stopped. What they call the Battle of the Bulge. Yes, we were pushed back, but it does not mean we are defeated."

Jurgen picked it up saying, "Not as long as the fire of National Socialism burns within us."

"Walter says 'burns within our breast.'"

"He thinks we might want to see an exhibit of war souvenirs at Hudson's, a department store downtown."

"Guns and samurai swords?"

"The usual stuff Americans bring home to show they were in the war. Or what they bought off someone if they weren't. Helmets with bullet holes. Maybe you'll see your Iron Cross the Yank took from you. Walter said he'll drop us off and pick us up in a couple of hours. You know by now," Jurgen said, "Walter's a coward. His claim to fame, he looks like Himmler."

"And takes himself seriously," Otto said. "He snaps on his pince-nez he becomes the lunatic's twin brother. Walter is as mad as Heinrich but not as naughty. He wants so desperately to be a real Nazi and I can't help him." Otto said, "Jurgen, I have to get away from this place."

They walked to the back of the house, Otto in his new double-breasted gray suit, his homburg cocked at a conservative angle, the suit and hat Walter's gifts to him. Jurgen wore a tweed jacket that had cost Walter thirty-nine dollars, the felt hat he got for six-fifty.

There he was by the car, gunmetal gray shining hot in the sun, the Ford sedan always polished. What Jurgen was wondering as they approached the car, how he might get a duplicate key to the ignition. Though in an emergency he could hotwire it.

From Farmington, in Saturday small-town traffic, Walter turned onto Grand River Avenue, telling them in German the road was a straight line southeast to downtown Detroit, twenty-two miles to Woodward Avenue and the J.L. Hudson Company. From the backseat Jurgen looked out at miles of farmland, pastures, and planted fields not yet showing a crop, the Ford rolling along at thirty-five miles an hour. Gradually there was more to see, filling stations and a few stores, now used-car lots as they passed Eight Mile Road, the city limits, while Walter explained meat rationing to Otto, in German.

Jurgen was thinking that if Otto insisted on leaving, he should go with him, keep him out of trouble, if that was possible. Or, if he wanted to go, let him, and stop worrying about him. But first, at least try to convince him he should stay here to wait out the war. He did hear what Walter was telling Otto when he stopped thinking and paid attention.

How the United States produced 25 million pounds of meat a year, the armed forces and their allies, England and Russia, getting eight million pounds of it, leaving 17 million pounds for the 121 million meat eaters in America, and it amounted to two and a half pounds a week for each meat eater, counting a child and a person who was ill as half a meat eater. Walter said, "The motto butchers must live by is 'Sell it or smell it.' Meat goes bad. If you hold out meat for good customers and they don't come in? Throw it away. You have to sell meat on the basis of first come, first served. But if we have enough meat that everyone in America can have two and a half pounds a week, why are there meat shortages? Because when German U-boats torpedo and sink ships carrying meat, hundreds of thousands of pounds of it going to the war in Europe, they then have to send more. And where do they get it? From the seventeen million pounds meant for butcher shops and I put a sign in my window NO MEAT TODAY. The government won't reveal that German U-boats caused the meat shortage, it's a military secret. It becomes a mystery to the meat eaters. They cry and complain 'Why is there no meat for us? Why are we giving our meat to the Russians?'"

He told Otto, "Go to a high-class restaurant or a nightclub and order a steak. Don't faint when I say it will cost you as much as seven dollars. You believe people will pay that much for a porterhouse steak? They do, because so many are making money working in war plants. Some of them eat out three times a day. You can buy black market meat almost anywhere. A chuck roast with a ceiling price of thirty-one cents a pound? Maybe you pay seventy-five cents a pound if you must have it. Pay the price, you don't have to give the butcher stamps from your ration book. People don't think buying black market meat is a bad thing to do. It was the same during Prohibition, people drank illegal alcohol because it wasn't the business of the government if they drank or not."

Jurgen said, "What happens if you get caught selling meat on the black?"

He saw Walter look at his rearview mirror.

"The government penalizes you, makes you stop doing business for a time, thirty days, sixty days. If they want, they can put you out of business until the war is over."

Walter spoke to Otto in German, to Jurgen in English.

He brought them all the way on Grand River Avenue, stopped for the light at Woodward where downtown was waiting for them: crowds crossing both ways in front of the car, people waiting at the curb for buses, in safety zones in the middle of Woodward for streetcars, and Walter said in English, "There is the J.L. Hudson Company over there, I believe the world's second-largest department store. Notice it takes up the entire block. When the light changes I'm going to drop you off over there on the corner, where you see the clock above the entrance to Kerns, another department store, though it doesn't compare to Hudson's. Exactly two hours from now I'll come by. Please let me find you waiting there, if you will. Under the clock." He said to Jurgen, "Go in Hudson's and ask where is the war exhibit show. You ask, please, not Otto. All right?"

They strolled among cosmetic and perfume counters, hosiery, costume jewelry, women's gloves and belts, coming to umbrellas now, across the aisle from men's neckwear and suspenders, and Jurgen stopped. He said, "There," looking up at the poster on the square white column that rose above the counter where neckties were displayed. Now Otto was looking.

BE SURE TO SEE
THE *DETROIT NEWS* & J.L. HUDSON'S
WAR SOUVENIR SHOW
In the Auditorium on the 12th floor!

"Aren't they proud of themselves," Otto said in German, "showing what they took from our comrades lying dead."

Jurgen turned his head to see a salesgirl in Gloves and Belts watching them. She couldn't have heard Otto, but someone would if he kept ranting in German.

"You know how to say pain in the ass?" Jurgen said. "It's how you're still acting. If you don't want to look at war souvenirs, tell me in English. I don't care if I see them or not."

"I would like a whiskey, a big one," Otto said, "and to dine in a good restaurant. My needs are simple."

Jurgen said, "Don't move," and walked over to the counter where the girl sold gloves and belts.

Otto watched him talking to her, the girl wide-eyed to show she was listening and would answer his question, Otto thinking he could use a girl like that to give him a bit of comfort, smile and touch his face with her hand, tell him she would do anything for him, anything at all. He had not been with a girl in more than two years, since the Italian girl in Benghazi.

Jurgen was coming back. Otto waited. Jurgen said, "The dining rooms are on the thirteenth floor, the Georgian, the Early American, and the Pine Room. Take your pick."

Eight

Honey could not believe the way the two of them kept talking, paying no attention to her: Kevin Dean the FBI agent and Carl Webster the U.S. deputy marshal, older but not that old, facing each other across the table and talking about an island in the South Pacific, Los Negros, where it turned out they'd both served but not at the same time: Kevin with the First Cavalry, ashore only two days when he was severely wounded by a Japanese grenade; Carl in the navy with a Seabee outfit, Construction Battalion Maintenance Unit 585, when he was shot, twice, and blamed Kevin for leaving two Nips hiding in the bush.

Honey sat facing the entrance to Hudson's Pine Room, full of shoppers having lunch. For a while she turned her head from one to the other as they talked back and forth. Now she found herself looking more at Carl, an old pro with a gaunt face who wasn't even forty.

Kevin said, "I don't see how you got shot, the island was secured."

Carl said, "You know what a Duck is? Not the one you eat, the kind you drive. She goes on land or water, looks like a thirty-foot landing craft with tires. We're coming back from the supply depot on Manus, the main island, with stores and a hundred and fifty cases of beer. We take the Duck into the water for forty yards and we're back on Los Negros. A minute later there's rifle fire, four shots coming out of the bush and I'm hit. Right here in the side, the fleshy part, the first time in my life I was ever shot. The two guys with me hit the deck. One of 'em, George Klein, had fallen in love with Lauren Bacall the night before watching *To Have and Have Not* on a sixteen-millimeter projector. It's the picture Lauren says to Humphrey Bogart, 'You know how to whistle, Steve?' If he wants her for anything. 'You put your lips together and blow.' The other one aboard the Duck, a fella named Elmer Whaley from someplace in Arkansas, me and Elmer were sucking on Beech-Nut scrap during the trip. I got hit and like to swallow the wad of tobacco. I remember I said, 'Boys, it's dense growth out there. We have to wait for the Nip to come to us.'"

Kevin said, "You were armed?"

"We had carbines with us."

"In case you saw Japs?"

"Your people told us the island was secured and we believed it. No, we brought the carbines along for fun, fire off a few rounds. The only trouble, our weapons were up in the bow. We couldn't get to 'em without showing ourselves. But for this trip I also had my .38, the one I'd been using in the line of duty for the past seventeen years."

"The .38 on a .45 frame," Kevin said, "the front sight filed off."

"Filed down so she'd pull like she was greased."

"That was in the book. The same gun," Kevin said, "your wife used to shoot Jack Belmont that time he was stalking you." He said to Honey, "Remember I told you about it?"

She said, "I think so," not sounding too sure.

"I looked him up," Kevin said. "Jack Belmont was on the FBI's most wanted list in 1934." He said to Carl, "He's the one his daddy was a millionaire?"

"Oris Belmont," Carl said, "sunk wells in the Glenn Pool south of Tulsa and came up a multi-multimillionaire. Jack Belmont was harum-scarum from birth. He tried to blackmail Oris for having a girlfriend. That didn't get him anything, so he set one of his dad's storage tanks afire and Oris had him sent to prison. Jack came out of McAlester and started robbing banks, show his dad he could make it on his own. Why Jack had it in for me I'll never know, but he came to my dad's place near Okmulgee stalking me. Jack got to where he was aiming a .45 at me, I'm not even looking, and Louly, bless her heart, shot him three times."

Honey remembered Kevin telling her about it, but without the details, like why she had Carl's revolver. And something about Louly being Pretty Boy Floyd's *girl* friend? Honey was thinking maybe she should read the book about Carl.

Kevin was saying, "There was another guy Louly shot, wasn't there? Another bank robber?"

"That was Joe Young they called Booger," Carl

said, "suppose to've been in Pretty Boy Floyd's gang, what he told Louly, but never was. Louly happened to be with Joe Young at a tourist court the time we showed up to arrest him."

Honey thinking, Wait. She *happens* to be there with Booger?

Carl was saying, "He opened up on us, Joe not wanting to go back to prison. We answered and there was an exchange of gunfire. Louly's in there with him, an innocent party to what was going on. She saw she was liable to get shot, bullets ripping through the door and windows. While I'm trying to get the cops, local police, to stop firing, Louly pulled a revolver from her crocheted bag and shot Joe Young, put him out of his misery."

Kevin said, "She packed a gun?"

"It was one Joe gave her. He'd told Louly he was gonna show her how to rob a bank."

Honey thinking, Do you believe this?

"I told her, after, the Oklahoma Bankers Association was prepared to give her a five-hundred-dollar reward for putting her friend out of business. She said Joe wasn't ever her friend, but did admit she had a crush on Pretty Boy Floyd. Louly met him, she was still a kid, the day he married her cousin Ruby. Then wrote letters to him while he was at Jeff City doing time. She made up a story, that Joe Young stole her stepdad's Model A and abducted her, took her to the tourist cabin. I told her, stay with that and you won't go to jail. But then the newspapers got hold of it, 'Sallisaw Girl Shoots Abductor.' Reporters started talking to Louly, wanting to hear her story, and before you know it the headline was 'Girlfriend of Pretty Boy Guns Down Mad-Dog Felon.' After a while she got over it, tired of people thinking she was Floyd's sweetie, bothering her all the time."

Kevin said, "And you married her."

"Not till she grew up. Now she's a U.S. Marine teaching jarheads how to shoot a Browning machine gun."

"You left off, you're still on the Duck," Kevin said.

"I hear the Nip coming through the growth," Carl said. "I see an Asiatic face in a dirty cap appear above the gunnel. I shot him as he's bringing up his rifle. We thought he was by himself, but now there's another one aiming a rifle at me, his face pressed against the stock. I shot him about a second before he fired and it threw him off. I got hit in the leg 'stead of between the eyes."

"That got you home?"

"By then I'd served my country and had a tattoo and a Purple Heart." He said to Kevin, "They must've given you one of those."

"Yes sir, I got a Heart. After that I was invited to attend FBI training."

"That's all, they didn't give you a medal?"

"Not for ending up in a VA hospital."

"They gave me a Navy Cross," Carl said, "for doing the two Nips. I think because nothing was going on at the time, the island, you keep telling me, being secured."

Carl missed Kevin's helpless look. He'd turned to Honey Deal.

"I can't wait to hear you tell me about Walter."

She liked his eyes and the way he was looking at her that had nothing to do with Walter. She said, "If you all are through telling war stories, why don't we order? I have to get back to being a sales-girl, put on my smile."

Carl said, "I was hoping we'd have time to talk."

She said, "I could meet you after work for a drink," and saw a gleam come into his soft brown eyes.

Carl said, "Tell me when the last time was you saw Walter."

"The day I walked out, November ninth, 1939."

"You think about him?"

"Hardly ever."

"You want to go with me when I see him?"

It stopped her. She saw Walter staring, he opens the door and she's in his life again. He looks stunned. Well, confused.

"Really?" Honey said, wanting to smile but held off. "What would I do, introduce you?"

"I think you'll make him nervous," Carl said. "I'll get him talking, ask him questions. You watch, jump in when you think he's lying."

Kevin said, "I'm there too, aren't I?"

"The only trouble," Carl said, "if you're with us—Walter's already told you he's never laid eyes on Jurgen and Otto, and he'll stick to it, realizing it's why I'm talking to him. I want to edge around the two Krauts and take him by surprise, get him admitting things before he knows it, while Honey stares and has him fidgeting. But what you can do for me," Carl said, "find out if Walter's at the butcher shop or the farm."

Honey watched Kevin, the poor guy not knowing whether to cry or act like a cool federal agent. What he did, he stuck to the job saying to Carl, "You don't know where anything is around here."

Honey said, "I know where the butcher shop is. Give me the address of the farm and I'll see Carl gets there."

"All right, fine," Kevin said, looking at Carl, "if that's how you want to do it."

Taking it like a man, Honey thought and looked at Carl, wanting to say, We work pretty well together, don't we? What she said was, "Are we having lunch or not?"

Carl ordered the chicken potpie.

Kevin asked the waitress if he could have the Canadian cheese soup and, let's see, a club sandwich, toasted, no mayonnaise?

Honey was hungry but chose the Maurice salad for now. She saw herself with Carl until he went back to Oklahoma.

Nine

The elevator stopped twice on the way up to let people crowd on, Otto and Jurgen pressed against the back of the car by the time they came to thirteen. Otto waited while people in front of them walked off the car with some purpose, knowing where they were going, but not the two old ladies in front of him. Otto saw the wide-open entrance to a restaurant, people at rows of tables that reached to windows showing sunlight, Otto thinking he would like a table back there to look out at the city, the streetcars, the crowds of people, uniforms among them but not that many. They called this city the Arsenal of Democracy. Oh, really? He saw nothing to tell him these people were at war. Jurgen had gotten off and Otto saw him now standing with the hostess. The two old ladies made it out of the elevator and came to a stop and Otto stopped. He saw Jurgen looking over the room of tables with the hostess pointing her pencil, a good-looking woman, her hair done . . . Jurgen turned and now he was looking this way at the elevator, then holding up his hand to tell Otto *Halt*, Jurgen shaking his head. Otto turned and stepped in the elevator again. Jurgen had seen someone he didn't expect to see, didn't *want* to see, and that was enough. He was coming now, his face, his expression, telling Otto nothing. Now he was stopped by the two old ladies in front of him, Otto watching from the elevator as the door closed and the Negro girl at the wheel turned the handle of the circular control and said as the car rose, "Fourteenth floor. Beauty salons, Hudson's Americana Salon and the Executive Barbershop. Employment office, employees' cafeteria, and the J.L. Hudson Company hospital."

Otto said to her, "Where are the books?"

On the mezzanine, tables and tables of books, nearly all by American authors. This was acceptable to Otto, he believed Americans wrote the greatest variety of readable books found in any language, all kinds of novels by authors who kept you turning pages. One of his favorites, about the confident gentleman who addressed his friend as "old sport." He also liked the author who used a blunt way of writing his stories set in Spain and Africa, not North Africa, East Africa, where the tall, handsome American on safari with his wife had "bolted like a rabbit" in the face of a full-grown wounded lion coming at him. He and Jurgen had both read the story while in the Oklahoma prison camp. Jurgen didn't understand the wife turning on the poor man, insulting him to his face. "Because he proved himself a coward," Otto said. Jurgen said, "But it wasn't his job to kill lions." Otto remembered saying, "What does the white hunter with the cold blue eyes tell him? 'In Africa no woman ever misses her lion and no white man ever bolts.'" Otto liked the woman using her husband's cowardice as an excuse to sleep with the white hunter, Robert Wilson, who brought a double-size cot on these trips, anticipating the strange behavior of American women. Otto liked the guns too, the white hunter's big-bore .505 Gibbs, and the 6.5 Mannlicher the wife used on her husband once he had redeemed himself and she realized she had lost him, shooting Francis Macomber "two inches up and a little to one side of the base of his skull." He called her Margot. Otto would see himself having a drink with Margot, smiling, toasting her with his glass.

He came to a table laden with green and gold copies of a book, *Forever Amber*, some of them upright, the woman on the cover of the novel looking at him, showing Otto bare shoulders but not much in the way of breasts. Now he was aware of a woman on the other side of the table watching him as he looked at the woman on the cover who must be Amber, though the blond ringlets made her look so innocent.

"Amber St. Claire," the woman across the table from him said and then recited, "uses her wits, beauty and courage to . . . well, become the favorite mistress of the merry monarch, Charles II."

Otto raised his eyes to this one in a black suit with trousers, a young woman, much more interesting than the one on the book cover, this one up to something.

Otto said, "Is it a good story?"

His accent didn't make her hesitate.

"It was banned in Boston, and you haven't read it?"

Otto said, "No," and smiled at her. He felt good and couldn't help smiling.

She wore round glasses in thin black frames, red lip rouge, no jewelry, no blouse beneath the slim, the very slim black suit he knew was expensive. She was tall, still a girl without being girlish, clean dark hair to her shoulders. He liked the easy refinement about this one he believed was up to something.

She said, "Are you a Vicki Baum fan? She's just out with *Once in Vienna*. . . . "

"I don't think I've ever read a book," Otto said, "written by someone named Vicki."

He watched her stroke her hair from her face with the tips of her fingers lacquered bright red, then toss her hair and he liked the way she did it, though it was only a gesture. He watched her turn to pick up a book from the table behind her and come around to him saying, "Werner Richter's *Re-educating Germany*. You know Richter?"

"He was Weimar, pre-Nazi," Otto said, "from olden times." He said, "Tell me your name."

She said, "I'm Aviva Friedman."

"Really?" Otto said. "You're a Jewess?"

"And you're a Kraut, a Nazi?"

"I'm an officer in the SS," Otto said, wanting to smile.

Aviva said, "Oh dear."

And now he did, he smiled because he felt good knowing he could talk to this woman, this girl who was up to something.

Otto said, "You remind me of a woman I knew in Benghazi. She was Italian." He smiled again and removed his homburg and laid it across two copies of *Forever Amber.* "I was in love with her."

"That's right, they're on your side," Aviva said, "the Italians."

"For whatever good they do us."

She said, "You look much younger without the hat."

"I *am* young, and free," Otto said, looking at his watch, "for the next one and a half hours. Then I'm taken back and told not to leave the premises."

She kept staring at him.

"You're a German prisoner of war."

"And if you tell anyone," Otto said, "I'll put the Gestapo on you. I told you I'm in the SS."

"Did you ever send people to death camps?"

"I was in North Africa with Rommel, commanding tanks."

"The Italian girl you think I resemble, she was there?"

"Yes, in Libya. She was a nurse at the hospital. She placed a dressing on my chest, where it was burned, and I fell in love with her."

"You're like what's his name, in *A Farewell to Arms.*"

"Frederic Henry," Otto said. "Are you sure you aren't Italian?"

"You know the nurse in real life," Aviva said, "wasn't an English girl, like the one in the book."

"No, I believe she was Polish," Otto said.

"I know what I bet you'd like," Aviva said, "*Leave Her to Heaven*." But right away said, "No," turned to the table behind her, came around with a book saying, "*The Prisoner*, by Ernst Lothar." She turned the book over to read from the back cover, "'From the Normandy beachhead to an American prison camp in Colorado, the story of the unmaking of a Nazi.' What do you think?"

Otto said, "Tell me what you're up to."

She said in an offhand way, "I'm curious to know what you read."

"For what reason?"

"I knew you were German. I should say I knew you weren't American and I guessed you were a Kraut."

"I don't care to be called that."

Aviva said, "I don't care to be called a Jewess. What are you, Lutheran?"

"At one time, yes."

"What do you call women who are Lutheran, Lutheranesses?"

Otto said, "You have a point. But what do you care what I read?"

"First tell me your name."

"Otto Penzler."

"Otto, I was making conversation, that's all. You're an interesting-looking guy. Then I hear your accent, I find out yes, you're German, and I thought oh, wow, I should get to know this guy."

"Why don't you think I look American?"

"I don't know, the way you carry yourself. You don't act like an American."

"But why do you want to know me?"

She seemed to have to think about her answer.

"I don't live here," Aviva said. "But when I come to Detroit I always stop at Hudson's. I love this store, and the book department, the tables and tables of books. I came to Detroit this time to buy the typescript of a play by Bertolt Brecht."

"Which play?"

"You know Brecht?"

"The Communist playwright."

"He digs Marx," Aviva said, "but he's never been a card-carrying Communist. You know his work?"

"*Mutter Courage und ihre Kinder.* I saw the one he did with Kurt Weill before they burned his books and threw him out of Germany, *Die Dreigroschenoper.* You see it, it's the *Threepenny Opera.* What is he doing now?"

"He's in Hollywood working on movies," Aviva said, "Fritz Lang's *Hangmen Also Die* with Brian Donlevy. It's about the assassination of Reinhard Heydrich, Himmler's alter ego. Brecht wrote the story, not the screenplay. When you write a screenplay there's always someone telling you what to write, and he's not good at writing to order. But the main thing Brecht's doing, he's getting ready to show his new play." She stopped and came around to the end of the *Forever Amber* display to be closer to Otto. She said, "Can I trust you?"

"Aviva," Otto said, and had to smile at her. "Can you trust me—you can do anything you want with me. Don't call the police and I won't send the Gestapo after you."

"Tell me," Aviva said, "they let you out for the day, the afternoon. Don't tell me you escaped, okay? If I can trust you, Otto, I've got a job for you. Translating Brecht's play into English."

"What does he call it?"

"*The Caucasian Chalk Circle.*"

Otto said, "*Der kaukasische Kreidekreis,*" mumbling the words. "What is it about?"

"I have no idea. It's sort of based on a Chinese play five or six hundred years old, *The Chalk Circle.*"

"Brecht is a friend of yours?"

"No, the guy I've been doing business with, he's in the army, in Hollywood fooling around and met Brecht. I think he sold him something. They're having drinks at Brecht's house, some kind of party going on. A copy of the play is sitting on the coffee table the whole while. Brecht got sloshed and went to bed."

Otto said, "Yes?" starting to smile.

"Pete had his eye on the script the whole time. He left with the script under his jacket and called me from his hotel. Asked if I'd be interested in buying the play."

"Why did he think you might want it?"

"We've got something going. Pete's in army transportation, he's a Detroit mob guy who somehow got drafted. For the past year he's been selling me paintings and art objects he and his guys smuggled out of France. All the stuff the Nazis stole, Pete took a lot of it off their hands."

"Important works of art?"

"Some, but it's all marketable."

"This is what you do, you fence stolen goods?"

"I find art collectors who look at my catalog and get a hard-on. I sell paintings that hung in the Louvre to people living in New York and Palm Beach, at a discount. I still make a pile of money and the collectors give me a big hug."

"How do you get into this business?"

"My dad got it going. He was a captain in the merchant marine, retired now, he's almost seventy. I called him to see if we should buy a play by Brecht, one that's still unknown to the world. Dad said he'd check with book collectors, see how much any of them were interested. I could tell he liked the idea. He said, 'Offer Pete five hundred, but don't go over a grand.'"

Otto said, "You got it for . . . ?"

"Two-fifty. I told Pete we'd be happy to give him a percentage if we get any interest in it. You play it straight with this guy."

"If you're going to sell it," Otto said, "why do you want a translation?"

"I'd like to know what it's about."

"You could go to prison."

"Everything I sell comes out of Europe. Good luck trying to trace it back. Pete's guys bring it into the country. I don't do any of that."

"And now you go home?"

"What I'm thinking," Aviva said, "you ought to come with me. You could start doing the translation on the boat."

Otto said, "The boat?" He loved this girl already.

"A forty-foot Chris-Craft. It's tied up at the yacht club on Belle Isle."

"You have a crew?"

"I'm the skipper," Aviva said. "I have a gook—excuse me—a Filipino boy who handles the lines and serves drinks in a white jacket. We head down the Detroit River past Ford Rouge and the steel mills to Lake Erie and we're almost home." Aviva said to Otto grinning at her, "Have you ever been to Cleveland?"

The first thing Walter said to Jurgen getting in the front seat, "Where is Otto?" Walter anxious, looking for Otto in his homburg in the crowd waiting for the light to change. Now cars behind them were blowing horns. Walter didn't move. He looked at the rearview mirror and said, "Be quiet!" But now he did put the Ford in gear and began to crawl past the block-long front of Hudson's.

"We were separated," Jurgen said.

"How could that happen? You were careful?"

"He got on an elevator without me," Jurgen said.

"You were arguing?"

"The door closed before I could get on. There's nothing to worry about, Walter. He'll be along. Circle the block, I'm sure we'll see him."

"I knew something like this would happen," Walter said. "Why I was against you going out in public, your pictures in every post office in the country."

Jurgen said, "Yes, but do we look like those lost souls? I hope not."

It took Walter ten minutes to drive several blocks past signs that refused to allow him to turn, finally coming roundabout past the corner again, Walter straining to find Otto in the crowd.

"Do you see him? No, because he isn't there. You let him out of your sight and now he's gone. We'll read about him in the newspaper, escaped prisoner of war arrested by the police."

"If he's caught he won't tell on you. We know you're up to something with the lovely Vera and Dr. Taylor who doesn't speak. Why won't you tell us about it?"

"I can tell *you*," Walter said, "but not with Otto present. I worry he's going crazy."

"He's always been crazy," Jurgen said. "It got him an Iron Cross in North Africa. I think he could get by here, with a little luck." Jurgen believed he could tell Walter almost anything. "Otto can be charming, if he has a good enough reason. I'm not going to worry about him."

Not with Carl Webster here.

Relentless Carl, not only knowing Jurgen would be in Detroit, but also having lunch where he and Otto were going to dine. Not the Georgian or the Early American restaurant, or the cafeteria in the basement the girl operating the elevator told him about, no, in the Pine Room.

Carl coming closer and closer.

How did he do that?

It was funny, because Jurgen wasn't surprised to see him sitting there. Startled, yes, for a moment but not actually that surprised. He knew that Carl, sooner or later, would be on his trail.

He could see himself sitting down with Carl, talking, getting along. A bar would be a good place, the Brass Rail they passed on the way to Hudson's. Or a nightclub he saw advertised in the paper, Frank Barbaro's Bowery. It offered entertainment, a romantic baritone, dinners from a dollar and a half up. What else? The room was air-cooled for your comfort.

Sometime after the war.

He would have to be on his toes now, wondering where he would see Carl next.

Ten

Carl liked the way she offered him a drink when he came to pick her up, Honey saying he could have anything he wanted as long as it was rye. He liked her in the black sweater and skirt and the way the slit in the skirt opened as she walked to the kitchen. She returned with drinks and offered him a Lucky, telling him in a semiserious tone, "I'm sorry, but I seem to be out of Beech-Nut scrap." Carl smiled, appreciating her effort, her memory even more. She paid attention to what he said.

Now they were at opposite ends of the cushy sofa with their highballs and cigarettes, both sitting back with their legs crossed: Carl showing a cowboy boot, old but polished, Honey a plain black pump hanging from her toes, showing Carl the delicate arch of her foot. She asked him if he always wore cowboy boots.

"About all my life," Carl said.

"Because you live in Oklahoma?"

"They're my shoes," Carl said. He asked if she was nervous, about to see Walter again.

"I'm looking forward to it," Honey said. "I can't wait to see how you handle him."

"Was he ever mean to you, lose his temper?"

"He never hit me, if that's what you're wondering."

"Does he own a gun?"

"He had a shotgun he'd take to Georgia, and go bird shooting."

"You never went along?"

"He'd meet his friend Joe Aubrey."

"The one with the chain of restaurants," Carl said. "I read the sheet the Bureau has on him. He has a plane?"

"A Cessna. He'd fly up here from Georgia," Honey said, "take Walter for rides and show him how to work the controls. That was in '39. I don't know if he's been up here since."

"He comes to see Walter a couple of times a year," Carl said. "Or Walter takes a bus to Griffin, south of Atlanta. Saves wear on his tires. You met Joe?"

"I stayed out of his way," Honey said. "I considered Joe Aubrey as big a lout as Fritz Kuhn. I've always felt Joe would love to shoot somebody."

"Why's that?"

"He hates colored people. I'd be surprised if he hasn't taken part in lynchings."

"He's never been arrested."

"He hates Jews and what he calls Commonists."

"How about Vera Mezwa?"

"She came after my time with Walter. Vera and Dr. Michael George Taylor. I don't know either of them."

"You think they're German agents?"

"Kevin does and he knows more about them than I do. I think they're serious about working for the Nazis. They like the idea of *sieg heil*ing each other and having secret meetings. But where do they get information about war production?"

Carl said, "From newspapers?"

"That's what I think. They send information written in invisible ink and that makes them spies. I think the FBI keeps waiting for them to actually do something subversive, wishing they'd hurry up and make a move before the war ends."

"Kevin told you about the Afrika Korps guys."

"The ones you're positive are here," Honey said. "You don't want to come right out and ask Walter about them directly. You said you want to edge around the two guys, try and surprise Walter into giving them up."

He liked her remembering what he'd said at lunch, about edging around. "Will you stare at him?"

"Blow smoke at him. You can torture him," Honey said, "it's okay with me. I'll help you."

Carl said, "Pull out his fingernails?"

"I don't know—he bites them down so close, gnaws on them like a squirrel. It'd be hard to get a purchase. You have a gun, don't you? Stick the barrel in his mouth and ask him what you want to know. Walter's the most serious person you'll ever meet in your life. Tell him something outrageous with a straight face, he'll buy it."

"Kevin said you told him a couple of pretty funny jokes that sailed right by him."

"Walter analyzes jokes. But he has no imagination, so he doesn't think they're funny. He won't accept the grasshopper that goes in a bar and orders a drink. Or a guy being in love with a sheep. But there was one I did tell him—I might not've mentioned to Kevin—and Walter surprised me, he sorta laughed."

Carl glanced toward the window as Honey said, "About a guy who tells his friend he's got an excruciating pain in his bum."

"Tell it in the car," Carl said. "I want to see Walter's place while it's still light."

They were on Ten Mile now, a narrow road that needed patches of blacktop, open fields on both sides, the Pontiac heading into the sun. Carl said, "The guy tells his friend he's got an awful pain in his butt."

"And the friend," Honey said, "tells him he has piles and what kind of cream to use for it. The guy tries the cream but still has the awful pain. He runs into another friend and tells him about it. This one says no, creams don't work. He tells the guy to have a cup of tea, then take the tea leaves and pack them up his behind like a poultice. The guy does it, has a cup of tea every day for a week and stuffs the leaves up his heinie. The guy's still in terrible pain, so finally he goes to see a doctor. The doctor tells him to drop his pants and bend over. He looks up the guy's keester and says, 'Yes, I see you have piles. And I see you're going to go on a long journey.'"

Honey grinned watching Carl, Carl laughing,

smiling as he looked at her and then at the road again still smiling, saying he could see the little doctor with a flashlight, down behind the guy bent over the examining table.

"I know," Honey said, "you can't help picturing the doctor. I see him the same way, a little guy. I told Walter the joke and couldn't believe it when he smiled. Then laughed—no, he chuckled a few times. I had to ask him, 'You get it?' Walter said, 'Do I understand the doctor is reading the tea leaves? Of course.'"

"Maybe Walter's been to fortune-tellers," Carl said.

"Or he has piles," Honey said.

They turned off Ten Mile onto Farmington Road and Carl said, "That must be the house up ahead."

A pickup truck pulling an empty stock trailer came riding hard across a field raising dust, approaching them on Honey's side of the road and Carl braked and shifted down. The truck came to a stop at the edge of the road they were on and Honey said, "Oh, my God," as they rolled past. "I think that's my brother driving the truck."

It turned onto Farmington Road, Carl watching it in the rearview mirror, and saw it turn again as it came to Ten Mile.

"When'd he get out of Eddyville?"

Honey, sideways in the seat to watch through the rear window, came around to Carl.

"You know about Darcy?"

"Not as much as I'd like. His file's right next to yours at the Bureau."

Eleven

Walter came in the side door that led to the kitchen and went to the sink thinking of Otto, still thinking of Otto since trying to spot his homburg in the downtown crowd of people. Jurgen had been helping Darcy bring the three cows and a heifer out of the stock trailer and work them into the pen joined to the barn, the abattoir. Darcy spoke to Jurgen for a few minutes and left with his trailer. Jurgen would be in the barn now, he was no trouble. Otto was the problem.

They came home without him and Madi said in English, "Where is the Nazi?" To the old woman they were "Jurgen and the Nazi," the Nazi demanding she and Rudi speak to him always in German and asked them one question after another, like an immigration official, to keep them talking. Rudi didn't mind talking to him, the two sitting at the kitchen table with a bottle of whiskey talking about the war, the Nazi telling Rudi of North Africa and Italian women.

She asked Walter, "Where is he, the Nazi?"

Walter saw hope in her eyes. He told Madi, reasonable with her since she was his aunt, they would have to wait and see if Otto could find his way here from downtown.

"He tell the police he's lost," Madi said, "they put him in jail? You should pin a note on his coat that say where he lives."

This was earlier.

Peeled potatoes in a pan of water waited for Madi to light the burner. Walter could smell the pork roast in the oven. He drew a glass of water at the sink, stepped over to the oven to open the door, and threw the water over the roast. Madi came in from setting the table in the dining room and caught him. It wasn't the first time. She would ask in English why he wet the roast. Walter would tell her it was burning. Madi would ask why he thought she wanted to burn a roast? More than half a century cooking every day of her life she had never burned a roast.

"You want me to cook for you good dinners? Stay out of my kitchen. Go see your visitors."

Walter was drying his hands on a dish towel.

"What visitors?"

"The car drove up to the house while you throwing water on the roast."

Walter left the kitchen, still holding the dish towel, moved around the dining table set for two, himself and Jurgen, to stand at one side of the dining room window. He moved the blinds apart and saw the Pontiac parked in the drive, no one in it.

The bell chimed.

Going into the living room Walter told himself this would be about Otto. They found him. They want to know if he lives here. Here? No, they inform him—this was better—they told Otto to stop but he kept running and they were forced to shoot him, and want you to identify the body. The FBI. They had already asked him if he knew Otto, and asked him again and again. They might try to trick him this time. All right, he would say as he always did, "Who?" and shake his head. "I never heard of this man."

Walter unlocked the door thinking if they wanted him to identify Otto dead he still wouldn't know him. He wouldn't have to worry about him either, ever again.

He opened the door.

It wasn't about Otto.

No, because he was looking at Honig standing not more than a few feet away, Honig smiling at him and saying, "Hi, Walter." The man with her said his name and showed his identification in a leather case—not FBI—with a badge pinned inside, a star in a circle. The name, Carl something, meant nothing to Walter. My God, no, he was looking at Honig for the first time in more than five years.

Carl glanced at her. He said, "You're right," and looked at Walter again. "I've never seen two people look more alike. Mr. Schoen, you're the spittin' image of Heinrich Himmler." Now he brought a folded copy of a *Time* magazine cover from his coat pocket. Carl opened it, looked at Himmler's portrait and handed the page to Walter. "This was two months ago. He's starting to look less like you. More like he's dead. I don't think they needed to put the crossed bones under his chin."

Walter didn't say a word. He looked at the illustration and folded the page in his hands.

"It's amazing," Carl said, aware of Walter's hands folding the page again and folding it again into a small, tight square. "Honey told me you're Himmler's twin brother. I look at you, Mr. Schoen, and I have to believe it."

Walter nodded, once. He said, "It's true," and looked at Honig again. "Heinrich and I were born in Munich in the same hospital on the same day and at exactly the same time and, for a reason I cannot explain, we were separated."

"You had the same mother," Carl said. "I mean if you're twins."

"Yes, Heinrich would have been born of my mother."

"What about *his* mother?"

Walter said, "You mean a woman who poses as his mother. Heinrich once said if the Führer asked him to shoot his own mother, as an act of unconditional loyalty, he would do it. Why not? The woman isn't his real mother." He looked at Honig. "Remember we spoke of this, wondering about her?"

"A lot," Honey said.

Carl said, "You tried to locate her?"

"I wrote to the hospital in Munich several times. I ask if they have a record of Heinrich Himmler's birth. They have never answered me."

Carl said, "Your mom didn't bring both of you home from the hospital?"

"How would I know that?"

"You never asked her about it?"

"By the time I was older, and learned the accepted version of Heinrich's birth, she had passed away."

"You didn't ask your dad?"

"Of course I did. He said, 'Are you crazy?'"

"You don't remember playing kick the can with Himmler when you were kids?"

"Look," Walter said. "There are questions I can't answer. The proof of our being twins is our identical appearance and the fact of our being born on the same day at the same hour—"

"But you don't remember him."

"I never *saw* him."

Carl said, "Walter, it's okay with me if you're Himmler's twin brother. No, what I've been wondering, looking at your spread, if you planned to fatten up that heifer in the stock pen. She goes about eight-fifty now? Give her twelve pounds of corn a day mixed with seven pounds of ground alfalfa hay, you can put another two hundred pounds on her by the end of summer. I know some families in Oklahoma operate home-kills and do all right."

Carl shifted his weight from one foot to the other and bent over enough to squeeze his left thigh.

"Walter, you mind if we sit down someplace? I'll tell you about a cow outfit I worked when I was a boy. Damn, but I have a war wound bothers me when I'm on my feet too long. I got shot twice but managed to nail the bugger."

Walter was squinting at him now, looking confused.

Carl liked the way it was going.

He said, "Put your mind at ease, Wally, it wasn't a Kraut I shot. Was a Nip taking a killer aim at me."

Honey didn't get into it until they were seated in the living room in old red-velvet-covered furniture Honey thought was depressing. Walter hadn't stopped looking at her. She said, "Why don't you turn on some lamps, Walter, so we can see each other. Or open the blinds."

Walter said, "Of course," turned on one lamp and then another, both with twenty-five-watt bulbs, the kind Honey remembered the cheapskate always used. She felt good being with Carl. She loved show-offs who were funny—Carl saying the Nip was taking a killer aim at him. They sat together on a settee opposite Walter in his armchair with an extra cushion to let him sit higher, the fili-greed back of the chair towering over him. Walter's seat of judgment. Much bigger than his chair in their old place, Walter sitting hunched over the ra-dio. This is what he'd be like if she'd stayed with him: wearing the same gray wool sweater but-toned up, the same Nazi haircut she called a nutsy cut; the same—no, his rimless glasses didn't pinch on—and if she let him get close she knew he'd have the same bad breath. But not the same heel-clicker she met in front of church.

Honey said, "How's your sister, she still a nun?"

"Sister Ludmilla," Walter said. "She's a Cistercian of the Strict Observance now. They never speak."

"I thought she was an IHM sister. Doesn't she teach school in Detroit?"

"She's still here but left that order for a much different life, as a Cistercian. I congratulated her having the will to live a life of prayer and silence."

"She seemed normal," Honey said, "the times I met her. You get her to join, Walter, so you wouldn't have to talk to her anymore? I remember her telling you Jesus is more important in your life than Hitler."

Carl said, "Ask him about your brother."

She was still looking at Walter. He heard Carl but Walter's expression didn't change. Honey said, "We saw Darcy driving out of your property with a stock trailer."

"Yes, of course," Walter said, "Darcy Deal is your brother. He came to the market and introduced himself, offered to supply beef for my slaughtering business. Your brother's an outspoken fellow, isn't he?"

"He's an ex-convict," Honey said. "He tell you that?"

"Yes, of course. He asked me, would I give him the opportunity to engage in a legitimate business."

Carl said, "Where's he get the steers?"

Walter shrugged. "At stockyards, where else? He always shows me the bill of sale."

"I imagine," Carl said, "the government inspectors drive you nuts dropping in the way they do."

Walter shrugged again. "Yes, but the meat has to be graded. It's the law, so you put up with it."

Honey took his shrugs to mean he wasn't concerned; they could ask him anything they wanted.

Carl was saying, "This one fella I knew in home-kill, he'd process a few head in between the inspectors coming by. Get the meat out in a hurry to hotels in Tulsa."

Walter said, "I believe you are an officer of the law?"

"Deputy U.S. marshal, Wally. I'm not FBI."

"But you could arrest this person if you wanted?"

"I don't work in that area."

"But you came here to question me, didn't you? See if I'm selling meat on the black market?"

"No sir, I'm investigating the numbers racket in war plants. Ford Highland Park, Dodge Main in Hamtramck, Briggs Body. Organized crime, they send their guys in the plants to take bets and sell dream books. I remembered Honey lived here so I called her up."

Honey took his arm and squeezed it with both hands, smiling at Walter. "We met on a train one time."

Carl said, "Honey told me her brother was working for you . . . I wondered if you wouldn't mind my taking a look at your operation. I've worked beef in my time. My dad has a thousand acres of pecan trees."

"You're not investigating me?" Walter said.

"All I'm interested in," Carl said, "I'd like to see how you process a cow up here. I don't mean right now. It must be close to your suppertime, but when you can spare me an hour."

Walter kept staring at him.

"You're none of my business as a marshal," Carl said. "Hell, seventy percent of the people, housewives, buy a lot of their meat without stamps and pay whatever the butcher says is the price. Hell with those OPA-fixed prices. Walter"—Carl taking his time—"I'd fatten up my herd for a year, cut out a bunch and take 'em to Tulsa in my stock trailer. Stop on the way back for an ice-cream cone. My dad's property wasn't too far from a camp holding guys from the Afrika Korps. They said the only reason they surrendered they ran out of gas." Carl took time to grin. "But they seemed to be doing all right in captivity. The government hired them out to do farmwork if they wanted. The government let my dad took a bunch of 'em to gather pecans, hit the branches with bamboo fishing poles to shake 'em loose. They'd bring their lunch from the camp, sit under the trees eating their sausage and pickles, cold bratwurst sandwiches. Once in a while I'd come by and get in a conversation. I'd say, 'What's stopping you guys from walking out of here? Wait for the guards to fall asleep. But even when you do bust out you're back by dinnertime the next day.' I'd say, 'Man, all the Germans living in the U.S., you don't have any relatives would hide you if you got away?'"

Walter said, "You tempt them to try to escape, so you can shoot them?"

"Come on, Walter, I'm fooling with them, trying to understand what they think about being locked up. You see them in the chow hall three times a day eating like wolves, you understand how important food is. It's the reason when they do escape, get a few miles down the road from the camp, they turn around and come back."

"There must be some," Walter said—sounding to Honey like he was being careful, picking his words—"who escape with the intention of returning home to Germany, if they see the possibility of it."

"I know there was a German flier back in '42," Carl said, "almost got to Mexico. He's the only one comes to mind."

Walter said, "I read in the newspaper about two officers who escaped from a camp." Walter still careful. "I believe it was four or five months ago?"

"Last October," Carl said. "Yeah, they were picked up."

Honey saw Walter stopped cold.

He said, "Are you sure?"

"They broke out of Deep Fork, near my dad's place."

"This is in Oklahoma?"

"Yeah, the camp's called Deep Fork, named for a creek that runs through there. The one officer had a girlfriend lived nearby. He'd slip out and visit her every once in a while—you know, to get laid—and was counting on the girlfriend hiding them. She did for a couple of days, but must've got nervous and blew the whistle, turned them in."

"I must be thinking of two others who escaped," Walter said. "The newspaper reported a nation-wide search was on for these two."

"That'll sell papers," Carl said, "but they're the

ones I'm talking about. They made half-ass civilian suits from uniforms and drove out of the camp in a truck delivers movies."

Walter said, "Well," sounding to Honey like he was giving up. But then he said in an offhand way, "Do you happen to know their names?"

"It was a while ago," Carl said. "The girlfriend had a weird name I'd never heard before, but I can't remember hers either."

Walter said, "Why didn't I read the two officers were captured?"

Not giving up if he could help it. Honey waited for Carl to explain, if he could.

"I think there was a question of whether they should prosecute the girlfriend," Carl said, "for giving comfort to the enemy, if you know what I mean. But since she did turn them in, the U.S. attorney decided not to prosecute, keep her neighbors from throwing eggs at her and cutting off her hair. No more news about the escape was good news for the girlfriend. Pretty soon the papers stopped asking about the two guys."

"The ones you say were captured," Walter said. "Where are they now?"

"Back in camp. The one guy's Waffen-SS. I think they're the SSers in the military. The regular SS are the guys who run the extermination camps, shove live people into gas chambers. Am I right about that, Wally?"

"Do you have to call me that?"

"What? Wally?"

"My name is Walter."

"You ever go by Walt?"

"It's *Walter*."

"I tried calling him Walt," Honey said, "he had a fit."

"How about a nickname?" Carl said. "What'd your mom call you when you were a kid?"

Honey knew but waited for Walter. He shook his head and Honey said, "His mom called him Buzz."

"Where'd that come from?"

"He was his sister's little buzzer," Honey said, "the one that quit talking. She was learning English and had trouble saying *brother*. He told me his dad never called him anything but Valter."

"I was wondering," Carl said, "you asked if I knew their names, the guys that escaped?"

Walter hesitated. "Yes . . . ?"

"What're the names of the guys you were thinking of?"

Honey squeezed his arm as he was raising it, slipping his hand into a coat pocket.

She thought Walter would stall, blow his nose or start coughing, at least clear his throat.

He didn't, he said, "I hesitate because it's been so long since I read about them in the newspaper. I thought if you said their names it would refresh my memory. But you offer me no help."

Honey watched him shrug, then look up as Carl stepped toward him, a marshal's card in his hand.

"This is my Oklahoma card, but I put the Detroit FBI office phone number on it. In case you remember the names of those boys. You understand I live down there. I knew 'em pretty well."

Twelve

They were on Ten Mile Road again driving back to Honey's, what was left of a red sky behind them. Carl turned on the headlights. Honey, comfortable, her legs crossed, lighted a cigarette and held it out to Carl, a trace of lipstick on the tip.

He said, "Not right now, thanks," and turned to look at her. "You were funny, talking to him about his sister."

"His sister the sister," Honey said. "I thought we did all right." She opened the vent window and flicked the ash from her cigarette. "I loved Walter asking if you happened to know their names."

"He had to ask, didn't he?"

"You said you didn't remember, but they were picked up in a couple of days. Now he was confused. Wait a minute—are we talking about the same guys?"

Carl said, "I was hoping he'd ask if I meant Jurgen and Otto. If he'd said their names I would've handcuffed him to that ugly chair he was sitting in and taken a look around. That's not a bad place for the Krauts to hide out."

Honey was grinning now. "You threw it back asking *him* for the names. That was beautiful, it sounded so natural. But he got out of it and didn't seem too concerned after that."

"He thought he was off the hook. He gave himself away when he asked if I happened to know their names, like he was only curious."

"I thought you'd tell him, get right to it. But you didn't."

"If I had, what would Walter say? Never heard of 'em. But who else were we talking about, busted out of a camp in Oklahoma last October?"

Honey said, "That doesn't mean they're with Walter."

"If they aren't, he knows where they're staying. The G-men'll get a warrant that says something about suspicion of subversive activity. We'll put Walter on the rack, stretch him out and ask about the spy ring."

Honey said, "You're only interested in Jurgen and Otto, aren't you?"

"The Bureau thinks they could be helping the spies. It's okay with me. We locate the two boys, I'm taking 'em back to their home in Oklahoma."

He glanced at Honey. "You see how Walter was looking at you?"

"He still loves me."

"I could've stepped outside, give you a chance to reminisce."

"Tell him a joke?"

"Ask him how he's doing. His piles still acting

up? You're right, that's why he thought your piles joke was funny. He's dropped his drawers in the doctor's office, knows the scene."

"Walter hasn't changed one bit. He was born an old man and he's stuck with it."

"You want to see him again?"

"For what?"

"He looks like he needs a pal, somebody he can tell his innermost thoughts to."

"See if I can get him to spill the beans?"

"What do you think?"

"How would I approach him?"

"He still loves you, tell him you're sorry for the way you walked out, not saying anything, not giving him a reason. You were just a kid, still immature."

"Do I have to kiss him if he wants to?"

"I think once you two're alone you'll know what to say. Keep talking, it'll come to you."

"Where does this take place, in his meat market?"

"Find out when he's out here and drop in. You don't have to ask him for a date." Carl stared at his headlight beams on the country road. "We can have supper if you want. Get hold of Kevin, see what he's doing."

Honey said, "Are you afraid to be alone with me?"

He looked over. She was taking a cigarette from the pack. "You want me to come right out and tell you?"

She said, "Of course," and flicked her lighter.

"I don't think it's a good idea, you and I start keepin' company."

She snapped the lighter shut and drew on her cigarette before saying, "If that's how you feel, okay, let's call Kevin."

It was quiet in the car for a couple of minutes, Honey waiting for Carl to say something. It was his turn.

He surprised her.

"When you told Walter we met on a train—"

"I thought of it as I said it."

"You ever meet somebody on a train?"

"I sat in the club car on the way to New York, for the Bund rally. Walter stayed in our seat to take a nap. He can sleep sitting straight up, like he's at attention. I had a cocktail and began thinking of myself as a mystery woman, the guys in the club car wondering who I am. I'm wearing sunglasses and a nifty cloche down on my eyes, I must be *some*body. A couple of different guys offer to buy me a drink, I say no thank you. I'm reading *Newsweek*. Finally a guy sits down next to me I think is interesting. He's in his forties, not bad-looking. He's wearing an expensive pinstriped suit. He tells me he's a real estate investor in New York City, and for the next couple of hours he buys me cocktails, whiskey sours in the afternoon, while he guesses what I do and why I'm going to New York."

"Did you tell him?"

"He wanted to see me. I told him to stop by the German-American Bund rally at the Garden, he'd get to hear Fritz Kuhn talk about Jews and Communists."

"The real estate guy's Jewish?"

"Yes, he is. So then I had to tell him about Walter and the reason I married him."

"What'd he say to that?"

"He still wanted to meet me, so we did. We met for a drink and talked. He wanted me to leave Walter and stay with him in New York."

"He's married?"

"Divorced."

"You trusted him?"

"He said I woke him up. Made him feel alive again."

"I imagine so," Carl said and waited while Honey took her time.

"I went back to the Garden to see Walter *sieg heil*ing Fritz Kuhn and I thought, What's wrong with me? Outside of being young and dumb."

They were quiet again.

She said, "You know Kevin's had his supper by now."

Carl said most likely, his eyes on the road.

"Are you taking me to supper or dropping me off home?"

"We'll stop somewhere."

"I ask since you don't care to have fun with women other than your wife."

"If I can help it," Carl said.

Thirteen

Jurgen watched the Pontiac creep past the front of the house, a green four-door, out of his view for several moments, now it appeared on the far side of the house and the trees in the yard, turning onto the road Darcy had made coming through the field with his trailers of cows. Jurgen watched the Pontiac coming across the barn lot now to creep past the stock pen. Then stop and back up. So the ones in the car could look at the cows? He watched the window come down on the passenger side and saw a young woman's face, quite a lovely face, smoking a cigarette. He couldn't see the man who was driving. Only his hat.

He remembered a green four-door Pontiac at the camp in Oklahoma. Watching through the fence to see who was in it. As he was doing now, watching from the cattle entrance to the barn, the chute where the cows and heifer in the pen would be prodded inside later tonight to lose their hides, their heads, their hooves, and finally all their parts.

He watched the Pontiac make a wide turnabout

and leave the yard in Darcy's tracks across the field, turn on to the main road and come this way, again out of view on the front side of the house. Jurgen waited. The Pontiac didn't come past the house. It must have turned into the driveway that circled and came out again. But the car didn't appear. It told Jurgen they had looked over Walter's cows and now they were going to drop in for a visit.

He didn't think they were friends of Walter's.

Walter had only three friends he ever talked about: Vera Mezwa, the Ukrainian countess, and her houseman Bohdan; Michael George Taylor, the doctor who supplied Vera with invisible ink; and Joe Aubrey, the official of the Ku Klux Klan who owned restaurants and a light plane. Months ago he had asked Walter, "You've told them about Otto and me?"

Walter said, "You know what happened to Max Stephan and the Luftwaffe pilot."

Jurgen said, "'Loose lips sink ships.'"

Walter said, "What?"

The girl in the car was too young to be Vera Mezwa. The guy driving, only his hat visible on the other side of the lovely girl, but something familiar about the way he wore it—of all the ways there were to shape a felt hat—and thought of the marshal, Carlos Huntington Webster, Carl at the table in the department store with another man and a girl who could, *yes*, very possibly be the girl in the car smoking a cigarette. He liked her beret. If this was the same girl, the one driving could very well be Carl, Carl coming closer each day. He had thought earlier, Where will you see him the next time?

Here, where he was standing at the chute entrance to Walter's slaughterhouse. Jurgen stepped inside.

Walter's cutters would arrive after dark and set to work on the cows and the heifer, have sides of beef hanging before morning. Darcy would arrive in his snub-nosed refrigerated van he'd bought at auction, and get the sides out of here before any government inspectors showed up with their meat stamps. He'd take the load to Walter's market where they'd hang and chill for twenty-four hours before Walter dressed them out. There were sides usually hanging in the barn's chill room, from cattle bought at legal sales for inspectors who dropped by unannounced.

"That's what they do," Darcy said, "sneak up while you're trying to make a living."

Jurgen had never met anyone like Darcy Deal, a former convict—they had imprisonment in common—who worked now as a cattle rustler and looked the part in his sweaty cowboy hat and run-down boots with spurs. Darcy had a hard, stringy build and seemed to prefer looking mean. Jurgen was hesitant the first time he approached him.

"Do you ride a horse?"

"You askin' if I can?"

"When you rustle the cattle."

"I work afoot. Shake out a rope on the cow, put a feed bag on her and lead her to the truck, if I don't use a trailer."

"Then why do you wear spurs?"

"I walk in a bar, they hear my spurs jingle jangle jingle they know who I am." Darcy grinned, three or four days' growth on his face. "My boots are about worn through, but I never once had these can openers off 'em."

Jurgen said, "I like the sound they make, that *ching . . . ching*, with each step you take."

"You hear it," Darcy said, "look out. They's a cowboy come in the bar."

Jurgen smiled. "Instilling fear in the hearts of the customers, uh?"

Darcy said, "Somethin' like that."

Jurgen asked him, "Do you know who I am?"

"You're one of the Kraut prisoners broke out of somewhere. Walter says you stole a truck and drove out the front gate in it." Darcy said, "I never tried to escape. I looked at gettin' out in two years and I did, got paroled, but then busted my foreman's jaw—we're workin' down in a mine and he give me some lip—so I was thrown back in to finish my time. This prison's on a hill, two thousand yards from the Cumberland River, if you ever got a chance to see it from inside. Eddyville, named for a Civil War general."

Jurgen was thinking, General Eddie Vill?

"General H. B. Lyon," Darcy said. "Eddyville's where he was from."

Jurgen said, "Well, we both know what it's like to be a prisoner, don't we?"

Darcy said, "You don't hardly have any accent."

"I try to improve my English."

"What'd you do in the war?"

"I commanded a tank in the desert of North Africa, sat in the turret with field glasses and directed fire. Our sixty-millimeter gun could destroy a British Stuart at more than a thousand meters. Other times I flew a single-engine reconnaissance aircraft, looking for British tanks they would try to conceal, covering them with Bedouin tents."

"Is that right?" Darcy said, sounding interested, though Jurgen doubted the cowboy knew what he was talking about.

Darcy said, "You must've killed some people."

Jurgen said, "Well, when we hit a tank it would often go up in flames. Sometimes one or two of the crew would get out." He paused and said, "We would machine-gun them," and paused again. "But not always."

"I been shot at," Darcy said. "Haulin' ass out of a pasture. I pick up steers from growers that set their price of beef high and wait for buyers who don't mind payin' it."

Jurgen had to think about this. He said, "The butcher is told how much he can charge for a pound of meat. But the grower, or the feeder, can ask any price he wants?"

"That's how she works."

"It doesn't seem fair."

"Don't knock it, it's why we're in the black market business makin' a good buck."

"I'm surprised Walter has the nerve."

"You kiddin'? Walter's fuckin' the United States government, breakin' the law in the name of A-dolf Hitler, 'cause Walter's a hunnert percent Kraut."

"You don't care he's your enemy?"

"Walter? The enemy's over across the ocean, Walter's my partner."

"So you don't care you're breaking the law."

Darcy looked surprised. "It's what I do. How I make my livin'. I round up cows in the dark of night. It don't have nothin' to do with the government, my gettin' back at 'em for puttin' me in jail. Man, I'm an outlaw. I been one since I was a kid. I stole cars, I sold moonshine, I hit guys and the fuckin' court'd call it 'assault to do great bodily harm.' Damn right, guy gives me lip, I'm suppose to take it?"

Jurgen was nodding. "Yes, of course, you're an outlaw. You don't need motivation to steal cows in the dead of night, other than it makes money for you."

"So I can eat," Darcy said. "Listen, take a ride with me in my truck. I'll show you how to rope a cow and put her in the trailer. Tell you what to say to her she won't start mooin' at you. You're keepin' an eye on the house, light showin' in a window upstairs. You're not nervous, but you wonder what the hell they're doin' they're not in bed asleep."

"Or they're in bed," Jurgen said, "and enjoy to become intimate with the light on."

"My favorite place to screw Muriel," Darcy said, "was on the squeaky glider on the front porch of her mom's house. Was before we're married. You ever met Honey?"

Jurgen shook his head.

"You ought to meet her. She's the smartest girl I ever knew and she's my sister. No, she *use* to be the smartest till she married Walter. He hasn't told you about her?"

Jurgen shook his head again. "You're married?"

"Sorta. I hardly ever see Muriel."

"Children?"

"Listen, I spent every night of a year trying to knock Muriel up. It must be a female thing she can't have children. But if you want to go out with me some night, become the world's first Kraut rustler, lemme know."

Jurgen said, "I don't have a cowboy hat."

Darcy said, "I got hats, partner. What size you wear?"

Darcy stopped at a bar in Farmington and had a few shots with beer chasers thinking about his sister, wanting to know what she was up to visiting Walter. And who the guy was with her. Darcy hadn't called Honey since he'd come up here, he was still getting around to it. He said, Shit, go on over there and introduce yourself to your sister and see if the guy's with the law.

It was dark by the time he left the bar and drove past the house, pulling his trailer.

The car Honey'd been in wasn't in the driveway. He cut through the field to the barn lot. The only cars here belonged to Walter's Kraut meat cutters. Shit. He could say to Walter, "My sister come to visit you, huh?" Get him to tell what was going on. He'd take a leak and stop in the barn first. See how the cutters were doing and kid with 'em. Those old guys and their six-inch blades they kept sharpenin', they could take the coat off a cow, Jesus, like it was buttoned on. There was only one area of their dressing down a cow where he disagreed with them. How they killed it.

Jurgen was watching the guy acting as the stunner this evening, holding a .22-caliber rifle in one hand he pointed at the cow's forehead, no more than a few inches from the end of the barrel, and shot it and the cow buckled in the chute, not dead but stunned, knocked cold.

Coming up behind Jurgen, Darcy said, "You see the cow lookin' up at the stunner? She's thinkin', The fuck you doin' with a .22? Use a man's gun. You want to kill me, fuckin' kill me, man. Get her done."

Darcy, still talking, moved up next to Jurgen.

"Cruelty to Animals says you got to stun the girl, so she won't feel it when you hoist her up head-down and slice through her arteries and *look out*, take a quick step back. You aren't wearin' that rubber apron 'cause it's rainin' out. Split her down the middle from asshole to brisket, pull out her tummies, her bladder, her kidneys. Pull the esophagus up through her diaphragm and it frees the organs hooked on to come loose. Take out all the nasty stuff—"

"The offal," Jurgen said.

"That's correct, what she was gonna make cow pies out of. Hell," Darcy said, "all the time you spend in here watchin', it tells me you're thinkin' of becomin' a butcher once you're free."

"I'm free now," Jurgen said. "What I want to do is go out West and be a cowboy."

* * *

Walter came in while they were talking about going out on a dark night, what Darcy called "the
owl hoot trail," Jurgen serious, wanting to know if
they could ride horses, do it as they did out West.
Jurgen serious but sounding like he was kidding.

He saw Walter approaching, Walter looking
excited for a change, telling them, "Honig was
here."

Jurgen said, "The girl in the car," to Walter,
"your former wife?"

Walter said, "Yes, Honig," and said to Darcy,
"Did you see her?"

"Out there on the road," Darcy said, "but I
wasn't sure it was her."

"They came in the back," Jurgen said, seeing the
Pontiac again, "and turned around."

"My sis," Darcy said. "I told you about her,
Miss Sunshine? Use to be Walter's old lady." He
said to Walter, "What'd she want, see if you become American yet? I didn't recognize that guy she
had with her."

"He's a federal officer," Walter said, "but is not
with the Federal Bureau." Walter's hand went into
his pocket as he turned to Jurgen. "He's looking
for you and Otto."

"He told you his name?"

Walter's hand came out of the pocket holding
Carl's card with the gold star engraved on it.

Jurgen could feel it between his fingers, taking
the card and seeing DEPUTY U.S. MARSHAL CAR-
LOS HUNTINGTON WEBSTER and thinking, You've
found me.

He would be seeing Carl again and liked the idea of it, talking to him, smiling at things he said, but didn't want to go back to Oklahoma, not until the war was over and he could look up that marshal who had worked with Carl Webster, the one who'd been a bull rider in the rodeo before he became a marshal. Spend time with guys like that, and Carl Webster. Watch them and learn how to spit. There was a lot of spitting involved with chewing tobacco.

"He didn't want to search the house, the grounds?"

"It was time for supper," Walter said. "He was hungry, so he left . . . with Honig."

Jurgen thought he was going to say "with my Honey."

"But he's coming back," Jurgen said.

"We have to believe that," Walter said. "He knows you. You must have told him you lived here at one time and of course have friends here?"

Jurgen nodded.

"Yes, he'll come back. I'm going to speak to Helmut," Walter said, looking at the three cutters. They stood by the cow now hanging head-down, all three of them sharpening their knives. "Helmut, Reinhard and Artur, excellent men. Helmut will take you with him when he leaves."

Jurgen said, "I'm going to live with Helmut?"

"No, you're going to stay with the countess, Vera Mezwa. Helmut will deliver you. I'll drive into Farmington to call her on a pay phone, tell her you're coming. I think she won't mind taking care of you, have something to do for Germany at this depressing time, something that will please her."

"It sounds like you're giving me to her as a gift, something to cheer her up." He thought Walter was smiling but couldn't be sure. "Is she really a countess?"

"She's Ukrainian. Married a Polish count."

"Killed in the war."

"Yes, a hero. They sent his wife here, trained in military intelligence. Vera Mezwa was the most important German agent in America."

"How old is she?"

"I don't know. Older than you."

"Is she attractive?"

"What difference does it make what she looks like? She's going to hide you."

Jurgen believed a woman with the name Vera Mezwa, a countess, a German espionage agent, could not be as boring as Walter. He was ready to move on.

Fourteen

Vera Mezwa's eyes and Jurgen's eyes met on the same level. She took his hand, stepped close and kissed him on one cheek and then the other, Jurgen feeling her lips brush his skin and they were eye to eye again, Jurgen knowing she was glad to have him here but not making a show of it. He could tell by the way she took his arm saying, "Come, let's sit down and be comfortable," her English bearing the hint of a Slovak sound. He had known Ukrainians in Hamtramck, a part of Detroit, who spoke English trying to sound American. She said, "Tell me what you like to drink."

Her manner confident, the leader of a spy ring, but with a wonderful scent that softened her before his eyes. He saw her lying on a bed naked and imagined muscle beneath the curves of her body, but with the breasts of a bodybuilder, and could tell she dyed her hair, preferring the raw tint of henna and a deep-red lip rouge, quite startling against her pale, powdered features. She was a handsome woman in the style of Central Europe and he liked her immediately.

"Whatever you're having," Jurgen said, confident it would be a drink with alcohol.

Her heels brought her eye to eye with him, her age would be somewhere in her late thirties, perhaps forty. Her age didn't matter to either of them. The living room furniture was formal, dull. Jurgen imagined it already here when she moved in. They took cigarettes from a silver dish, Vera lighting them with her Ronson, Vera sitting with him on the sofa, Vera facing him, her legs drawn up in a wool skirt, a shade of rose that matched the sweater she wore and was loose on her body, nothing beneath the sweater, pearls displayed in the open neck. Her head raised and she was looking past Jurgen.

He turned enough to see a young man wearing a white apron over his T-shirt and red neckerchief standing in the room waiting, his hands on his hips, shoulders somewhat slumped, a slim young fellow standing relaxed as he waited.

Vera said, "Bo, the vodka in the refrigerator, please."

Jurgen watched him turn without a word and go off through the dining room. He believed the young man wore his full head of blond hair in bangs and over his ears in the style of Buster Brown.

"Bo's my houseman," Vera said, "Bohdan Kravchenko. He was my husband's steward aboard ship when my husband, Fadey, was running the blockade during the siege of Odessa, June to October 1941. Perhaps you know already Fadey's ship was sunk and he went down with it. Bo was in my employ when Odessa fell to the Romanians you pushed ahead of your troops. An *Einsatzgruppen*, one of your death squads, found him and put him in a labor camp with Jews, Communists, Romas, and made him wear a pink triangle that identified Bo as a homosexual. The Jews' color was yellow."

Jurgen said, "He escaped?"

"Finally," Vera said. "But first Bohdan gave all his food each day for ten consecutive days to an inmate, a man who somehow was in possession of a butter knife and didn't know what to do with it. Bo honed the small knife on a stone until he had the edge he wanted. He cut the throat of a guard who made him kneel down and open his mouth and the SS thug would try to piss in it from two meters away. Bo crept into the guards' barracks, found the pisser sleeping and sliced open his throat, and two more while he was at it, without making a sound. He would have been shot whether they found he killed the brutes or not, they were shooting everybody. We left Odessa—I brought Bo with me to Budapest dressed as a woman and finally to America as part of the agreement I made with the German espionage service."

Vera stubbed out her cigarette and lighted another.

"Listen to this. One night at the Brass Rail, downtown, he tells the sissies he's getting drunk with he works for a German spy. The Federal Bureau hears of it. They ask Bohdan would he like to work for them, become an agent of the United States and spy on me. Or, be locked up as an enemy alien and sent back to the Ukraine after the war.

Bo hopes someday to become a citizen of the USA and he said yes, of course, and asked how much they would pay him. They asked him how much he valued his freedom. That was his pay. He tells me about it, he's going to spy on me. I asked him, 'What are they giving you, a medal?' No, nothing. I said, 'Why don't you become a double agent and spy on them for me?' I said, 'Don't we have a good time together? Don't I let you wear my jewelry?' It's all costume. We make up things he gives them that sound to be true, so they'll keep him in their employ. But they already knew things about me. That I was recruited by Miss Gestapo herself, Sally D'Handt, a famous agent for the Germans. That I went to spy school in Budapest and was accepted into Division One of Abwehr, the Intelligence Section. How could the Federal Bureau know all this about me? I was impressed."

Bohdan came to them with a frosted bottle of Smirnoff and aperitif glasses with stems he carried upright between his fingers.

"Bo, I'm telling Jurgen what you do for the Federal Bureau."

Bo places the glasses on the cocktail table.

"We love making up stories to tell them. How I overhear Vera talking on the phone about saboteurs planning to blow up the tunnel to Canada."

"And the Ambassador Bridge," Vera said.

Bo filled the three glasses and sat across the cocktail table from Vera and Jurgen, close enough to pick up a vodka, drink it off and pour himself another.

Vera said, "Tell Jurgen what you'd do if you were Walter."

"If I had to go through life looking like Him-mler? I'd cut my own throat. With a butter knife I have, a keepsake." He winked at Jurgen.

"Be nice," Vera said. "Captain Schrenk is to be held in respect." She said to Jurgen, "If Bo turns the music on and asks you to dance, tell him thank you but you'd rather not. Bo sometimes is impulsive."

"With the kind of impulses she likes," Bo said.

Jurgen watched Vera drink a shot of vodka, re-fill the glass and turn to him. "What are you wait-ing for?"

He raised his glass, took the swallow of vodka and let her fill the glass again.

"You know you bombed Odessa to rubble."

"I've never been to Odessa," Jurgen said.

"You know what I mean. Our home escaped the Stukas because we lived three kilometers east of the harbor. You marched in pushing the fuck-ing Romanian Fourth Army ahead of you to do the dirty work, and what did you find? Nothing. The fucking Russians had gone, taking everything they could carry. It's what they do, they're loot-ers. They used to check out of hotels with towels in their bags, pictures if they can pry them off the walls. The Romanians are another story. They come to Odessa and begin murdering Jews. They shot them, they hanged them from light poles on the main streets. They put them in empty storage buildings, as many as twenty thousand, locked the doors and machine-gunned them through holes they made in the walls. Then they set the buildings afire and tossed in hand grenades. Do you believe it? In case any of the Jews were still alive."

Bo said, "Tell about the Death Squads."

"The SS," Vera said. "The war came to Odessa and my life changed, from one of relative leisure to the appearance of leisure." She gestured. "This home. My husband was in the shipping business, coastal freighters that traded among ports on the Black Sea. Fadey got along with the Soviets, gritting his teeth, offering bribes when his bullshit wasn't enough. He had only complimentary things to say about Josef Stalin, that pockmarked midget. Do you know how tall he is? The Russians say five foot six. Oh, really? He wears lifts in his shoes or he'd be no taller than a five-foot pile of horseshit. It's the reason he's killed ten million of his own people. His mother sent him to a seminary to become a priest, but God rejected him."

She kept talking, Jurgen listening.

"I told you the siege began in June 1941? My husband Fadey became a blockade runner like Rhett Butler. Slip out of Odessa and cross to Turkey, neutral at that time, and return with guns and food supplies. Turkish wine also, I couldn't drink. Fadey was with elements of the Soviet fleet. Stukas dove on them and sank two destroyers, *Bezuprechnyy* and *Besposhachadnyy*, also a tugboat and Fadey's ship. He put out to sea and I never saw him again, my husband, taken from my life."

Jurgen waited a few moments.

"The Germans killed your husband?"

"Or was it a Soviet gunboat sunk his ship?"

"I was told your husband was a Polish cavalry officer, killed in action."

"That's the story they gave me. I arrive in Detroit the widow of a Polish count no less, who met his end heroically, fighting tanks with horses. I come with social position, one that's more acceptable than the widow of a Black Sea gunrunner. I asked at the spy school if the count knew what he was doing. They wouldn't say. I asked if there was such a person. They still wouldn't tell me. On my passport I'm Vera Mezwa Radzykewycz, Countess. Do I look royal?"

"Indeed," Jurgen said. "But the widow of a gunrunner isn't a bad story. It could have attracted support."

"I told you I was contacted in Budapest by Sally D'Handt, a turncoat Belgian who became a spy for the Germans. Now she recruits for military intelligence, gathers lost souls into the Abwehr. You've heard of Sally? She's famous." Jurgen shook his head as Vera said, "Blond hair like Veronica Lake's, very theatrical. She told me with great solemnity it was a Soviet gunboat that sank my husband's ship. She said they were ordered to because the repulsive Josef Stalin didn't trust anyone."

"Did you believe that?"

"The Soviets were always at us. Sally asked if I had ever been to America. Yes, when I was a girl. Would I like to go back now, during the war? I said I would love to. Now the turncoat Belgian cunt actually made tears come to her eyes, she's so moved. Close to crying as she tries to smile to show her joy that I agree to come here. It's the look Joan Fontaine gives Cary Grant in *Suspicion* when she realizes he loves her. Or, the look that says the moment the camera stops rolling she and Cary will be in her dressing room fucking each other's brains out. It's that kind of look on Miss Gestapo's face as she murmurs, 'Vera, you are exactly the woman we need to gather intelligence from the very arsenal of our enemy, the city of Detroit.' Or did she say, 'the so-called Arsenal of Democracy'? Now I'm not sure."

Vera shrugged in her loose sweater. Now she decided to have another cigarette.

"From Budapest I came to Detroit by way of Canada. I took the place of an agent who turned in her own spy ring once the FBI began picking on her, Grace Buchanan-Dineen. She called herself 'Grahs' and was the only agent I know of, besides Ernest Frederick Lehmitz, who used invisible ink in messages to her contacts. Lehmitz reported on ships leaving New York for Europe until he was caught and sent to prison."

Jurgen said, "Was this Grahs's house?"

Vera smiled. "That would be funny, wouldn't it? The German spy house. No, Grahs lived downtown, on the river. I was given the house on a lease that runs until June of this year—"

"You have only two months?"

"Wait. I was given a five-thousand-dollar bank account and a thousand a month to cover expenses."

"That sounds rather generous."

"Last year it was reduced to five hundred a month. This year the checks have stopped coming, the last one was in February."

Jurgen took a cigarette from the dish. Vera reached toward him snapping her lighter.

"You're out of funds?"

"Don't worry about it."

"What will you do?"

She looked at Bohdan. "We talk about it."

"Constantly," Bo said, pouring a vodka. "I tell Vera to become a rich man's concubine and I'll be the eunuch."

"You're not German," Jurgen said to her. "Why are you working for German Intelligence?"

"She hates Russians," Bo said.

"I dislike them. The only part of this war I don't mind," Vera said to Jurgen, "you and the fucking Russians killing each other. I'll tell you something. In 1940, '41, all the young grenadiers in newsreels looked sexy to me. You were attractive, proud of yourselves, you had ideals you believed in. You sang, you marched, you sang while you marched. I remember thinking this was very bad light opera. But the upbeat mood of it was catching. I liked the purity of it, a new Germany full of healthy young men and women with Nordic features and platinum hair. In that crowd I knew I'd stand out like a film star. But, did I want to trade one police state, Stalin's, for another? Have to be so careful of what I say? How can I look at the super-Nazis goose-stepping down the street and not think them ludicrous? I thought, Well, the Germans are a strong, self-willed people, they won't stand for Adolf and his gang too long, having the Gestapo in their lives. After the war it will change back to the way it was."

"What about the killing of Jews," Jurgen said, "do the people accept it?"

"They turn their heads."

"But they know about the death camps."

"They can only wait until Germany is beaten and Adolf is tried before a world court. Everyone knows the end is coming. I hear: we can't win. We should settle for peace now and try it again in ten years. I hear: America will demand unconditional surrender. Germany will have to give up the land it stole, the countries. Give up everything, or the Russians will be turned loose on them."

Jurgen was shaking his head. "We won't have a choice."

"I try to rationalize," Vera said, "how can I work for this war-loving, Jew-baiting Führer? I see a story about Henry Ford and learn he's critical of Jews. He warns of the international Jewish conspiracy, which I take to mean communism, what else. We know he's opinionated. Henry Ford believes sugar on grapefruit causes arthritis. But in his factory he's a genius. Why is he so against Jews, as a race? I think he resents Jews because they tend to be smart. He knows that some of them, like Albert Einstein, are even smarter than he is. He won't admit it so he condemns all of them as a race."

"I read about Ford," Jurgen said, "before the war and was quite surprised."

"My point is, there are a variety of prejudices against Jews. Henry Ford was a pacifist while America was neutral," Vera said. "He refused to build aircraft engines for England. Two years later he's producing an entire four-engine bomber, a Liberator, every hour of the working day. It's what they're doing at Willow Run, putting together more than one hundred thousand different parts to make a bomber. To make a Ford sedan took only fifteen thousand parts. That's the kind of information I store in my poor brain. The Willow Run plant is more than a half mile long. It's put together with twenty-five thousand tons of structural steel. Ninety thousand people have jobs in that one plant. At Chrysler, on the other side of Detroit, they make tanks by the thousands. Packard and Studebaker make engines for planes, and Hudson makes anti-aircraft guns to shoot down the other side's planes. Nash does engines and propellers and General Motors makes some of everything America needs to make war. They can produce three million steel helmets"—Vera snapped her fingers—"like that, at a cost of seven cents each."

"Now we have to admit," Jurgen said, "we didn't come close to judging them correctly, as an opponent."

"Your Führer was too busy strutting before the world to notice," Vera said. "Do you know what I've been doing, what my contacts used to ask for? They wanted the names and locations of companies that produced light metals. They believed if we could destroy all the aluminum plants in America they wouldn't be able to produce bombers. They wanted me to stop the Allies from bombing Germany. They're going crazy over it, bombs dropping on them twice a day. Abwehr Two are the saboteurs. They were told in directives, 'For God's sake, cut the fucking source of power to the plants. Turn them dark, quick.'"

"Were any of them successful?"

"You would have read about it."

"No major feats, like stealing the Norden bombsight?"

"That was 1938, the year Fadey and I got together. I tell them about a fast new welding process at Fisher Body. At the Chrysler arsenal they've reduced the finishing time on antiaircraft guns from four hundred hours to fifteen minutes. I ask if they want details and get no reply. They're down in their bomb shelter."

"How do you send it?"

"I want to tell them to subscribe to *Time* magazine. Himmler was on the cover again in February, his third appearance since April twenty-fourth, 1939. Walter will frame it, hang it on the wall. Himmler will hate the piece but order a hundred copies . . . I give the information I send—say it's about the location of a new Alcoa plant—I give it to a man who comes by when I call a number. He goes off somewhere and transmits the message in code to a German shipping company in Valparaíso, Chile, and from there it's sent to Hamburg."

"How do you remember April twenty-fourth, 1939?"

"Vera has a fantastic memory," Bohdan said, "but has to see the words or figures written."

"If you tell me something I should remember," Vera said, "I write it down so I have something to look at when I wish to call it to mind."

No one spoke for several moments. In the silence Jurgen could hear, very faintly, Glenn Miller's *"String of Pearls"* on the radio in the kitchen. He said, "There's a federal agent, a marshal by the name of Carl Webster, who's after me."

"Yes, I read that in Neal Rubin's column," Vera said. "You're the one he's after?"

Jurgen said, "I thought Walter would have told you about him."

"Walter lives in his own world."

"If Carl knows about Walter, he knows about you."

"You're on a first-name basis with this policeman?"

"We know each other."

"And you think he'll come here looking for you. Would you care to give yourself up, the war nearing its end?"

"No, I wouldn't."

"I don't blame you. But if your friend wants to search my house, what do we do with you?"

"I'll leave," Jurgen said.

Vera took her time. She said, "Let me think about it."

It was quiet again, a silence beginning to lengthen, as Bohdan said, "Well, now we're coming on to teatime."

"We can let the vodka be our tea," Vera said and looked at Jurgen. "Why don't you go up and rest. I put magazines in your room I know Walter wouldn't have, or even know they exist. Have a nap, come down at six for cocktails and a supper Bo will prepare for us." She turned to him. "What do you have in mind, or would you rather surprise us?"

Jurgen was watching Bo. For a moment Bo's expression said he was tired of this happy home life routine. But then he did come alive and seemed keen to answer Vera.

"I can't surprise you, Countess, the way you come in the kitchen sniffing. But let's see if I can stimulate Jurgen's appetite."

"I hope I didn't sound like I was flirting," Bo said, on the sofa now with Vera, her fingers feeling through his cap of Buster Brown hair, brushing his shoulder now with her hand.

"I think you have dandruff."

"I set my mind to play a *goluboy* and everything I say sounds provocative."

"You're very believable," Vera said, remembering the afternoon Fadey came home hours early and almost caught them in the bedroom naked. He called her name from downstairs, "Vera?" By the time he came in the bedroom Bo had become a drag queen in one of Vera's frocks, hands on his hips, looking at himself in the mirror. Vera, now in a skirt and sweater, stepped out of the closet to see Fadey staring at Bo.

She said to Bo now, "Do you remember what I said?"

Bo grinned. You said, 'He loves to wear women's clothes, but he's still the best fucking cook in Odessa.' I wanted to kiss you. And Fadey accepted it."

"He didn't care one way or the other."

"I don't know how you thought of that so quickly. You hear him downstairs and I'm a sexual deviant in the same moment."

"You *know*," Vera said, "there are times when you do sound girlish. But then you began putting it on—"

"It was fun."

"Yes, until people notice you, maybe your shipmates. It doesn't take much. You hold your hand the wrong way looking at your nails." She put her arm around him, drawing his slender body, his ribs she liked to feel, close to her. "The death squad comes by and someone on the dock points you out. 'He's one.' You try to tell them you have a reason for acting the way you do, to prevent someone's husband from shooting you. And they pissed on you." Vera began caressing him, touching his face, moving her hand over his hair. "My poor baby. I'm so sorry."

"I could stop acting like a queen."

"Not yet. You're my secret weapon."

"I didn't think Jurgen would be a problem, but he is."

"I'm not going to worry about it, if I have to give him up, I will. Walter, I don't know, he doesn't say much. But now he has something he wants to tell us. What he's planning to do for Hitler's birthday, the twentieth."

"What is it?"

"He won't say. He'll tell us tomorrow night, here. He'll bring that loudmouth from Georgia if he flies up. I called Dr. Taylor, told him he'd better come. Keep up with what's going on."

"I hope Joe Aubrey can't make it," Bo said. "The weather has him socked in. No, he takes off. Fuck the weather, he's a ferocious, two-fisted little fellow and no storm is going to stop him. But it does, he crashes and burns to death. Wouldn't that be neat?"

"Except he's taking the train this time," Vera said. "The one I've been thinking about is Dr. Taylor."

"He doesn't say a word," Bo said, "as his eyes silently move over us, missing nothing."

"He doesn't speak very much at a meeting. But he could be talking to the Federal Bureau. I think if he has to," Vera said, "the doctor will tell on us rather than go to prison. Or have his sentence reduced."

"What would you like me to do about it?"

"I'll let you know tomorrow night, after I watch these people. See if I like any of them."

"See who has money to give us," Bo said. "We know the loudmouth could spare some. You could vamp him, give him one of your lines."

"No, I couldn't. His cologne makes my eyes water."

"Mine too. I thought it was Joe's breath. Get him to write you a check for German Relief, the starving people of Berlin, made out to cash." Bo squirmed against Vera to lay his cheek on her breast. "Tell me when you're out of money, I'll go stand on the corner."

"Don't say that. Please."

"Six Mile and Woodward Avenue, partway up the first block. Catch some trade going home to the suburbs, where the people with money live."

Vera took Bo's jaw in her hand and turned his face to look at her and see the judgment in her eyes.

"Never, ever, tell me what you could be doing when you're not with me. I don't want to hear it. You understand? Not even kidding, or I'll cut you loose." She kept looking at him, their faces close, and kissed his mouth, Vera gentle now, her voice soft saying, "You understand? You're my love. I want to feel you belong to me, no one else. Be nice to me," Vera said, "I'll make you happy. I'll let you wear my black sequined dress tomorrow night."

Bo twisted around to sit up.

"You mean when your spy ring's here?"

"It's up to you," Vera said.

"The black with sequins?"

Fifteen

Carl phoned Louly every week at Cherry Point, North Carolina, the marine air base, so he wouldn't have to write letters. He'd listen to her get on a subject like marching, how marines loved to march and had their own snappy way of calling cadence, more like sounds than words, not making any sense. She said, "Why is marching so important? In boot you march everywhere you go. Even now, visitors come up from Washington, congressmen, we're out on the parade passing in review, doing right and left obliques, to the rear march, showing the visitors, goddamn it, we're marines."

Louly sounding like a dedicated jarhead.

"We even marched a lot," Carl said, meaning the Seabees. "You're in the service, it doesn't matter which one, they march your ass off. I think it's to get you doing what you're told on the beat. You're in combat, you get ordered to move, you don't stop and think, you move."

So his wife would think he was as Semper Fi as she was.

Toward the end of the conversation Louly would say, "You staying out of trouble?"

Carl would say, "I don't have time to get in trouble. How about you?"

"We stay in the barracks we play hearts or read. We go out, we have a few beers and listen to gyrines try their dopey lines on us. The officers who've been in combat think they're hot stuff and act real bored. I tell them my husband's shot more people who wanted to kill him than any of you, without even leaving Oklahoma."

"What about the two Nips I got? On an island supposed to be secured?"

That time Louly said, "Don't worry, I tell them about your scoring a couple of Nips."

He'd feel good after talking to Louly. Her enlistment was up in the summer and he'd tell her he couldn't wait to have his sweetie home. He'd start looking for an apartment in Tulsa.

This time, talking to him in Detroit, Louly said, "You staying out of trouble?"

He said what he always did about not having time, but with pictures of Honey Deal flashing in his mind, Honey wearing her black beret, in the car and at dinner, Honey's eyes on him as she sipped her dry martini, straight up.

Louly said over the phone, "I love you, Carl," and he said, "I love you too, sweetie," remembering not to call her honey.

There were two anchovy olives in Honey's martini.

She said, "I take one of the olives in my mouth, like this, crush it between my teeth and sip the ice-cold martini, the silver bullet. Mmmmmm."

He said, "They get you feeling good in a hurry."

"Yes, they do."

"If you aren't careful."

She said, "Even if you are."

Her eyes smiling at him.

He dropped Honey off at her apartment after they had supper. She thanked him. Hoped she'd see him again sometime. She didn't ask if he wanted to come up.

See?

She was fun to be with, that's all. She flirted a little bit with her eyes, certain things she said, but that didn't mean he'd ever go all the way with her. He had a good-looking wife who'd shot two men in her time and taught twelve hundred gunnies to love their .30-caliber Browning. Louly was all the girl he had ever wanted, and had sworn at the time to remain faithful to her. He had no intention of ever committing adultery with Honey. If that's what she was game for and it looked like it might happen, Honey being what you'd call a free spirit, with bedroom eyes and that lower lip waiting there for him to bite, the girl acting like there was nothing wrong with free love.

Carl told himself there was no possibility of his ever going too far. Even if he'd be seeing more of her now. Pretty much every day, now that he'd lost his guide to Detroit, Kevin Dean reassigned to bars blowing up.

He phoned Honey from the FBI office where he'd spent most of the day. She sounded busy but

calm answering questions thrown at her by sales-
girls, sounding like she was in charge over at Hudson's Better Dresses; so all he said was his plans
had changed and he would like to talk to her about
what they'd be doing. He could give her a ride
home after work, save her taking the streetcar.

Honey said, "Carl, you're my hero."

He said, "Shit," once he'd hung up.

At the hotel cigar counter he picked up a copy
of the *Detroit News* and went through the paper
until he found Neal Rubin's column. Carl saw the
heading and said "Jesus Christ" out loud and then
read about himself.

What's America's Ace Manhunter
Doing in Detroit?

There is a remote chance you know why Carl
Webster is known as "the Hot Kid of the Marshals Service." It was the title of the book about
him that I reviewed for the *News* ten years ago.
I liked the book, but can't for the life of me remember why he's called the Hot Kid.

The question now is, what's Carl doing in
Detroit? He works out of Tulsa, Oklahoma. In
a column last year that I called "America's Most
Famous Lawman," I told of Carl's specialty:
going after German prisoners of war who have
busted out of camp and are on the loose. Carl is
an expert tracker, our Ace Manhunter.

That's Deputy U.S. Marshal Carl Webster in
the photo, taken in the lobby of the Detroit FBI
office. He's looking at mug shots of wanted fugi-

tives. It's too bad that flash of light on the glass makes it impossible to identify any of the bad guys.

I would be willing to bet Carl Webster is after one of them. Possibly even two. *Jawohl?*

Neal Rubin filled the rest of his column with Esther Williams, telling what it was like to have lunch with Esther at the London Chop House. He called it "The next best thing to going swimming with her."

Honey got in the Pontiac saying, "Did you see Neal Rubin's piece? I think he's great, his style is so . . . conversational. He doesn't act like he knows everything, the way most of those guys sound, with their inside stuff. You notice you were the lead item? You upstaged Esther Williams."

"I saw it," Carl said.

"Does it blow your cover?"

"I never had any to begin with."

"I could tell it was you in the picture."

"How? The guy shot me from behind."

"The way you wear your hat," Honey said, and sang the next lines to him in a low voice. "'No, no, they can't take that away from me.' What's the new thing you'll be doing?"

"It's Kevin. They put him on an investigation that came up." Driving out Woodward in traffic, he told her about it.

"If a bar owner doesn't want to do business with these guys that supply jukeboxes, mob guys, they try to intimidate the owner, blow up his bar. They aren't experts at handling dynamite, they leave clues. The mob also tries to sell the bar Canadian whiskey they've heisted, no tax stamps on the bottles in violation of federal law. The FBI gets on it and that's what Kevin's doing, poking around in bars that were blown up and smell awful."

Honey said, "Are we going to have dinner?"

"Yeah, if you want."

"Let's have a drink and talk first, at my place."

Sixteen

Honey made highballs in tall glasses, rye and ginger ale, while Carl opened a can of peanuts saying he'd spent most of the day at the FBI office. He was coming to the tricky part now of what he wanted to tell her.

"They sat me down and said I was to forget about Jurgen Schrenk for the time being. They're pretty sure the Detroit spy ring's up to something. They're meeting tonight at Vera Mezwa's and the Bureau wants to be sure I don't get in the way. I asked what the meeting had to do with Jurgen. They said that's where he's staying now, at Vera's. I said, Otto's with him? It sounded like they'd forgotten about Otto, the SS major. They said they believed he was still at Walter's."

"I'd love to meet Vera," Honey said. "Kevin showed me pictures of her doing her lectures. She's attractive, has her own style, knows how to fix herself up, writes letters with invisible ink. She knows Jurgen?"

"The Bureau," Carl said, "believes he's involved

in whatever Vera's up to, it's why he's at her house. But what kind of job would they give an escaped prisoner of war? I said what if they don't know about Jurgen? Walter's never mentioned him. He knows what happened to Max Stephan when he showed off the Nazi pilot, so he's kept Jurgen under wraps. But now he calls a meeting to introduce him to the gang."

"Why?" Honey said.

"I was asked that. If Walter was so careful before, keeping Jurgen a secret, why would he expose him now? I said I didn't know, but I'd talked to Walter last night."

"They were surprised."

"They said oh, is that right? I told them Walter knows I'm after Jurgen and Otto. He's afraid I'm gonna come out to the farm looking for them."

"How do you know that?"

"Why were we out there last night? I told them I must be the reason Walter got rid of Jurgen, sent him to stay with Vera, let her hide him for a while."

"You think she knows about you?"

"If she's any good. But if she doesn't realize I'm closing in, Jurgen will point it out to her. Now what does she do, hide him or throw him out? She can't hand him over. What's she doing with an escaped Nazi POW?"

"You told this to the feds?"

"I said she knows you guys would come down on her. And before you're through wringing her out she knows she can kiss her spy act good-bye. But, I told them if Jurgen feels she's nervous about the situation he'll leave, disappear. They want to know how I can be sure that's what he'd do. I said because he knows he's better off on his own than having to count on people who're strangers to him. I know he'd have serious doubts about Walter. Walter's scared to death to have Jurgen around."

"They ask how you know that?"

"I said Jesus Christ, I've met Walter. I know what kind of man he is. I sized him up as I would any offender I'm after. I said the thing to do before you lose Jurgen, go on in the house and bring him out handcuffed. Vera too." Carl paused to let Honey wait for what he'd say next, but she beat him to it.

"They ask you what an old boy who wears cowboy boots knows about people in espionage?"

"Only the way they put it," Carl said, "was why don't we let the scenario play out a little more, not spook the spooks."

"What scenario?"

"Whatever they think is going on."

"How do they know Jurgen's at Vera's?"

"Bohdan Kravchenko. He's been working for the feds since Vera came here."

"Kevin told me about him, yeah, Vera calls him Bo."

"Kevin says this Ukrainian tells them spy stuff without telling them anything. There's a meeting tonight, but Bo doesn't know why it was called. The Bureau guys admit he could be stringing them along, but he's all they've got. I mentioned before, I think Walter's gonna present Jurgen to the gang."

"But you don't know why, if he's kept him a secret until now."

"He has a reason this time or he's showing off. Look, everybody, here's an honest-to-God Nazi superman I brought to the party."

Honey said, "If you think Jurgen will disappear by tomorrow—"

"That's where I'm stuck. What do I do about it?"

"Don't they have agents watching the house?"

"That's why I can't barge in."

"I have to assume," Honey said, "the FBI guys know what they're doing. Don't they?"

"They do, only their scenario's different from mine."

"You're afraid Jurgen's gonna slip by them," Honey said, "and you'll have to start all over. What's he like?"

"Jurgen? He's a nice guy, he's smart, he's funny. He can do different accents."

"How old is he?"

"I think he's twenty-six."

"What's he look like?"

"He has dark blond hair, blue eyes, he's five nine and a half, one forty-five, he's always tan, his legs, 'cause he likes to wear short pants."

"Is he good-looking?"

"Girls like him, they think he's cute. I'd see girls that worked in the administration building, just outside the gate, watching him through the wire fence. One of them pulling on the front of her blouse like she needed air. He had a girlfriend at that time, a hot young babe, he'd sneak out of camp to visit."

"You mean he'd escape. What did the hot babe do?"

"It was an experience," Carl said, "to know her. She went from the debutantes' ball to a cathouse in Kansas City, became a very expensive call girl and got rich, saved it, didn't get into opium. She's gonna write a book, says I won't believe some of the things happened to her in her life. I think she was sixteen working in the cathouse. Shemane had a sideways look she'd give you." Carl grinned. He said, serious now, "She's a redhead."

"You liked her," Honey said.

"I already have a redhead."

"But you lusted after her. Was she famous?"

"In Kansas City."

"Will she name names in her book?"

"I told her don't get any good guys in trouble, that's all."

Honey said, "Tell me what you want to do."

"About Jurgen?"

"About now. What do you want to do?"

They had their drinks and cigarettes sitting low in the sofa, both of them sunk into the cushions that crushed to fit their shapes, close enough to reach out and touch each other.

Carl said he needed a guide since he'd lost Kevin for a while. If she'd like to fill in he'd write a letter to get her off work for a few days and pay her for her time. Or have someone in the FBI office write the letter.

"I call in sick," Honey said, "it's no problem. Yeah, I'd love to take you around. I have a car a friend's letting me use while he's at Benning jumping out of planes. He's an instructor, airborne. It's a 1940 Ford Coupe, but I don't have any gas stamps. The guy's just a friend of mine."

Carl said he'd get her stamps, but they'd do their running around and maybe surveillance in the Pontiac. He had maps he'd show her.

Honey said, "Wow, maps." She said, "I'm thinking we should go across the street for dinner. The Paradiso, right there, I think is the best restaurant in Detroit. Outside of the Chop House. It's Italian, but not heavy on the tomato sauce Italian. Really good scaloppini and Tosca, the house salad's terrific, and they have collard greens like back home. I told them they ought to have grits on the menu. Whenever I fix calves' liver and bacon I make a little gravy to put on the grits."

Carl said, "I crumble bacon in my grits."

Honey said, "Are you hungry?"

"I'm not in any hurry."

"The trouble is, if you're hungry and you eat first, and then decide what you want to do or just let it happen, there are certain things you'd be too full to, you know, throw yourself into."

"Certain things," Carl said.

"I went with a guy from Argentina during another entire year of my life, after the entire year I spent with Walter. Those two were night and day. Arturo, the guy from Argentina, could order dinner in five languages and choose just the right wines. He said only one restaurant in Detroit had a decent wine list, the London Chop House, so that's where we went. We'd come back to his digs at the Abington, kick our shoes off and have cognac and coffee. The Abington had a dining room, but we only used it if we were too tired to go out. This is when Art would start fooling around in his Latin way, very serious about it, after the dinner and three different kinds of wine."

"You drank three bottles?"

"Once in a while we'd finish them off. The first time we went out together he said he came to Detroit six times a year for meetings at GM."

"How'd you get together?"

"We started talking. A young woman from Grosse Pointe, I'll call her, very tailored, brought him along while she tried on dresses. We talked for maybe fifteen minutes and he asked me out. I said, 'What about your girlfriend?' He said, 'She's my mother,' deadpan, and we went out."

"Did he buy her a dress?"

"She had two that she liked. I thought he'd show off and tell her she could have both. No, he said he didn't care for either of the dresses. The tailored young woman handled it. She said, 'Okay,' and was just a little bit cold."

"And he never saw her again."

"I don't know, I never asked about her, or what he was doing at General Motors."

"He told you he came to Detroit six times a year."

"Never stayed more than a week, and wanted to see me each time he came. I said, 'You're asking me to sit and wait for the phone to ring?' He called me every day from Buenos Aires." She sipped her drink. "We worked it out. I liked him, he was fun, he was thoughtful. He came every month for five days whether he had a meeting at GM or not. I thought that was sweet."

"Did he want to marry you 'cause his wife didn't understand him?"

"I think he was married and had kids, but it never came up. He was Latin and fun at the same time. I called him Art. Or I'd call him a Latin from Manhattan and he'd say 'You can tell by my banana.' He was a terrific dancer." She was quiet a few moments. "He had something to do with auto racing. He took me to the Indy 500 the year we were seeing each other. Walk along Gasoline Alley, he knew just about everybody, and you could tell they liked him. Mauri Rose won that year, qualified at a hundred and twenty-one miles an hour and led thirty-nine laps out of two hundred." She said, "After Pearl Harbor, December of that year, I never heard from him again."

She told him she was going to change, get out of the suit she'd been wearing all day picking up lint and put on a dress. "The paper's right there." She said, "Decide when we should have dinner," giving him a look. Or maybe not, he wasn't sure. She said, "I'll be, oh, fifteen minutes or so."

It made him think of Crystal Davidson eighteen years ago going into her bedroom while he was waiting for Emmett Long. Crystal telling him, "Don't get nosy," but left the door open. It wasn't a minute later she stepped into plain sight wearing a pink-colored teddy, the crotch sagging between her white thighs. She thought he was from a newspaper. He told her, "Miss, I'm a deputy United States marshal. I'm here to place Emmett Long under arrest or put him in the ground, one." A line he'd prepared for the occasion.

Now he was looking through the front section of the *Free Press*. He remembered saying to Crystal, "What you want to do when Emmett comes is pay close attention. Then later on you can tell what happened here as the star witness and get your name in the paper. I bet even your picture." Crystal said, "Really?"

Carl looked at the paper again and read a couple of stories he thought were funny. He got up from the sofa and began reading aloud from the paper as he approached the hall, Honey's bedroom on the left, the bathroom on the right. "'A woman was shot in her fashionable eastside home by a jealous suitor. The suspect said he did it because she had trifled with his affection.' You think those were his words?" Carl said, looking up now at the bedroom door standing open.

Honey still had on the skirt to her suit but was bare otherwise, her breasts pointing directly at Carl. She said, "I can't imagine anyone saying that."

Carl looked at the paper again—Jesus Christ—and read another news item. "'Barbara Ann Baylis was bludgeoned to death with an iron frying pan in her home in Redford Township. After several days of grilling, her sixteen-year-old son, Elvin, admitted he had slain his mother in reprisal for a scolding.'" Carl looked up.

Honey hadn't moved.

She said, "Don't you love the way they write? The boy goes insane, screams at his mom and beats her to death with a skillet. 'Cause she scolded him?"

Carl said, "I can imagine the scene"—closing the paper—"the boy going into a rage."

Honey said, "Have you decided what you want to do?"

Carl said, "I was thinking we could have supper then drive by Vera Mezwa's. Check on the cars there for the meeting and get the license numbers."

Honey still hadn't moved to cover her breasts.

She said, "That's what you want to do, check license numbers?"

Seventeen

Bohdan came in the kitchen with Dr. Taylor's glass, empty but with dregs, a maraschino cherry, orange rind and bits of melted ice Bo dumped in the sink.

He said to Vera fixing a cheese tray, "The doctor's turning into a chatterbox. He said the most I've ever heard come out of him at one time. All by himself in the parlor reading *Collier's*, he licks his thumb getting ready to turn a page, very deliberate about it. He hands me his empty glass, he says, 'I've told Vera a hundred times sweet cherries simply don't agree with me.'"

"I forgot," Vera said. "I forget everything he tells me almost instantly." She repeated, "'I've told Vera sweet cherries simply don't agree with me.' What's that, ten words? It's about average for him. Unless he's telling us what the Jews are cooking up."

"You left out he's told you a hundred times, that makes thirteen words, but I haven't come to the good part. Really, he couldn't seem to shut up. I took the glass and said, 'Doctor, it will be my pleasure to fix this one myself.' He looked up and did a doubletake. I turned to walk away and he said, 'Bohdan?' with that sort of British accent he puts on, though not all the time. He waited for me to turn to him and said, 'You look very handsome this evening. You're doing something different with your hair?' I said no, it's the same, and shook my head so my hair would bounce around. I said, 'How do you like this outfit on me? It's pure cashmere.' He said, 'Oh, you're wearing a skirt,' as if he'd just noticed. I said, 'Do you like it?' He said, 'It's very chic, I like it with the sandals.' He asked me to turn around, but didn't say anything about my fanny."

"His drug must be kicking in," Vera said. "I told you he takes Dilaudid. That druggist, the one who flirts with me, said it's more potent than morphine. The doctor prescribes it for a physical infirmity, his gallstones." Vera was cutting wedges of hard and soft cheese for the tray, with soda crackers. "Walter will pout because there's no King Ludwig beer cheese, or Tilsit."

"There's Tilsit in the fridge."

"That's mine, I'm not putting it out." She said to Bo, "You decided against the black dress."

"I love it, but it's not me. The shoulder pads. I look like a footballer in drag."

"This way you're a little boy in drag. The pearls would look nice."

"I'm easing the group into what I might do more often. Oh, Jurgen came down. He's wearing his sports coat but no tie in sight. He could use a scarf, or one of my bandanas. I introduced him to Taylor. The doctor rose to his feet and saluted."

"The Nazi salute?"

"The snappy one. But then looked embarrassed, sorry he'd tried it. Jurgen gave him a rather pleasant nod. He'll have a whiskey with ice, no ginger ale. I'll take care of the doctor."

"I'm waiting for Joe Aubrey to see you," Vera said. "Walter called. Joe took the train this time. Walter, his faithful comrade, met him at the station. I don't understand their friendship, Joe is so crude."

"But he's the one with money."

Vera closed her eyes and opened them. "I can't imagine kissing him."

"But if it gets you what you need—be brave, it won't hurt you. Take off your dress and ask if he'll make out a check payable to something German, Dachau? They need funds too, you know, repair the gas chambers, do a little redecorating."

"In what amount?"

"One hundred thousand simoleons. Life will be bliss for at least ten years."

"This is too spur of the moment."

"Vera, take off your undies and get out the invisible ink. The bedroom's dark. He writes in whatever amount the cheap fuck wants in invisible ink and we write over it what *we* want." Bo said, "Listen, why don't you seduce him tonight?"

"Please—"

"He's here. He goes home, how do you get to Griffin, Georgia? Ask him to stay. You want to talk to him about going into some business, wigs, expensive wigs made of human hair. I see the little Oriental girl crying as they cut off her beautiful hair. Tell Mr. Aubrey I'll drive him to Walter's after, 'after' being whenever you've finished with him. He won't stay the night, knowing Walter would give him the silent treatment, not offering a word, but willing to give his left nut to know what happened. So when you're through fucking Mr. Aubrey, let me know."

"Please, I don't like you to use that word."

"I love it when you're a prude. You can't say the word but go wild doing it."

Jurgen stood with his drink waiting for Walter to arrive and deliver his statement, his plan, whatever it was, to a gathering of ersatz spies, Vera the only genuine one, a paid—at least at one time—espionage agent of the Abwehr, but never with her heart in it. She'd said to him last night, "There is nothing I can do for your people, it's too late." She said, "To tell you the truth I would have been more comfortable working for the British a few years ago, in 1938, '39, when Germany began taking whatever it wanted. I've had to rationalize like mad to send information to Hamburg, trying to help the cause of your Führer." Vera said, "I've given up. Still, I don't want you to be caught. You're here because Walter can't be responsible for you and work on his plan. That's the reason he gave me."

"It's enough," Jurgen said. "But once I meet your associates I can't risk staying. I don't know these people."

She told him about Dr. Michael George Taylor, an obstetrician who saw quite a number of German women in his practice. "He tells them, goes to their ladies' groups and tells them about the tremendous leap forward the Nazis have made in the history of man. He doesn't say what they've done for women, if anything. He loves Germany because he hates Jews. Don't ask him why, he'll recite his speech on the international Jewish conspiracy. I think what he tells anyone who will listen is seditious rather than treasonable, though he did give me information, at least a year ago, about a nitrate plant in Sandusky, where he's from originally, in Ohio. In the late thirties the doctor lectured on *Mein Kampf* for ladies' clubs. Imagine the glazed expressions on the faces of the women." Jurgen smiled and Vera said, "Yes, but Dr. Taylor doesn't try to be funny. He's serious, he's afraid, he worries. If he's arrested I'm quite sure he'll give us up." She said, "Did you ever read *Mein Kampf*?"

"I've never felt it necessary."

"Last summer in my backyard the doctor pissed on the American flag. No, he set fire to it and then pissed on it."

"To extinguish the flame."

"The fire was out," Vera said. "I think he simply had to piss."

He liked Vera and liked being with her; she was warm to him. He knew if he stayed she would take him to bed before long. Unless Bohdan was providing the love, the going-to-bed love. At this time he liked Bo and admired his skirt and sweater, like a baby step into pure decadence, if that's what he wanted to do. Jurgen hadn't yet made up his mind about Bo. What all his duties were. What he might be up to. It didn't matter to Jurgen; he wasn't going to wait around to find out.

He wished he could help Vera. Think of something she could do with her life, use her personality in some way, when the war was over. If she didn't go to prison. Bo swore, kissing his Black Madonna holy medal, he had not told the G-men anything they could use against Vera. But Jurgen thought he must, from time to time, tell them things that happened. Good liars spoke in half-truths.

Walter came in with Joe Aubrey, they approached Jurgen and Joe Aubrey gave him a salute that was stiff, military, and told Jurgen meeting him was a special honor, something he couldn't wait to tell his grandkids.

Jurgen said, "Oh, you have grandchildren."

Joe Aubrey said, "My first wife was barren, my second wife frigid, and my third wife's gonna get traded in she don't have a duck in the oven by this time next year."

"You could see a doctor," Jurgen said, "find out it isn't your fault your wife can't conceive."

"All I have to see," Joe Aubrey said, "is a good-lookin' high yella, high-assed Georgia-Hawaiian in Griffin with a light-skinned boy looking dead-on like yours truly when I was a tad."

Jurgen paused to make sure he understood.

"You're his father."

"Don't say it too loud now."

"You support him?"

"Twenty dollars every month. I told his mama, 'You see he behaves. He's going to that nigger college in Atlanta, Morehouse, when he's of age.'"

Joe Aubrey looked off and then turned to watch Bo talking to Dr. Taylor.

"My goodness, will you get a load of Bo-Bo, finally showing he's a girl at heart. Look, he even stands like a girl, one that's kinda lazy."

Now he was walking across the Oriental carpet in the middle of the sitting room to join Bo and Dr. Taylor, Aubrey saying, "Hey, Bo-Bo, you had knockers you wouldn't be a bad-lookin' broad, you know it?"

Now the doctor was telling Aubrey to leave him alone. "Why do you have to be so crass? Bohdan isn't bothering you, is he?"

Joe Aubrey turns on the doctor, Jurgen thought and watched him do it, Aubrey saying, "What're you, Doc, on the fence? Tired of looking up the old hair pie all day, so what's the alternative? How 'bout a boy dresses like a woman, looks like a woman, acts like one . . . Doc, I know you have a wife name of Rosemary. How's it work, you go either way?"

Dr. Taylor was saying something about his wife Jurgen couldn't hear. He felt someone come up next to him. Vera.

"Why can't he behave himself?"

"He holds Negroes in disdain," Jurgen said, "but fathers a child by a Negro woman."

"What don't you understand?"

"He called the woman high yellow. If 'yella' means yellow."

"You know what a mulatta is, or a quadroon?"

"Ah, I see."

Vera started to move away and he touched her arm.

"Are you afraid Joe Aubrey will give you up?"

"Joe talks without hearing what he's saying. He could give me up without realizing it. And Dr. Taylor . . . Dr. Taylor the drug addict."

Jurgen listened, but now was distracted. He said, "Let me speak to your guests," and walked across the room to join Vera's spies: Bohdan with the palm of his hand to his mouth; Walter frowning with all his heart. Frowning when he told Jurgen he was being moved to Vera's so Walter could concentrate on what he planned to do for the Führer. Still frowning as he admitted yes, Carl Webster had come to see him and lied, saying Jurgen and Otto had been caught and put back in the prison camp. *Why?* Jurgen said, "To confuse you. Get you to say no, we're still free." Jurgen could feel Carl coming closer in his cowboy boots, with each stride. He remembered Carl saying, "I like to hear myself walk." Hardly ever saying what Jurgen expected. He missed talking to Carl, missed his company, this federal lawman from Oklahoma who believed Will Rogers was the greatest American who ever lived because there wasn't ever anyone as American as Will Rogers. He was funny and dead-on accurate when he took shots at the government, and he was always a cowboy. Carl said, "You could tell he was the real thing by the hundred-foot reata he carried around, could do tricks with, throwing his loop over whatever you pointed to and never had to untangle it. Jurgen was thinking that if he ever saw Carl Webster again, even if Carl had him handcuffed, he'd ask him how one became a cowboy.

He heard Joe Aubrey telling the doctor, "The reason you don't talk much 'less it's about Jew boys, you know you sound like a woman. You use words like *lovely* and *precious* you never hear men saying. Or you come off creepy having all those drugs in your medicine cabinet."

Jurgen reached them.

He said, "Gentlemen, Walter Schoen is ready to give his address. He's going to tell you about all the women he's been screwing for the past five years or so and give you their names. Vera will introduce Walter in a moment. Dr. Taylor, have a seat, please. Bohdan, if you'll turn these chairs around . . . And, Mr. Aubrey, come with me, please. I want to see how you make your mint julep."

"With rye? Are you kiddin'," Joe Aubrey said, "and no mint? I swear, Vera's the cheapest rich broad I ever met."

Vera began with a quote from her predecessor assigned to Abwehr's Detroit station, Grace Buchanan-Dineen.

"You will recall that when the Justice Department threatened Grahs with acts of treason, and she allowed them to plant a recording device in her apartment, Grahs said, 'I was technically involved in the spy ring, yes, but I never considered myself morally guilty.'"

The statement made no sense to Vera. If turning in her spy ring wasn't an immoral act, what was? It was a cheap out, getting the woman twelve years instead of a rope around her neck. Still, Vera used the quote. She made herself say to the group seated in her living room, there was no reason for any of us to feel moral guilt, fighting the good fight, working for the cause of National Socialism. But, she said, as the end of the war draws near, our efforts have proved to be, well, insufficient, despite the Führer's inspiration, Vera said, wanting to bite her tongue. Even our brave saboteurs, two months from the time U-boats put them ashore, were tried by a military court and convicted. Six of our fellow agents were hanged, the remaining two, the informers, languish in prison. Vera had to pause and think before telling them the indictment against the thirty defendants last year for sedition ended with prison terms. We are told we have a right to free speech, but when we stand up for the truth, say that Communists control the American government, that Franklin Roosevelt, the cripple, gets down to kiss the ass of the midget Josef Stalin, we are imprisoned.

"I recall one of the defendants in that trial," Joe Aubrey said, "invented what he named a 'Kike Killer,' a short round club that came in two sizes, one for ladies."

Maybe she could get him to write the check and not have to kiss him or do anything else.

"This evening," Vera said, "could be our last meeting. There are no recording devices in my house, or any one of us likely to inform on the others, despite the ruthless efforts of the Justice Department. Let's refill our glasses, toast our future"—looking at Walter now—"and hear what our Detroit version of Heinrich Himmler is so anxious to tell us. Walter?"

* * *

They had turned off Woodward and were creeping along Boston Boulevard, the street divided by a tree-lined median and big, comfortable homes on both sides.

Honey said, "I can't read the house numbers."

"The one with two cars parked in front," Carl said. "The Ford belongs to Walter," the cars shining in the streetlight, "and a Buick."

"That's all?" Honey said. "What about the one we're coming to?" Another Ford, three houses from Vera's on the same side of the street.

"That's FBI surveillance."

"How do you know?"

"It's where you'd park to watch the house."

They crept past the car, Honey sitting taller to have a look at the black four-door sedan.

"There's no one in it."

"I'll bet you five bucks the house is under surveillance."

"Okay, turn around, and we'll go back."

Now she was telling him what to do. At the Paradiso, the restaurant, she kept telling him what to order, like the collards. In charge now since he'd chickened out. Would not jump on her when she showed him her bare breasts, Jesus, using them like a buck lure, and they'd gone out to eat instead of falling in bed. She didn't act pissy or disappointed, she was making fun of him by giving him orders. Carl turned at the next opening in the median and started back toward the house. Now she told him, "Park behind Walter's car."

"What're we doing?"

"I thought we'd drop in on the meeting."

Carl pulled to the curb and stopped.

"You believe they'll invite us in?"

"Don't you want to see Jurgen?"

"When they tell me I can pick him up."

"What if he's gone by then?" She said, "You know what? I'll say my ex-husband asked me to stop by and I brought a friend. We'd never met any spies before."

Carl said, "You're having fun, aren't you?"

"Or, I'll go in and you can wait here."

"How about this," Carl said. "You get out of the car you're on your own."

Honey got out and stood holding the door open.

She said, "I'll tell you about it tomorrow." Closed the door and waved her fingers at him in the window.

Eighteen

Jurgen was seated with Vera on the sofa, more than half the living room from where Walter was standing in the opening to the dining room, a row of candles on the polished table lighting him from behind. He had placed a few newspaper and magazine pages on the table and now was ready to begin.

"All of you know of the enigma that shrouds the birth of Heinrich Himmler and myself." He paused.

Vera groaned. She said, "Please, God, shut him up."

"I think he memorized his opening," Jurgen said, "and forgot what comes next."

"Their date of birth," Vera said.

"I was delivered into the world," Walter said, "the seventh day of October in the year 1900."

"On the same day," Vera said.

"On the same day," Walter said, "as Heinrich Himmler, the future *Reichführer* of the SS."

"In the same hospital," Vera said, her eyes closed.

"But not in the same place," Walter said.

Jurgen turned his head to Vera. She was again watching Walter, saying, "What's he doing?"

"Heinrich was born at home," Walter said. "Two Hildegardstrasse in an upstairs flat. I also was born at home. However I was taken to hospital with my mother the same day where we were both cared for. My mother had suffered complications giving birth to me."

Vera turned to Jurgen. "He wasn't born in the hospital."

"I have never lied to you," Walter said. "I believed I was born in that hospital and came to believe Heinrich was also, as my twin, because so many people said to me from the time I was a lad, 'Aren't you Heini Himmler? Did you not move to Landshut?' Or, someone says to me, 'I saw you this morning in Landshut.' It's north of Munich fifty miles. 'What are you doing here? Isn't your father headmaster at the school?' Now I'm living here, and by the thirties I see photos of Heinrich in German newspapers. Heinrich reviewing SS troops with the Führer. I look at the pictures of him and I think, my God, Heinrich and I are identical. I began to consider other similarities. Both of us born in Munich on the same day. Could we look so much alike and not be twins, born of the same mother? Why were we separated, kept apart? I began to believe Heini and I were put on this earth with destinies to fulfill."

"Not unlike the Virgin Mary," Vera said.

"In April 1939 I was asked by several of my Detroit friends, did I see myself on the cover of *Time*, the magazine. I was already reading about this rising star of the Nazi Party who must be my twin. Now he was gaining international attention. Heini was dedicated, conscientious. So was I."

"Dedicated to what," Vera said, "cutting meat?"

"He suffers from an upset stomach," Walter said. "At times so do I."

"Gas," Vera said. "Quiet, but telling."

"At one time he was a devout Catholic," Walter said. "So was I. He believed that allowing oneself to be sexually aroused by women, who by their nature could not control themselves, was to be avoided before marriage. So did I."

Jurgen said, "I can't see Heinrich with a woman."

As Walter was saying, "Heini's wife, seven years his senior, gave him a child, a daughter. I'm told he first noticed Marga—who referred to the Führer's exterminator as 'my naughty darling'—because of her beautiful blond hair. The woman I married was much younger than I and, unfortunately, quite immature. Honig also had blond hair. My one regret is that she did not provide me with a son before she walked out of my house." Walter paused. "I saw Honig the other night, the first time in five and a half years." He said, "She looked the same as I remembered her. Perhaps her hair was more blond." He stopped and stared into the room at his audience: Jurgen and Vera, Bohdan and Dr. Taylor, Joe Aubrey in an armchair by himself. Walter continued, saying, "Heini believed in unconditional devotion to duty. So do I." He paused and was thoughtful as he said, "Why did I believe for so long we were identical in every way, one of us an imprint of the other?"

"Because you wanted to believe it," Jurgen said.

"Because I wanted to believe I have a destiny as meaningful as Heini's, who has set out to eliminate a race of people from the world by means of *Sonderbehandlung*, a special treatment, murder in the gas chamber. First in Europe, then comes here and turns his *Einsatzgruppen* on America, his death squads. They say, now that Heini is head of the SS and the Gestapo, Reich Minister of the Interior, Reich Minister of Home Defense, head of military intelligence, Germany's chief of police, he must follow the Führer as the next master of the Third Reich. But think about it. Would the Führer in his wisdom choose the most hated man in the world to succeed him? A man so detested he would be rejected even by the Nazi Party? Heini has said people may hate us, but we don't ask for their love, only that they fear us. He tells his SS, we must discuss the plan for extermination, but never speak of it in public. He said they can look at a thousand corpses in one place, mounds of dead bodies the result of their work, and know they remain good fellows. Heini is responsible for the murder of Jews, Romas, priests, homosexuals, Communists, ordinary people, in numbers estimated to exceed, easily, ten million."

Vera and Jurgen watched him, not saying a word.

"I cannot," Walter said, "compare my destiny to Heini's. I have in mind the extermination of only one man."

He turned to the dining table and began looking through pages from magazines and sheets of notepaper.

"Himmler," Vera said.

"You're joking."

"Walter is Himmler's ghost double, his doppelganger. When someone's doppelganger appears it means the someone he looks like is going to die. It happened with my husband, Fadey. The day I learned he went down with his ship, Bo was trying on one of Fadey's suits, very loose on him. He put on Fadey's hat the way Fadey wore it and was impersonating him, the gruff way he spoke."

"And Fadey walked in."

"Not this time. Fadey never saw Bo mimic him, but I think Bo was still his doppelganger."

Jurgen nodded toward the dining room and Vera turned her head to see Walter in his black suit and pince-nez ready to continue.

"I have photographs and my notes here, and a map you can look at later if you want. What I intend to do is assassinate the president of the United States—"

"Frank D. Rosenfeld," Joe Aubrey said and started laughing, putting it on. He said, "Walter, how you gonna do it, sneak in the White House?"

"The Little White House in Warm Springs, Georgia," Walter said. "I have learned Roosevelt has been there since March thirtieth, resting, restoring his energy. I was counting on him remaining in Warm Springs through the twentieth of this month, Adolf Hitler's birthday, but I'm going to move the date of the assassination to the thirteenth. Once I'm successful, the name Walter Schoen will have a place in American history to rival that of John Wilkes Booth."

Jurgen said, "Who's John Wilkes Booth?"

"And will be remembered longer," Walter said, "than the name of the man who murdered ten million. I say this not in a boastful way." Walter paused and said, "What was his name again?" Walter smiled and turned it off.

"Who was the one he'll be as well known as?"

"Booth," Vera said. "He shot Abraham Lincoln. Ask Walter how he's going to do it."

Joe Aubrey was already saying to Walter, "How you gonna get near him with Secret Service and marines all over the place? You know Rosenfeld's been going there for twenty years? See if that warm mineral water—why they call it Warm Springs—always eighty-eight degrees Fahrenheit day or night. See if it'll help his polio-my'litis ease up. You know he wears steel braces on his legs, has 'em painted black, or he wouldn't be able to stand up, like he does from the ass end of a train, the observation car. There's a lot of people go down there for the water. I been to the springs, it isn't fifty miles from Griffin, up on Pine Mountain."

He said to Walter, "Even before you told me, I had an idea you were after Rosenfeld. You come visit and get me to fly down there. All this time you're scouting the area."

He said to the others, "You can get in trouble you fly over the Little White House. They warn you, get out of here. You don't leave fast I'm told they shoot you down."

Joe Aubrey turned to Walter again. "How you gonna do it, buddy, show up in an iron lung? You don't halt when they tell you, you'll hear machine-gun rounds dingin' off your breather. Walter, tell us how you plan to assassinate the man."

"I'm going to rent a small plane," Walter said, "fill it with dynamite, light the fuse, dive straight down like a Stuka into the Little White House and blow it up."

No one in the room spoke.

Jurgen and Vera were sitting up now. Jurgen said to her, "He's going to kill himself."

Vera raised her voice. "Walter, why do you wish to end your life?"

"It's my gift to the Führer."

"Please, what has the Führer done for you?"

Joe Aubrey said, "I taught Walter to fly in my Cessna after he pestered me to death. Now he tells us he wants to be the only German-American ka-mikaze pilot in World War Two, so people will re-member him, Walter the Assassin. Walter, you ever hear about the Jap kamikaze pilot that survived? Chicken Nakamura?"

Vera said to Jurgen, "What's today, the elev-enth," and to Walter, "When are you leaving?"

"Tomorrow. I'll fly down with Joe. I'm counting on my friend to get me the dynamite and rent a plane, since I don't have a license."

Vera got up from the sofa and went to Walter,

wanting to touch him. She put her hand on his shoulder. Walter staring at her through his *pince-nez*, submissive, sad? Perhaps confused. She said, Walter, if you could fly your plane to Moscow and use it to kill the Evil Dwarf, ahhhh, it would be a gift for humanity. The world would rejoice, even the Bolsheviks. Trust me, Walter, it's true. But to kill the president of the United States, now, the war in its final, what, weeks? What would be the good of it?"

"I told you," Walter said, "it's my gift to the Führer."

"You want him to show his appreciation?"

"It isn't necessary."

"Give you the Knight's Cross posthumously. Or to a member of your family, your sister who never speaks?"

"Knowing I've served the Führer will be enough," Walter said.

"But will Adolf appreciate your gift, the Red Army about to descend on him? What happens to your meat business, your slaughterhouse?"

Bohdan said, "Vera?"

She looked at him sitting with Dr. Taylor.

"What Walter might consider," Bo said, "develop an act where he does Himmler monologues in an SS uniform, the hat, the one with the skull and crossbones on it."

Vera gave him her cold stare.

"I'm serious," Bo said. "The material's way overdone, and with funny punch lines where you least expect. Walter does it without cracking a smile."

Vera said, "Yes . . . ?" Thinking about it now.

"Walter does it for American audiences?"

"Who else? After they win the war. You could represent Walter, act as his agent."

"He's serious," Vera said to Walter, Walter frowning at her. She gave his cheek a pat and turned to Jurgen on the sofa, Jurgen with raised eyebrows showing her an open mind. Vera moved to him with a faint smile thinking, Thank God for Jurgen.

The front doorbell rang with a *ding-dong* chime.

Then again.

It stopped Vera at the sofa. She looked at Bo. Bo looked back at her but didn't move from Dr. Taylor's side. Vera gestured toward the door. She watched Bo give the doctor's hand a pat as he got up from his chair.

"Vera, are we expecting anyone?"

Now Joe Aubrey was on his feet.

"Lemme handle it. Nobody comes in this house without a warrant signed by a federal judge."

Vera was thinking if it was the police, the FBI, all right, it was over, out of her hands. She watched Aubrey go to the front entrance, release the double lock and open the door.

Walter said, "My God, Honig?"

Joe Aubrey turned to Vera, not sure what to do.

Honey walked past him into the foyer.

She had a nice smile ready for the faces staring at her, picking out Vera Mezwa, the head German spy Kevin had told her about, and the young guy in the sport coat—not the one wearing a skirt—who must be Jurgen, the German POW watching her with a pleasant expression; he seemed calm for a guy on the run. Joe Aubrey looked familiar, from the Bund rally in New York years ago. The other two must be Dr. Taylor and the houseman, the one Carl had called Bohunk, but the guy didn't look bad in the gray sweater and skirt. Weird but kind of attractive. They didn't look to Honey like a ring of German spies having a meeting, but that's what they were.

She stuck out her right arm in the Nazi salute to show she'd come in peace, with no intention of causing trouble, and said, "*Sieg Heil*, y'all. I'm Honey Deal."

Nineteen

I have no reason to deceive you," Honey said. "A federal marshal dropped me on your doorstep and left, not wanting to disturb you or with authority to do anything else. But I risked being denied entrance knowing that Walter Schoen, my former husband, was here and I'm anxious for Walter to hear what I have to say. Seeing him again the other evening, after so many lost years, I remembered how thoughtful he was during the year we were married." She turned her gaze on Walter saying, "What I've come to do, Walter, is tell you I'm sorry, deeply sorry for the rude, unforgivable way I walked out of your life."

She waited. No one said a word.

Do it, Honey thought and crossed the room to Walter, arms at her sides in the trench coat, saucy beret snug on her blond hair, Honey suppliant, going to Walter for his forgiveness, Honey hoping she wasn't overdoing it. She reached out to him with both hands and he took them in his, his calloused, meat-cutter hands, his pince-nez catching flashes of light as he looked at his people and brought his gaze back to Honey. She would tell Carl sometime tomorrow, in a quiet tone, *I saw the lost years welling in his eyes,* Honey leaving herself open for Carl to say . . .

Walter sniffled before bringing out his white handkerchief, sniffled again, took hold of his nose and blew it, wiped his nose and looked in the hand-kerchief. He hasn't changed, Honey thought and said to God, Please don't let him cut one, I don't play being shot anymore.

To Walter she said, "Would you like to introduce me to your friends?"

The one she was dying to meet was Jurgen from the Afrika Korps, but Vera got to Honey and took her by the arm to the kitchen, saying they needed to talk.

"We'll get you a drink since you *sieg heil*ed us. What would you say to a vodka martini?"

"You're too kind," Honey said.

"I could have used someone with your cheek," Vera said. "Tell me about the federal policeman who dropped you off. You want it dry?"

"Very. He's Carl Webster from Oklahoma. He fools you, you think he's a shit-kicker till you look in his eyes. Carl's a keeper, but he's married."

"Yes? That makes a difference?"

"Not to me especially. I'm with him I act a lit-tle like I'm on the make, but I'm not after him to leave home. I thought we might have some fun, but he's the kind, he gives his word that's it, it's cut in stone."

"Perhaps you're trying too hard."

"I don't have a lot of time."

"Yes, but you have to be subtle."

"He comes to visit, don't open the door bare naked?"

"You want him to think going to bed is his idea."

"I haven't given up." Honey sipped the martini Vera gave her and said, "You know what you're doing, don't you?"

"I hope so," Vera said.

Bohdan stuck his head in the kitchen. He said to Vera, "Let's not forget Mr. Au-bur-ree," in kind of a singsong, and to Honey, "Love your beret, it's classic," and was gone.

Honey smiled. "He's cute."

"Bo's my guardian angel," Vera said. "He was reminding me I have to talk to Joe Aubrey before he leaves. About going into a business."

"How can you stand that guy?" Honey said. "He never shuts up."

"He's Walter's friend," Vera said, "I see him only once in a while. But, my God, you were married to Walter an entire year? You must have come close to losing your mind. I tell him, 'Walter, you love the Nazis so much, why don't you go back to Germany?' No, his destiny is here. Finally tonight we find out what it is. How he'll change from Walter, the dullest man God ever made, to Walter the Assassin."

"He wants to shoot somebody?"

"Crash a plane into the man's house."

"And kill himself?"

"Yes, but for the Führer. On his birthday or close to it."

"Walter knows how to fly?"

"He knows how to take off."

"Crash a plane into someone's house for the Führer," Honey said. "Joe Aubrey's plane, that Cessna? He can't be going far."

"I thought it might be Himmler," Vera said, "from the way Walter was talking about him. You know Walter believed all his life that in some mystical way he was Himmler's twin brother."

"The first time we met," Honey said, "standing in front of church, I had to guess who he looks like. This was back in '38, but I knew who it was. I told Walter he looked exactly like Himmler and Walter bowed his head and said thank you."

"Well, this evening," Vera said, "Walter denounced Himmler, called him Heini most of the time. Walter believes that in America his name will become as well known as John Wilkes Booth. You know who I mean?"

"The actor who shot Lincoln," Honey said. "You're saying Walter wants to assassinate President *Roos*evelt?"

"I can't see him doing it," Vera said. "But listen, I have to speak to Joe Aubrey before he leaves. Tell me if you want to meet anyone besides Jurgen."

She expected Walter any second to walk into the kitchen and tell her how he's going to give his life for Hitler, hoping to do it on the Führer's birthday. What would she say? You don't want to just send him a tie?

Without being a smart-ass what would she say?

Well, if that's what you want to do, Walter. If you've made up your mind. Tell Walter it's the bravest thing she's ever heard of. Without overdoing it, stirring his emotions about *lost years*. She told herself to think, will you, before you say anything? Keep it simple. Tell Walter he's your hero and tell Carl, tomorrow, what Walter plans to do.

She'd have to get Walter to drive her home.

And thought, Oh shit, he'll want to stop and talk, hold my hand. It was embarrassing watching a Nazi-lover trying to be lovey.

And thought, No, he won't stop because Joe Aubrey will be in the car. Walter must've brought him, he always did. She'd let Joe sit in front, listen to him rant about the Klan for fifteen minutes and she'd be home. Only once, back in the Bund days, Joe Aubrey ever made a real move on her. Came up behind her and slipped his hands around her body to cup her breasts, alone in the kitchen, the house on Kenilworth near the market, grabbed her breasts and whispered in her ear, "You can do better'n Walter. You know it?"

She said, " 'Course I know it."

He said, "You ever thought of movin' to Georgia? You could work at Rich's in Atlanta, the best department store in town, and I'd fly up and see you."

She said, "Joe, I've given up my cute southern ways, acting ditsy in front of boys? I've learned I'm way smarter than most of them."

He was caressing her breasts now saying in her ear, "I know how to please a woman, get her moanin'."

Honey said, "You don't stop, I'm gonna grab your weenie and yank it so hard Walter'll hear you scream and come running out here to kill you."

What did that do? Got him excited. It was one of so many times she spoke before she thought it out. Still, it never got her in trouble, did it?

Jurgen came in the kitchen with his empty glass, smiling, showing his nice white teeth, telling Honey, "Since you came in this house I've been thinking of ways to get you alone and Vera offers you to me."

"Like she knows you're the reason I crashed the party," Honey said. "Do you know what I mean?"

"I think so, yes."

"I have to talk to you about what's gonna happen next."

Jurgen hesitated. "You mean when the war ends?"

"I mean now, tonight. I want to know what you're gonna do," Honey said. "If you've made up your mind to leave here tonight, slip off in the dark or what?"

"Let me think about this," Jurgen said. "You told Vera that Carl Webster dropped you off here. This policeman who wants to put me in the hoosgow."

"He can't," Honey said.

"You know the word *hoosgow*?"

"It's the jail in a Gene Autry movie."

"Yes, what cowboys call it, from the Spanish word *juzgado,* meaning a court of law. You know *hoosgow,* uh?"

"Listen to me," Honey said. "You're right, Carl would love to grab you and take you back to Oklahoma, but he can't. The Federal Bureau of Investigation's ordered him to stand back, leave you alone. They think you're helping out the spy ring and want to see their investigation play out. Carl told me he's cut corners in his time but has *never,* when a higher-up gives him an order. Has never disobeyed it, he said, and never will."

She didn't think it sounded much like Carl, but part of it was true. She wasn't sure he'd never disobeyed an order. If he did, she imagined that by the time he explained why, he'd tell a great story that ends with gunfire.

Jurgen said, "This is Carl's idea? To ask me what I'm going to do?"

"It's mine," Honey said. "Carl dropped me off but hasn't any idea what I'm doing. Actually what I thought of when I walked in and saw you. Carl would love to sit down and talk to you, and if you want, you can do it. I swear he's been told to leave you alone. You can walk up and give him a shove, he might growl but he won't handcuff you. He's been ordered not to"—she was starting to overdo it—"and I know he would love to see you again. How's that sound? Sit down with Carl and have a drink."

He seemed to like the idea, but was still suspicious, being on the run, a fugitive.

Honey said, "I imagine Vera would just as soon you weren't here. But don't leave unless you know where you're going. I mean to a friend who'll hide you, not to some hotel. If you don't have a friend, Jesus, outside of Walter, you must've been a loner when you lived here that time, more interested in what was going on than having buddies." She paused for a moment and said, "Do you trust me?"

"I don't know you."

"All I can say is take me on my word, it's good as gold." She said, "I'm willing to help you out, Jurgen."

"Become complicit in a German soldier's escape?"

"We're in the eye of the storm," Honey said. "It's calm in here. The FBI's leaving you alone. Carl can't touch you. It's like a time-out in football. You and Carl can get together, have a few drinks and talk, decide what you want to do next. You want to leave, Carl has to let you walk away."

Jurgen said, "Why are you getting involved in this?"

"Why'd I marry Walter?"

"Why did you?"

"Don't ask hard questions," Honey said. "I have a place where you can meet Carl and tell war stories to each other. Yes or no?"

"What you're telling me," Jurgen said, "I'm no longer important as an escaped German soldier?"

Almost sounding offended.

"For the time being," Honey said.

"But I might be a spy. So they have to wait to see what I do?"

Honey said, "If it was okay for Carl to pick you up, you think we'd be standing here talking? You'd be on your way to Oklahoma."

"But you say he doesn't know what you're trying to arrange."

"I told you, I hadn't thought of it yet."

"So you don't know what he'll say about it."

Maybe she was trying too hard.

"It's up to you," Honey said. "You want to come with me, I'll ask Walter to give us a ride when he's ready."

"Yes, and where would we be going?"

"To my place," Honey said, "my apartment."

See if that stirred him any.

Twenty

Bohdan and Dr. Taylor were on the sofa talking, Bo animated, using his hands. Vera wasn't
anywhere in sight, or Joe Aubrey. Honey couldn't
imagine them off together somewhere in the house.
There was Walter sitting by himself with his
schnapps, raising the glass to have a sip, but now
he saw her and came to his feet. Rehearsed, Honey
would bet, ready for her.

As she moved toward Walter, Bohdan and Dr.
Taylor were going to the front door together still
talking. She watched Bohdan open the door, put
his hand on the doctor's shoulder saying good
night and closed the door. Now he was looking
this way. Giving her a smile? Now he was flitting
up the curved stairway to the second floor, leaving her with Walter, Walter standing in her face
as she turned to him.

"I want to tell you what I'm going to do," Walter
said, "and what I would like you to do for me."

Honey thought of her dog Bits, hit by a car when

she was a little girl, and said, "Vera told me, Walter," with a catch in her voice.

"I think of Germany," Walter said, "at the time we were married setting forth on its conquest of Europe, a time that offered me the great adventure of my life, if I were to take advantage of the opportunity."

Honey, trying her best to look interested, wondered how long this would take. It was like trying to hold a smile while someone told a boring story that was supposed to be funny.

"Now the war is coming to an end," Walter said, "while I have given nothing of myself for Germany and the Führer. All that remains is that I give my life. It will be my gift to the Führer for his fifty-sixth birthday."

Honey said, "Walter . . ." But then what?

Walter said, "Honig," and it saved her for the moment. "As I prepare to sacrifice my life, there is something you can give me. In honor of our time together."

She said, "Really?" but saw it coming and wanted to tell him no, please.

"A son," Walter said, "to bear the name Walter Helmut Schoen after I am gone."

It stopped her. "Helmut, that's your middle name?" She said, "There isn't time, Walter."

"He will be conceived tomorrow."

"I'm not ovulating. I know, because you feel different when you can make a baby."

"We can try, Honig, and pray," Walter said.

He was talking about screwing her sometime tomorrow. She thought of herself in bed with Walter during the day. Their first time with sunlight on the shades pulled down. He'd have his first good look at her bush, dark as the roots of her hair. He'd see that too and scream at her, "You lied to me, you Gypsy slut." Strange? She thought of this first?

"Tomorrow morning," Walter said.

"I've got the curse."

"It doesn't matter."

"You can't conceive during your period."

"We try," Walter said. "Maybe God will help us. You know we met in front of the cathedral."

He was different. His voice was different, more German. He had made up his mind he was taking her to bed tomorrow morning. But it couldn't be tomorrow. She'd have Jurgen. Yeah . . . ? But would she be with him all day? Carl would come by. If there was a reason she *had* to see Walter tomorrow she could probably find the time. Whatever the reason. Though it wouldn't be to go to bed with him, old Mr. Serious, Mr. Speedy Von Schoen. She said, "Walter, don't ever make a promise when you've been drinking you're gonna do something."

"I've been thinking of it since I heard of Warm Springs, where polio victims and your president go to bathe in the mineral waters."

"He's your president too, Walter. Remember my saying that to you in front of the cathedral?"

Looking at her, his glasses glistening in lamplight, Walter said, "I still love you, Honig."

His eyes raised and Honey turned enough to see Bohdan coming toward them from the staircase.

He said to Walter, "Old friend, Mr. Aubrey won't be going back with you. He and Vera are talking business of some sort, I don't know what. When they've talked themselves out I can drive Mr. Aubrey to your farm. He likes to tease me—you know how he is—but I don't mind, it's all in fun." Bo seemed about to walk away but paused and said to Walter, "Old sport, it's a noble thing you're doing for the Führer. It will give him the strength to go on."

Honey watched Bo heading for the staircase, Bo throwing his head to make his hair bounce. She said to Walter, "I have to ask you a huge favor. Do you love me?"

"I told you, didn't I?" Walter frowning as he said it.

"I have to hide Jurgen. Can he ride with us?"

"Take him where?"

"My apartment. I'll put him in the storage room full of junk and spiders, and a cot he can sleep on," Honey said, "so you won't be arrested for helping him out. You can keep your mind on the assassination."

"But tomorrow," Walter said, "you'll be with Jurgen? How will I see you?"

"It doesn't mean I have to stay with him," Honey said, maybe going too far, as usual, but at the moment curious about Walter, if he was still a complete bore in bed. A thought flashed in her mind and she saw no reason not to say it. "Give me a call, let's see what we can arrange."

Vera was at rest in her bedroom wearing a gauzy yellow negligee Bo could see through, Vera standing by the window so he could look all he wanted. The room was dim, dramatic, Bo thought, almost theatrical, a bedside lamp holding Joe Aubrey in a soft glow, Joe sprawled on his back in the double bed, his naked body round and white down to his black socks and garters. Bo stood by the bed for a close look, Joe's mouth open, wet snores dribbling out of him, before crossing the room to the goddess on her love seat smoking a cigarette, a white ceramic ashtray resting on her crotch.

Bo said, "It worked, uh?"

"The amount he drank, he didn't need the goofball."

"It won't hurt him. Makes him go seepy-by is all it does. Tell me what he did."

"He gave me a check."

"I mean in bed, what did he do? Is he a muff-diver?"

"They all are, you give them a chance."

"So, it was painless?"

"For the first time in years and years I feel I should go to Confession."

"'Bless me, Father, I fucked a Grand Dragon,' 'You did? Tell me about it, my child.'"

"I'm too tired to scold you. No, because it was devious, a dirty trick, taking him to bed because we need money."

"You have the check?"

"In a safe place."

"How much did he give you?"

"I couldn't ask for what we need. I said, 'Put in the amount you feel you can give.'"

"Vera, please don't say that."

"Made out to the Bomb Victims Fund of Berlin."

"Tell me how much he gave you?"

"I said to him, 'Wait, I don't think that's the exact name of the fund.' I won't tell you what I was doing to him while he's holding his pen and his checkbook."

"You're both completely naked."

"Joe has his socks on. I told him, sign the check, I'd fill in the name later."

"He wrote in the amount?"

"He was much too anxious, getting ink on my breasts, but he did sign the check."

"Becoming groggy?"

"Not yet, but slurring."

"And failed to write in the amount?"

"I'm going to type it in," Vera said, "the amount, the date, and to whom it's paid."

"For how much?"

"Let's talk about it in the morning. You have to get Mr. Aubrey on the road."

"Time for Joe to go nigh-nigh," Bo said. "You know it's an awfully long ride out to Walter's."

"Stay with the plan," Vera said. "When you come out of the driveway, make sure the surveillance car doesn't follow you. They have the rear end of my Chrysler imprinted in their minds, they've tailed it enough times. I doubt they'll follow you, but be alert, they can radio another car to pick you up."

"In the middle of the night?"

"Bo, dearest—"

"I know, stay with the plan."

"You found the shovel?"

"A spade, but will do the job. It's in the trunk."

"I cleaned the Walther," Vera said.

"Which one?"

"Your favorite, the .380 PPK."

"You're a dear," Bo said. "I'd get rid of the Tokarev, that Russian piece of shit, it's so heavy. How does one carry it, keep it concealed?"

"My, we're testy this evening."

"I'm anxious to be going."

"You're wearing your girdle?"

"I hate it, it's so tight I can't breathe."

"We all have our crosses to bear," Vera said.

Twenty-one

One o'clock in the morning Bo came out of the driveway in the Chrysler and turned left around the median. Now he was approaching the FBI surveillance car, having a look at it through the line of trees in the median. It was Vera's idea: go left and they would have to turn around in the street to come after him. "If anyone is in it," Vera said. "I see it as a decoy. Sometime after breakfast an agent is dropped off to sit in the car and pick his teeth."

Joe Aubrey was a mess, but not a problem in his rumpled suit, his shirttail hanging out. Bo had said, "I'm not sticking his shirt down in his pants." Vera didn't care. Joe was groggy from the goofball, still drunk but miserable, what was left of him once Vera was through. He opened his eyes to streetlights and neon signs.

"Where we goin'?"

"To Walter's."

"He's way out'n the country."

"Yes, he is," Bo said. "Go seepy-by and let me drive."

Aubrey reached over to lay his hand on Bo's thigh. "You still wearin' your skirt? I'm gonna stick my hand under it, see what you got."

Bo said, "Mr. Aubrey, please," and gave the hand a slap. "Let's not be naughty." They were driving south on Woodward, only a few miles now from downtown Detroit.

"Man, I am in pain. I think I got laid, but I'm not sure."

"You did, after a fashion."

"That's the first hangover I've had in twenty years. I suck oxygen I keep in my airplane and it clears up my head."

They drove in silence for a while, Joe Aubrey lying back with his eyes closed through the downtown area now, past J.L. Hudson's, Sam's Cut Rate, past the big open square called Campus Martius across from city hall, past the Empress and the Avenue burlesque houses, and turned left on Jefferson Avenue, on their way to the bridge that crossed to Belle Isle in the middle of the river with its recreational areas, baseball diamonds, picnic tables, a zoo, horses to ride, canoes to paddle in the lagoon, and the river to swim in during the summer. Bo could see no sense in driving all the way to Farmington, a good hour from Vera's, when he could drop Mr. Aubrey off in the Detroit River, a popular grave for hundreds of souls during Prohibition, bootleggers bringing whiskey across from Canada, getting waylaid by the murderous Purple Gang if the police didn't stop them. It was a rough town, used to violence. Two years ago, 1943, a Negro sailor was thrown in the river from the Belle Isle bridge and it started a race riot that went on for days, property destroyed, cars turned over, troops called in . . . He'd drop off Mr. Aubrey, turn around and take Woodward north this time to Dr. Taylor's English-looking home in Palmer Woods, just off Seven Mile Road on Wellesley. He had not mentioned to Vera his plan to see Dr. Taylor tonight. But why not, while he was at it? He was thinking, Wouldn't it be lovely if Dr. Taylor were here, to join Mr. Aubrey on the bridge?

And immediately thought, Turn it around. Take Mr. Aubrey to Dr. Taylor's.

Bo U-turned on Jefferson beginning to rehearse what he'd do, ring the doorbell and say, Doctor, I'm very sorry to bother you . . . Mr. Aubrey desperately needs to use the toilet. We're on our way to Walter's. I'm afraid he's just a bit tipsy.

Just a bit—he hoped he could keep sleepyhead on his feet.

Dr. Taylor was wearing a maroon smoking jacket with black silk lapels and wide shoulders over his shirt and tie, the doctor still dressed. He stepped back from the door, his right hand in the pocket of his jacket. Bo recited his lines and Dr. Taylor said, "Yes, the powder room's right there."

Bo got Aubrey inside and closed the door, Aubrey wanting to know, "Where'n the fuck are we?"

Bo told him, "You have to piss, understand? Stand over the toilet and take out your dong and aim it. Wait. Mr. Aubrey, will you please fucking *wait*, you're pissing all over the floor." There was no way to stop him now; he should have sat him on the toilet. Bo said, "Lean over it with your hands on the wall, so you don't fall and hit your head." He stepped out of the powder room and closed the door.

Dr. Taylor, waiting for him, his hand still in his pocket, said, "It's a shame you didn't come alone. I have a rare cognac we could sip while we continue our talk."

The man was of no interest to Bohdan, his thoughts or his inclinations, the way he gave signs of intimacy but then seemed to lose his nerve. Bo said, "Do you have a gun in your hand?"

Dr. Taylor smiled bringing it out.

"You're very observant."

"A Luger?" Bo said.

"No, a Walther P38," Dr. Taylor said. "In the thirties it took the place of the Luger as the German military pistol. I do have a pair of Luger 08s that date back to the first war and, if you can believe it, an MP40 *Maschinenpistole*."

Bo said, "A Schmeisser?"

Dr. Taylor smiled at him again. "Where did you get that, from a comic book? Americans can be very ignorant. They call it a Schmeisser, but Hugo Schmeisser had absolutely nothing to do with the design or creation of the weapon, nothing."

Bo said, "May I see the Walther?"

The doctor extended it holding the barrel.

"Be careful, it's fully loaded. The safety is on the left side of the slide. It's on."

Bo shifted the P38 to his left hand. He raised the hem of the gray cashmere and brought out his Walther PPK from the band of the girdle he was wearing as sort of a holster and now had a pistol in each hand, his Walther not looking anything like Dr. Taylor's Walther.

"I see we both hold dear the law of self-preservation," the doctor said. "Do you know how many times my life has been threatened? Do you think I would dare answer the door at night without a pistol in my hand?"

"How many times?" Bo said.

"In letters I receive in the mail. In notes I find, here and at my office. In phone calls—I'm talking about actual threats against my life. Some might be from the same person, it's difficult to tell. One of the recent letters said, 'I am a little guy in that I am short, but I have a big gun. Quit spouting off about Jews or you will pay with your life.'"

"How interesting," Bo said, "he tells you he's short."

"Yes, isn't it strange?" The doctor said, "Oh, I see you're still wearing your skirt. You're so chic, but at the same time you make a delightful Buster Brown."

Bo said, "Thank you, Doctor," with a coy smile and bounced his hair.

He had decided how he would do the job.

He slipped the PPK again into the girdle beneath his skirt and could feel it against his tummy, Bo turning to the powder room with the doctor's P38 in his right hand now. He snicked the safety off, opened the door, and shot Joe Aubrey in the back of the head, *bam*, and saw part of the white wall spewed red before he could close the door again.

The doctor stood rigid in his maroon silk smok-

ing jacket, his eyes stuck wide open, his eyes raising then to the sound of a woman's voice calling
from upstairs.

"Michael?"

Bo looked toward the staircase. It would be the
doctor's wife, though he didn't see her yet, the upstairs dark.

"Answer her," Bo said. "Aren't you all right?"

The doctor called out, "I'm okay, Rosemary."

Bo saw her now, a pale nightgown coming out
of the dark, her hand sliding along the round ban-
ister, Rosemary joining the party, and Bo revised
how he'd finish the job. She reached the bottom of
the stairs and saw him in the lamplight. Now he
turned, extending the pistol, and shot Dr. Taylor in
the chest, shot him through the chest, a china lamp
behind him shattering as his wife screamed and Bo
shot him again.

Now she'll throw herself on his body and wail in
anguish, Bo thought, the way the women of Odessa
wailed running to the wall, their men lying dead
and the fucking Romanians eyeing the women as
they walked away. But this one has not had the
experience of people killed by gunfire. She seems
unsure if he was alive or dead. Really? A nine-
millimeter parabellum slug having torn through
his chest? Two of them. What did she expect him
to do, sit up? Ah, now she crept to her husband lying on the floor and went to her knees saying his
name, crying, confused.

Bo stepped over to hunch down next to her
and could see into her nightgown the way she was
crouched, so-so breasts hanging limp. He touched

her shoulder, then brushed her hair from the side of her face, telling her in a soft tone of voice, "He's dead, Rosemary." Now he placed the muzzle of the Walther against her temple, turned his face away and shot her through the head.

He used her nightgown to wipe the Walther clean and placed it in Rosemary's right hand, pressing her fingers to the grip. He noticed the diamond on her left hand, an impressive stone he believed he could twist from her finger. It occurred to Bo he could take whatever the doctor had in his billfold. Look in the bedroom for jewelry, cash, objects of value—the doctor must do well in his practice, a house this size.

Except he hadn't planned it to look like a robbery.

As soon as he saw Rosemary coming down the stairs he set the scene. She finds her husband and Mr. Aubrey doing nasty things with each other in the powder room. She has suspected her husband and now catches him going at it with Mr. Aubrey, shoots them both in a blind rage and turns the gun on herself.

He thought about it for several moments.

She's consumed with a feeling of unbearable shame.

Would the police see that?

Or she can't imagine spending the rest of her life in prison. Or she's insane. Or whatever way the police would see it, looking at the evidence.

What was the evidence?

Bo was thinking he'd have to take their clothes off. Dress Mr. Aubrey and now undress him, without getting bloodstains on Vera's skirt. At least unzip their flies. What was Mr. Aubrey doing? He had to piss. Bo hears him saying to Rosemary, "You're being a foolish girl. I'm going to piss and be on my way."

How did he get here?

He must have come with the doctor.

Yes? The police arrive and they see Rosemary has killed her husband and Mr. Aubrey. The police pose motives to explain why Rosemary, with her drooping dugs, is the killer. Why, why, why. Stuck with looking for her motive. Never seeing this as a robbery. Or even thinking of robbery as a possibility.

What he should do, give Vera a call.

In case he's overlooked something.

He would tell her he changed the plan. He *wanted* to tell her, proud of the way it worked out, improvising as he went along. Call her and get it over with. You changed the plan. Aubrey is not buried in a cornfield. You decided to take care of the doctor too. "Vera, you know he'll fold under FBI pressure. I thought, since I'm out running errands anyway . . . " Tell her, "The moment I saw Rosemary descending the stairs in her see-through nighty, I was inspired."

Make it sound easy and Vera will love it.

Vera was under the covers, the phone in bed with her.

She said, "Wait. Start over. Bo, I was sound asleep. You're at Dr. Taylor's?"

Listening to him, not once interrupting, she began to push herself higher on the pillows bunched against the headboard. By the time Bo, winding down, was describing his action as inspired, Vera was sitting up in bed smoking a cigarette. Before she said a word she reminded herself, *You need him.*

"Bo, I love it."

"I knew you would."

"You could be a playwright."

"You know I've always wanted to write."

"But you can't leave Aubrey there."

It stopped Bo in his tracks.

"Why? It doesn't work without Mr. Aubrey. He's the other man."

"But as soon as he's found dead, the check he gave me is worthless."

"Yes, but who knows when that will be?"

"Rosemary has a maid who comes every day."

"Go to the bank early, as soon as it opens."

"Bo, I'm making it out for fifty thousand. I'm not going to deposit the check of a man who was murdered the day before."

"What if I move Mr. Aubrey?"

"I don't know," Vera said.

"He gave you the check and went home to Georgia, as far as anyone knows."

"I'd still be afraid of it."

"Even if he's in the river, never to be seen again?"

"I don't know." She needed to think about it and said, "There's still Dr. Taylor."

"I could drop him off too."

"Give me a minute," Vera said. She slept naked and got out of bed this way, chilled as she went to the tea cart that served as her bedroom bar, poured a slivovitz and drank it down; poured another and brought it to the bed with her.

"If the doctor isn't there, and his wife is found dead—"

"A suicide," Bo said.

"Yes, but the police will suspect her husband killed her. Where is he? Has he fled? Bo, leave the doctor where he is. It's much simpler if Rosemary killed him and killed herself." Vera finished the slivovitz and lighted a cigarette. "Have you ever had a conversation with Rosemary?"

"I've asked her what she'd like to drink. She says, 'Oh,' and acts flustered. 'Do you have white wine?'"

Vera said, "I doubt if anyone who knows Rosemary will believe she killed Michael. But, I suppose that can be said of most women who kill their husbands. She's a timid soul. I can't imagine her firing a P38 or even knowing how."

"The doctor also has a couple of Lugers," Bo said, "and that bullet hose, the MP40 machine pistol."

There was a silence as Vera smoked her cigarette and imagined the scene in the doctor's house. Finally she said, "Bo, listen. I want only the doctor and Rosemary there. Who knows why she killed him. It will be announced on the front pages of Detroit papers, Wife Murders Her Husband the Doctor. After that, stories will be about the doctor's politics. What is he? An enemy alien born in Canada, a former member of the Bund and alleged member of a German spy ring. We won't know if the police suspect murder. They'll talk to neighbors, the doctor's hospital associates, his nurses, perhaps some of his patients, and before long they'll ask us how we happen to know Dr. Taylor."

"Only socially," Bo said, "he's so much fun."

"But if Aubrey's body is found in the house," Vera said, "it becomes a much bigger story because Aubrey's an infamous celebrity. They'll write entertaining features about his Klan activities, perhaps the only Nazi Grand Dragon in America. The investigation can go on forever, newspaper columnists offering theories. More light is cast on us as enemy aliens and the Justice Department is forced to take action. We'll be indicted, charged with acts of sedition, if not plotting to overthrow the government. We'll be offered a bond we can't possibly afford, and sit in a federal prison for months awaiting trial."

"But what do they have on us?" Bo said. "Nothing."

Bo sounding confident for her benefit. Vera knew him, his poses, his attitudes he could turn on and off. By now she could anticipate his reactions. If the FBI came for Bo, he'd run.

She said, "What would you do if they came to arrest you?"

"Run," Bo said. "Have it already worked out how we'd do it. I *know* they won't be after me without you."

She wanted him to mean it and murmured into

the phone, "This is when I need to feel my lovely boy against my body and whisper things to him."

"Dirty things?"

"What I want him to do to me."

"You're giving me what Americans call a boner," Bo said. "Stay in bed. I'll be home as soon as I dump Mr. Aubrey."

"The way we planned it."

"Yes, bury him."

"He's quite bloody, his clothes?"

"I suppose. I shot him and closed the door."

"You have to put him in my car, don't you?"

"I can wrap him in a blanket."

"Bo, don't take anything."

"I won't."

"Perhaps the Lugers. But you understand it isn't to look like a robbery."

"Leave the Schmeisser?"

"The doctor called it that?"

"I did. So he'd think I'm an oaf."

"Bring the Schmeisser if you want."

"Anything else?"

"Be sure to clean the powder room."

Vera had learned that if she screamed at Bohdan, sometimes only raised her voice, he'd sulk. He'd stop talking to her and she would have to wait for him to get over his funk or let him wear one of her cocktail dresses. She loved Bo; she did. When they were having fun in bed or on the floor or the stairway and Bo's mind was set on giving her pleasure, she adored him. This lovely boy from Odessa who killed with ease having seen hundreds and hundreds of people gassed, shot against walls, shot with pistols against their heads, hung from street-lights, locked in rooms and burned alive, all of it a part of Bo's coming-of-age. She would ask him, "Will you always love me, Bo?" And he would tell her she was his life, his reason for living.

She wished she'd had more time to spend with Jurgen, another lovely boy, at first thinking he might be a bore or a tragic figure after North Africa, instilled with war, and she would have told him to wake up, we've all been to war. But he was never tiresome. He let you know he was alive, happy to be in America, and he was inquisitive. He accepted her being a reluctant German agent and in another day or so they could have been in love. At least lovers.

But along came Honey, the cheeky *Sieg Heil* girl, not Honey Schoen, Walter's ex, Honey Deal. She had taken Jurgen away and by this morning would have eaten him up. Vera liked Honey from the moment she walked in the house, she sounded so American. "I'd marry Carl in a minute, but he's taken." Or when she said, "I act a little like I'm on the make, but I'm not after him to leave home." Honey just wanted to have fun. She thought Bo was cute.

Vera loved the way Americans spoke in their different accents and the expressions they used. One of her favorites was "on the make," which meant flirting. She loved Honey saying, "You think he's a shit-kicker till you look in his eyes." Telling so much in a few words about the federal policeman, Carl, the one Honey had her eye on.

The day they arrived in Detroit she told Bo, "We are going to listen to people, the way they pronounce words and the slang they use. We are not from the South or New York City, we live in Detroit and speak the way they do here."

At that time Bo said, "I have one. 'So is your old man.'"

"*So's*," Vera said. "*So's* your old man. You hear the difference? It's a rebuff."

Bo was a natural. He liked to imitate people on the radio, Walter Winchell, Gabriel Heatter, Jack Benny. He could do Rochester. Vera laughed because he was funny and she loved him, this boy who told her she was his life.

But if the time came he had to make a choice, give her up or go to prison?

He'd give her up.

In the courtroom Bo would gaze at her with tears in his eyes—he could do that, cause his eyes to fill—and testify for the prosecution. Bo would create for her daring acts of espionage, and the newspapers would make her a star, World War II's Mata Hari, without citing a single reference to what Mata Hari did for the Kaiser. Or did she spy for the French? Vera wasn't certain, perhaps both, but knew she was better-looking than the Dutch woman—huge thighs but no tits—whose stage name was a Malay word for "eye of dawn."

If offered the same choice, would she give up Bo?

Regretfully.

Though it would never come to that. Or Bo in a courtroom testifying against her. She would shoot him first.

Love in a time of war had only moments.

But awfully good ones.

Even Aubrey wasn't that bad.

Twenty-two

Carl's dad phoned at 6 A.M. waking him up.
"How you like De-troit?"

"All right. It's big. They say it's our third-biggest city, but I heard Philadelphia was."

"It don't mean a thing to me," his dad said. "How's the ho-tel?"

They'd go through this until his dad came to the reason he was talking to Carl long-distance.

"A guy called last night saying he was a buddy of yours and wondered where you were. Narcissa talked to him."

"What's his name?"

"Vito Tessa."

"Jesus Christ."

"No, I said Vito Tessa." His dad being funny.

"Didn't the name sound familiar? He's the kid gangster with the big nickel-plate and the zoot suit, the jitterbug, the night before I left."

"The one, his brother's Lou Tessa?"

"Yeah, it's another one of those brother things.

What'd Narcissa tell him, I'm in Detroit, uh? Or you wouldn't of called."

"Yeah, I guess she did. And where you're staying."

"I thought she knew better."

"He told her he was in the Seabees with you. How would he know that?"

"Every time I talk to a writer he wants to know what I did in the war."

"The kid gangster read up on you." Virgil said, "Wait a minute, Narcissa's standing here listening." Virgil came back on saying, "I told her one time shipmates stand together, and she believed the guy was a shipmate of yours. Hold it again." This time Virgil said, "Narcissa says he told her his name, Vito Tessa. And if we talk to you, let you know Vito Tessa is coming to see you. Why'd he say that if he's out to shoot you?"

"The brother tried to shoot me in the back."

"This one wants to try face-to-face?"

"I'm not sure. Marvin the doorman at the Mayo said, 'Uh-oh, the man's got a gun,' and I turned. Now we're face-to-face, but he didn't want any part of it. I don't know what he's doing giving you his name."

"Showin' off," Virgil said.

"But it doesn't mean he won't try to surprise me. I'm gonna have to call Tulsa police, find out who he is and why they turned him loose. They had him for possession of a firearm. I can't see the kid gangster with a license to pack. He might be smarter than I gave him credit, but not that different from his brother. Now I have to keep looking

over my shoulder while I track the Krauts and get
'em home. One of 'em I believe took off, Otto, the
SS guy, but hasn't been gone long." Carl said to his
dad, "Well, I guess my day has started."

He phoned Honey at seven, seven-thirty, and five
of eight, each time letting it ring in case Honey
was in the shower, Carl seeing her face raised
in the spray, eyes closed, soapy water streaming
over her sparkling clean breasts, but never got
an answer. He had decided the best thing to do,
keep Honey on as if she had never shown him her
breasts. Though it could get tricky talking to her
face-to-face, each knowing how close they came
yesterday to something happening, if not adultery. He'd try not to stare at her blouse and imagine the two girls in there, thinking they were a
size smaller than Louly's, but weren't what you'd
call small breasts, either. What Honey's had was
a look of their own, one he thought of as, you
know, perky, their pink noses stuck up in the air.
He liked this image that came to him, but couldn't
think of anyone he could tell and admit he made it
up. Maybe Narcissa.

He had stood in the bedroom doorway looking
at Honey. She didn't move or give him any kind of
sexy look. She didn't have to. She commented on
what he read to her from the paper, the same as
if she had all her clothes on, and asked him what
he wanted to do. No, she said, "Have you decided
what you want to do?"

The first thing he thought of was, You got to be kidding. But didn't say it. He didn't want to see her smile, encouraged. He had to be as cool about it as she was, and said let's have supper and drive by Vera Mezwa's, see who's there. Honey said, "That's what you want to do, check license numbers?" Standing there with her honkers staring at him. Honey started to smile, then was laughing, shaking her head. Carl grinned at her and at the two girls he would never see again and everything was almost back to normal. Honey got dressed.

Last night he'd said to her, "You get out of the car you're on your own," in a normal tone of voice, but laying it out, this is the way it is. What did she do? She got out saying she'd tell him about it tomorrow and waved her fingers at him. She was out of view trespassing around the house, appeared again on the other side, went up to the door, turned and waved to him.

What did he do after that—nothing. Came back to the hotel, had a drink at the bar, went up to his room and turned on the radio for news reports. The Russians in Vienna fighting house to house. Carl listening, Carl thinking of how to be himself with Honey without getting in trouble.

Last night Carl had stopped at the curb in front of Vera Mezwa's house to let Honey out, Honey having her way without acting snippy about it. This morning he turned into the driveway and cut the motor. Nobody was going to drive off while Carl was visiting, not Mrs. Mezwa, not her little helper and not the Kraut escape artist Jurgen Schrenk. Carl followed the walk to the front door, his hand raised in a gesture to the surveillance car across the street—not the empty one there for show—his acknowledging them saying there was no reason to call it in, we're all friends here, aren't we? But that's what the agents would do, radio the office. Carl rang the bell and heard the chime inside the house, waited and rang the bell again. He wasn't going anywhere.

The door opened and Carl said, "Bohdan Kravchenko from Odessa, a survivor of the siege. Nice going, buddy. I'm Carl Webster, here in no official capacity to see Miz Vera Mezwa, the lady of the house."

Bo had on a green smoking jacket with black lapels, his bare chest showing, and pajama pants. He said, "I'm sorry, but Mrs. Mezwa is not entertaining callers this morning."

Carl said, "I don't need to be entertained, Bohunk. Run upstairs and tell her I have the means to search the house if I need to."

Bo appeared to have turned to stone. He seemed to be trying not to move his mouth as he said, "May I see it?"

Carl pulled out the leather case he carried every day of his life and opened it to show his marshal's ID and his star.

Bo said, "That only tells me who you are."

Carl said, "It's all you need to know."

"But it's not a court order."

Carl said, "It's better."

* * *

They were both on the sofa at opposite ends, but turned to each other, Vera in a greenish silk dressing gown that was loose in front and she would let come open enough to catch his eye—Carl thinking these Detroit women came right at you. They were talking about Honey Deal.

Vera saying, "Yes, you dropped her off and she went home with Walter Schoen. That is to say I believe he drove her home. I can't presume to know his intentions. Honey, quite openly, apologized to Walter for the way she left him, rather abruptly, and I sensed he was encouraged to renew their relationship. At least to try. I noticed at one point while they were talking Walter was wiping his eyes."

Carl said, "No kidding."

He couldn't imagine her getting Walter worked up on purpose unless she was playing with him. Or she felt sorry for him, the reason she was being nice. Honey was out front in her way, not the least self-conscious. Carl believed she could walk out on a stage, face an auditorium full of strangers, and give a talk off the cuff. Tell about the funny thing that happened on the way there and make up the rest. Tell a few jokes. He felt he and Honey were alike in that they could talk their way in or out of situations. She always seemed herself, didn't need to put on any kind of act. He said to Vera, "She left with Walter. Just the two of them in the car?"

"As far as I know."

"What about Dr. Taylor?"

"You're familiar with everyone."

"What was he doing?"

"Talking to my houseman, Bo."

"I understand Joe Aubrey arrived with Walter."

"Honey told you that? Or, there actually *is* someone in the surveillance car?"

Carl smiled for a moment.

"Didn't Joe Aubrey go home with Walter? That would be three of them in Walter's Ford."

"I don't know, really. I had already said good night to my guests. They could stay and talk if they wished."

"Maybe Aubrey went home with Dr. Taylor."

"He might have."

Carl said, "Who did Jurgen go home with?"

Vera was smoking a cigarette, at ease. She said, "Poor Jurgen. I understand for five and a half months no one can find him, and the Hot Kid arrives. Tell me, what does it mean to be a hot kid?"

"You start out being lucky," Carl said.

"Twelve times," Vera said, "you were lucky with your pistol, shooting criminals?"

"What you do with a gun isn't luck," Carl said. "I'm talking about, in the line of duty having chances to look good, like you know what you're doing."

Vera liked that. She smiled at him. "The newspapers write the story and you become a hero."

"Once you get a name," Carl said, "and somebody writes a book about you, you get referred to a lot. A clerk in a store stops a robbery. They might say he made a lightning fast Carl Webster move and brought up a revolver. Last month I was interviewed about escaped prisoners of war like I'm an expert on it. They call me 'cause my name's familiar. Let's see what Carl Webster has to say. It was a piece in *Newsweek*."

"I saw it," Vera said. "'The Hot Kid's War.' Did you like what they wrote?"

"The writer and I got along pretty well."

"Your wife I see is a marine?"

"A gunny. Louly teaches firing a machine gun from a dive-bomber."

"Of the dozen people you've shot and killed in your career, were any of them women?"

"None. They were pretty much all wanted felons, bank robbers. One a cow thief caught in the act, but I don't count him."

"Why is that?"

"I wasn't a marshal yet. If you're counting people I shot in the line of duty."

"Do you ever regret taking their lives?"

Carl said, "Does Joe Foss regret shooting down twenty-six Zekes? He flew a Wildcat in the Pacific."

Vera said, "Yes, of course, why would it be different? Though I imagine Joe Foss never sees the faces of the ones he kills." She said, "Forgive me, I'm making conversation."

Bo came to the sofa looking only at Vera to say there was a call for the deputy marshal. "In the den," he told Carl, still looking at Vera, and turned away.

Carl said, "Was he asking you if it was okay?"

"You must have said something he didn't like." Vera waved her hand. "He wants you to follow him."

* * *

It was Kevin Dean on the phone.

"You're talking to Vera?"

"I'm looking for Honey," Carl said standing by the desk, shelves of leather-bound sets of books behind him, books he thought of as decoration, never opened.

Kevin said, "She doing you any good? I haven't seen her since I was reassigned. You have trouble calling her Honey?"

"No," Carl said. "Do you?"

"I did at first. In fact I still have trouble. It's what you call your wife or your girlfriend. Anyway, listen, the reason I called, Dr. Michael Taylor, one of the useless spy ring guys, was shot and killed last night. It looks like his wife Rosemary did it with a Walther P38 and then used it on herself, blew her brains out. The cleaning woman said the gun belonged to Dr. Taylor. She came this morning surprised to see the car still in the garage, the doctor hadn't left to go to his office, and found them in the living room."

Carl was thinking, If Kevin had trouble calling her Honey, it meant he hadn't gone to bed with her yet. He said, "The maid called the police?"

"Right away. Detroit Homicide got on the scene. One of the guys in the squad knew about Dr. Taylor being pro-Nazi, a member of the Bund back in the thirties, arrested on a misdemeanor, demonstrating in front of a synagogue. Homicide's keeping us up on what they find."

Carl was looking at Bo standing in the doorway, his back to Carl by the desk.

"Something else," Kevin said. "They're positive a third gunshot victim was in the lavatory, shot in the back of the head. They found traces of blood the shooter tried to clean up but did a half-assed job, so the evidence techs went over the entire lavatory and found bone fragments and brain tissue in the drain."

Carl told Kevin to hold it a minute. He said to Bo, "Sweetheart, instead of listening to the conversation, how about getting me a cup of coffee?"

Bo walked away without saying a word.

"Maybe the doctor," Carl said, "was in the can when she popped him."

"Taylor was shot in the chest. It was someone else."

"Who's missing?"

"Joe Aubrey."

"His plane's at the airport?"

"It never was. He took the train this time. He's having work done on the Cessna, in Atlanta."

"Where's Walter?"

"At his farm this morning."

"Alone?"

"That German couple's there. I asked the woman, she answered the phone, if anybody came home with Walter, she said no."

"You know Honey crashed the spy party."

"I heard, yeah. You believe it? I've been trying to get hold of her, but she hasn't been home or at work all morning."

"You still pickin' through bomb damage?"

"I'm on the homicide now. You want to look at the scene, I'll take you."

Carl said, "Is there any reason to believe the third one might be a woman?"

Kevin took a moment to say, "I don't know. I think they all assume it was a guy. But the wife, say she caught him with another woman." There was a silence. "No, if the wife did it, the other woman's body'd still be there. I'll find out and let you know."

"Or the third one," Carl said, "was the other *guy* she caught her husband with? But where did he go?"

Kevin said, "You're not thinking it could be Honey."

"Vera said Walter drove her home. I don't have any reason to believe Vera, but I do. I accept her lying about Jurgen."

"Well, Walter's at the farm. I spoke to him for a while. In the surveillance report for last night, Walter arrived with most likely Joe Aubrey, but it was hard to get a positive ID. They know Walter because of his car. Surveillance says he left with a man and a woman."

"You call him before or after you knew about the homicides?"

"After I went to the scene. I called him from there, asked him who he drove home. He said Honig Schoen. He dropped her off at her apartment. I said, 'Walter, there were three people got in your car when you left the meeting.' Walter said, 'You have a photograph of three unidentified people standing by a car at night somewhere?' He said whoever saw us was mistaken or lied. His wife was his only passenger."

"That's what he called her?"

"Which, his wife or his passenger? I asked if she was at the farm with him. Walter said no. But she promised to spend time with him today."

"She told him that?"

"Walter said he would see she kept her verd."

"So we know what she's doing now," Carl said. "She's hiding from Walter."

Vera hadn't moved from the sofa. Sitting with her again Carl thought of giving her knee a pat for no other reason than having the war in common, on different sides but they'd feel the same way about it. He said to her, "You think the war's done anyone any good?"

"I'll say no one, because I'm too tired to think of something that sounds wise, or enigmatic. Or stupid."

"What do you want to do when it's over?"

"Try not to be noticed."

"You worried about people telling on you?"

"My friends?"

"Your spy ring."

Carl looked up and there was Bo with a coffee service for one. He placed the tray on the cocktail table and poured a cup as Vera said to him, "This gentleman wants to know if I suspect you would tell lies about me to save your *dupa* from rapacious prison convicts."

Bo said, "What's wrong with a rapacious convict?" He served Carl, handing him a cup of black coffee. Carl said thanks and Bo said "*Koorvya mat*" in a pleasant tone of voice and walked away.

Vera was watching him. Carl said, "What's *koorvya mat* mean?"

"You thanked him—you didn't think he was saying oh, you're very welcome?"

"He was too sweet."

"I shouldn't tell you," Vera said, "but what difference does it make. *Koorvya mat* is Ukrainian for 'Go fuck your mother.' What did you say to him, before?"

"I might've raised my voice," Carl said. "You don't think he'll turn on you, huh?"

"If they frighten him enough, I wouldn't be surprised. But whatever he tells them will be highly entertaining. Bo loves attention." She said, "What will the others do if accused? Nothing. Joe Aubrey will continue to be Joe Aubrey. Dr. Taylor the obstetrician will inspect vaginas as he thinks up racial slurs, and Walter . . . Honey must have told you his astonishing plan."

It took Carl by surprise. He said, "Yeah, Walter," and said, "you think he'll pull it off?"

Vera started to smile. "You haven't spoken to Honey, have you? You're still upset she left you to come to my party. You know, you may not be smart enough for Honey. I saw the photo of your wife in *Newsweek*, in her uniform. She's quite attractive. I suppose she's pleasant. But if you haven't noticed, Honey is a rare human being, a free spirit who knows how to think. She's not simply in a rush to be entertained, try new things."

"You're saying I should leave my wife for Honey Deal?"

"I'm saying she's one of a kind. If you're afraid to spend time with her, then don't."

Carl said, "Let's get back to Walter."

"I won't talk to you about Walter. I'm sure he told Honey. Ask her what he's doing, as Walter says, to meet his destiny."

"You don't care that Honey knows?"

"It's too big for Walter," Vera said. "It's his grand illusion, Walter Schoen becomes a prominent name in the history of the world."

Carl said, "He wants to assassinate somebody."

"I'm not saying another word."

"I was thinking he might want to return to Germany for Adolf's last stand, but there's no way for him to get there. So it must be Walter's gonna shoot somebody like the president of the United States. Get him riding in that open car he likes. A fella by the name of Giuseppe Zangara, an anarchist, fired five shots at Roosevelt one time from no more than twenty-five feet away. In Miami, 1933."

Vera said, "He missed?"

"A housewife by the name of Lillian Cross bumped Zangara and threw him off his aim. He missed the president, but hit five other people standing there, one of them Anton Cermak, mayor of Chicago."

"Did she think five people shot," Vera said, "was worth not losing the president?"

"I've wondered that myself," Carl said. "One of these days I'll look Miz Cross up. In the meantime I'll see if I can find Honey—if her free spirit hasn't gotten her to run off."

Carl had put his cup on the tray. He picked it up

now, took a sip and put the cup on the tray again, the coffee served to him ice cold.

"You realize," Carl said, "you could be indicted for knowing about Walter but not saying anything? It's called misprision, concealing treasonable acts against the U.S. government. Even if you take no part in the act."

"I told you," Vera said, "it's his dream. Do you think I should go to prison for something Walter has no intention of actually doing?"

"You're still liable."

"Do you care?" Vera said. "You haven't asked if Jurgen is here."

"Is he?"

Vera said, "No," and smiled.

"How about Dr. Taylor?"

"What about him?"

"You think he might tell on you?"

"Dr. Taylor has no credibility. He continues to say Adolf Hitler is the savior of the world, and who believes that? No, the doctor is not a concern of mine."

Carl said, "You mean now that he's dead?"

Twenty-three

Vera came in the kitchen to see Bo hunched over the morning paper spread open on the table.

"Did you hear what he said?"

"I wasn't listening. He's a peasant."

"He knows about Dr. Taylor."

"It's not in the paper."

"He doesn't *need* the paper."

Vera's tone got Bo to look up at her.

"He knows policemen, federal agents. He asked if I was worried about the doctor informing on me. I said he's not a concern, and he said, 'You mean now that he's dead?'"

Bo said, "He knows already?" sounding surprised.

"You call him a peasant," Vera said, "with your prissy way. You serve him cold coffee. The man is the most famous law officer in America. They write stories about him in magazines. A book was written about him with photographs, you think he's of no concern."

"I thought his behavior crude." Bo shrugged

in his new smoking jacket. "What did you say to him?"

"I said, 'The doctor, he was in an accident with his car, and was killed?' I must've sounded stupid."

"I'm sure you were convincing."

Bo's gaze dropped to the newspaper and Vera said, "Look at me, I'm talking to you," and swept the paper from the table. "The police know another person was killed."

"Rosemary."

"I don't know how you could shoot that poor woman."

"I had no choice, she knows me."

"I'm talking about Aubrey, in the loo. They found traces of blood someone tried to clean from the wall, blood and brains, Carl said, and did a poor job."

"Since it was the powder room," Bo said, "he should have said I did a piss-poor job."

"I said to Carl, 'Who could it be?' astonished, eyes wide with innocence. Do you know who he said it was? Not who he thought it might be? Aubrey."

Bo frowned. He'd used soapy guest towels to clean up the mess, knew enough to take the towels with him, stuffed into Mr. Aubrey's pants once he got them pulled up. Then had to wrap Mr. Aubrey's head in a bath towel he got from upstairs when he went up to look around, found some jewelry he liked and the doctor's smoking jacket in green. Then he had to look for the Lugers and the machine pistol locked in a cabinet and had to pry it open but thought he did a rather professional job. He borrowed a blanket from Rosemary's warm bed he used to drag Mr. Aubrey across the tiled floor to the front entrance where, Bo decided to let Mr. Obnoxious wait while he cleaned the powder room and thought about driving all the way out to a cornfield near Walter's place at four in the morning when he was already in Palmer Woods, not a forest but there were patches of woods here and there.

"They're sure the third one's Joe Aubrey," Vera said. "Joe's the only one missing who was here last night."

"It couldn't be someone else?"

"I know it's Aubrey and Carl knows it's Aubrey you shot in the back of the head to make a mess. Did you think about where you should shoot him?"

"There was his head only a few feet away," Bo said, "while he's taking a whiz. Have you heard that one, for pissing? Mr. Aubrey was whizzing all over the floor."

"You must have touched Rosemary."

"I moved her hair aside."

"With the Walther?"

"No, the tips of my fingers. I was gentle with her. But she saw me, so I had no choice."

"You're very good at what you have to do," Vera said, laying her hand on his shoulder. She had been harsh with him and didn't want Bo to sulk, waste her time acting hurt. She stroked his hair saying, "To make you feel better, we have Joe Aubrey's check for fifty thousand dollars. If I can put it in an account and make withdrawals within a few days, we'll have our going-away money."

"And we can amscray out of De-twah," Bo said. "Can I lay my tired head against your tummy-tum?"

Vera took his face in her hands and brought his cheek against her body. "What we don't want to happen, they find Aubrey before we amscray. Can you imagine the interrogations we'd have to survive? Two of my alleged aides found shot to death?" She said, "That won't happen, will it, Bo?"

"That's not the problem," Bo said and waited for Vera.

She said, "There is always a problem, isn't there?"

"Walter could tell them I was to drive Mr. Aubrey out to the farm but we never arrived. Or as Kevin Dean would say, 'We never showed.' That girl Honey Deal will say, 'Oh, that's right, Mr. Aubrey. Didn't he go home with Bohdan?' That fucking marshal, you know what he called me? Bohunk."

"I wondered what he said to you. Honey thinks you're cute."

"She does? Well, Jurgen's with her now."

"Having him for breakfast," Vera said. "The girl's a man-eater."

"The FBI will ask him, 'Was Aubrey in the car with you?' Jurgen will say, 'No, he vasn't.'"

"Jurgen doesn't speak that way. But they left with Walter before you put Aubrey in my car. They can't be certain you took him *any* where."

"Do you want to leave it to chance?" Bo said.

"Maybe the police will find out I took Aubrey to see the doctor and maybe they won't. Meanwhile, Vera wets her panties every time the doorbell rings."

Vera said, "God," weary of this war business, "all the dead we've seen."

"Don't give up on me now," Bo said. "What's a few more?"

At least three. Four, with any luck.

"All right," Vera said, "when the police say to you, these other people told us you drove Aubrey to Walter's. If you didn't go there, where did you take Mr. Aubrey? What will you say to that?"

"I'll say, 'Where in the world did they get that idea? I didn't take Mr. Aubrey anywhere. By the time he left the party I was in bed.'"

"So how did he get to Dr. Taylor's?"

"How should I know?"

"But you were here with everyone. What kind of arrangement was made if Walter didn't take him?"

"Give them my theory?"

"If it makes sense."

"Well, the way I see it, Dr. Taylor and Mr. Aubrey had a thing going and made plans to meet somewhere after the party was over. Say, at a bar on Woodward or maybe in front of the cathedral, only a block away. Dr. Taylor picked up Aubrey and took him home so they could monkey around in peace, tease each other, and the doctor's wife Rosemary—I always thought of as a very sweet woman—heard them giggling, crept downstairs, caught the two old dears kissing and shot them with her husband's Walther. Then, so ferociously distraught by what she did, pressed the pistol against her temple and *kapow*, took her own life." Bo, still looking at Vera, said, "Her breasts were so-so."

Vera said, "'Ferociously distraught?'"

"Enormously depressed to learn her husband the respected doctor is a sissy."

"Where did she get the pistol?"

"She knew her husband was a scaredy-cat and kept it in his smoking jacket when he was downstairs alone at night."

"How do you know that?"

"Rosemary told me one time. Or, she brought the pistol from upstairs."

"You're wearing the smoking jacket he had on?"

"This is a different one."

"So they say to you, 'If Mr. Aubrey wasn't there this morning, what happened to him?'"

"I say, 'How should I know, I'm not a detective.'"

Twenty-four

A t Vera's Jurgen was quiet, he was pleasant, he was a cute young guy in a sport coat.

Honey brought him home, turned on a lamp, and he was an escaped prisoner of war standing in her living room. Maybe because Jurgen seemed at home in Vera's formal setting and Honey had never imagined a German soldier in her apartment. German soldiers were in the newspaper. Jurgen trusted her, had come willingly, and now she wasn't sure how this was going to work out. Arrange for Carl to see him tomorrow. They talk, maybe have a drink, and then what? Jurgen says *auf Wiedersehen* and Carl lets him walk away? After coming a thousand miles to get him? Or will he handcuff Jurgen and take him back to Oklahoma? What he's been dying to do for months.

And Jurgen will think you set him up. Lured him here for Carl. Telling him Carl can't touch you. Telling him to take your word, it was good as gold. Sounding like a nitwit, Little Miss Sunshine, when she was a little girl and the world was perfect except for her brother Darcy being in it, living in the same house. Or telling Jurgen it was safe because right now it was like being in the eye of a storm.

She'd be nice to Jurgen, not too nice but nice, and ask him if he was hungry, if he'd like a drink, if he wanted to listen to the radio or one of her records; she had Sinatra, Woody Herman, Buddy Rich, Louis Prima and Keely Smith.

"You don't have Bing Crosby? 'I'll Be Home for Christmas'?"

"I never cared that much for Bing. I have Bob Crosby and the Bobcats and my all-time favorite, Billie Holiday doing 'Gee, Baby, Ain't I Good to You.'"

"What about Bob Wills and Roy Acuff?"

Honey was already singing in a hushed voice, making it sound easy, "Love makes me treat you the way that I do, gee, baby, ain't I good to you," and said, "You like hillbilly music, uh?"

Jurgen said he started listening to Grand Ole Opry in '34, when he was here with his family.

He was comfortable with her. Didn't say a word about Carl coming to see him. Never mentioned his name. He believed what she'd told him, that he was safe with her, didn't have to worry about being grabbed and hauled back to Oklahoma, and it made her feel like a traitor, not sure at all now what Carl would do.

"There was another Tulsa marshal," Jurgen said, "I met at the camp, Gary Marion. He turned in his star because he missed the rodeo and he's back competing."

"Rides bucking broncos?"

"Rides homicidal bulls. The day I left the camp—"

"The day you escaped?"

"I got a letter from Gary he wrote while he was in Austin rodeo-ing. That's what he called it. Gary was never a trail-driving cowhand, but he wore the hat and rode bulls on the circuit."

"You want to be a bull rider when you grow up?"

"I have no plans to grow up. I had thought of being a cowboy and wear the hat and the boots, but if you can compete—ride wild horses and killer bulls for eight seconds at a time—you don't have to be a ranch hand, a working cowboy."

"And you get to wear the hat, and the boots like Carl's," Honey said. "Carl looks more like a cowboy than any cowboy I've ever seen, and he doesn't wear the hat."

She brought Carl into the conversation without thinking, pictures of him prowling around in her mind, but Jurgen didn't pick up on it. He said, "Your brother's giving me one of his hats."

"I hope it fits," Honey said. "Darcy has a tiny head." She looked at her watch and then at Jurgen, both of them on the sofa now. "It's late. I'm ready for bed."

"So am I," Jurgen said.

"I don't have a spare bedroom," Honey said, "but there's a double bed in my room you can have half of if you promise not to start any funny business."

He said, "Of course," but look at him grinning.

"I'm serious, no fooling around," Honey said and believed she meant it. "I'm not a girl who engages in any kind of intimate activity on a first date. Really, not till I get the feeling we might have something going. But I'm not censored by the Hays Office, so you don't have to sleep with one foot on the floor."

Jurgen said, "This is our first date?"

"You know what I mean."

What got it going, he touched her bare shoulder under the covers in the dark and Honey couldn't help turning to him saying, "Hold me." That was all she meant, she wanted to be held, she loved being held. But then once she was snug in his arms she let her hand roam over his body to see what this slim boy was all about, feeling ribs, a flat belly, let her hand slip down some more and now both of them were making sounds in the dark, making love with a dynamite kick that left them hanging on to each other out of breath, not a word spoken until Honey said, "I got to know more about you, Hun."

She wasn't going to answer the phone in the morning no matter how many times it rang, wanting to discourage poor Walter, having no idea if Carl would call or not. The phone rang nine different times before 8 A.M.

What Walter did, once he realized Honey wasn't going to answer the phone, he drove to her building and buzzed the apartment.

"It's I," Walter said. "Open the door."

He was here—she felt she had to let him in. Honey woke up Jurgen and told him to go back to sleep. "If you have to go to the bathroom, go, quick. Walter's coming up. Or stay in the bathroom, take a shower."

The first thing Walter said, true to form, he told her he had not had his coffee this morning. That got them in the kitchen, Walter at the table, and it gave Honey a glimmer of hope. He wouldn't try to jump her till he'd had his coffee. But then didn't seem interested in jumping her, talking so much about Joe Aubrey, wanting to know where he was.

Honey said, "What're you asking me for?"

"I picked him up yesterday at Michigan Central. He must be still here."

"Bo drove him out to your farm."

"They never came there. I called Bo this morning, Vera says he wasn't home, he went out. I asked her was he gone all night. Vera says she doesn't know what time he came home, she isn't his mother."

"You're sure he's not at the farm?"

Honey didn't know why she said that. It brought out the Walter she had been married to. "You still don't listen," Walter said. "I already told you they didn't come there."

"Well, maybe they *came* while you're wasting time yelling at me."

He said, "Where is Jurgen," in a quieter tone.

"In the bathroom."

"I'll wait for him to come out."

"Walter, if I don't know where Joe Aubrey is, how's Jurgen supposed to know?"

"I have to find him," Walter said. "I have to go to Georgia and set my timetable. I want to be there, ready, no later than tomorrow."

"Does Joe have a girlfriend here?"

"Whores."

"Then that's where he is," Honey said, "at a whorehouse in Paradise Valley. You know he likes colored girls. He took Bo along to see if he can get him to go straight. After a night with the girls they're still there, having their coffee, resting up. Do I have to think for you, Walter? You want to go to Georgia? Take the bus."

"That sounded like an entire year of marriage," Jurgen said, "the abridged version. Tell me why you married him."

"I don't remember."

"Walter's lucky. If he can't find Joe, he has an excuse for not assassinating your president. Do you like Roosevelt?"

"I've voted for him since coming of age."

He was grinning at her again.

"Would you like to go out West with me?"

Someone downstairs buzzed.

Honey's first thought, Walter was back.

But it was her brother, Darcy.

"I can't believe it," Honey said, "it's been years." She looked at Jurgen. "You know him, don't you?"

"Yes, the cattle rustler. He's giving me one of his range hats."

"You may as well say hi to him," Honey said.

* * *

Darcy walked in past her, his spurs *ching*ing, Jurgen catching his attention, Jurgen standing by the sofa in Honey's orange kimono. Darcy did pause to look at his sister and tell her, "I'd kiss you but I smell of rotten meat." He said, "How you doin', Sis?" and turned to Jurgen.

"Man, you sure get around. The last I heard you're livin' at Vera's. I'd see her now and then I delivered meat, but never thought much of her. She's not my type, too bossy. Tells me to bring her a leg-a-lamb and some chops instead of beef. I wanted to tell her she could be a prison hack, easy. That young swishy fella works for her, Bo? He reminds me of a con at Eddysville use to dress up like a woman in his cell. His name's Andy but looked a lot like Bo. We called him Candy Andy or Lollypop, the all-day sucker."

"You're here since last fall," Honey said, "but wait till you smell like rotten meat before stopping by?"

"Was October I got my release and come here to do business with Walter. Up till yesterday I'm busier'n that one-legged man y'all of heard about. I'm comin' down from Flint in the refrigerator van, two calves aboard startin' to stink to high heaven and my generator cut out on me. I hooked on the back of a semi with a chain the guy had and he towed me to a gas station. We stood around talkin' about the calves and meat rationin' till I went across the street to get somethin' to eat at a hamburger joint. I'm done, I start out the door, they's state police over there looking at my van. Here I am, I don't know are they checkin' on ownership or the smell comin' off the calves."

Jurgen said, "Didn't you buy the truck at auction?"

"Actually I swiped it off a lot in Toledo, down there with a buddy of mine. I told Walter I paid eighteen hunnert for it used and got him to go halves with me, so I'm not out nothin'."

Honey said, "Why'd the calves smell so bad?"

"They was already dead when I picked 'em up. They's layin' in a pasture and this farmer said take 'em if I could hoist 'em in the van. So they didn't cost me nothin' either. I thought I'd take the calves to Walter and have him look 'em over in case they had a disease. If Walter told me to get rid of 'em I would. But I could see him cuttin' out the livers and startin' to slice onions."

"You had to leave the van," Honey said.

"I had to get outta there. I hitched a ride back to Flint and took a bus and another one out to Walter's and he tells me he's done with the meat business. He's goin' down to Georgia to assassinate the president. I said, 'Where's that leave me? I been workin' my ass for you.' Walter says, 'Do what you want.' I started to yell at him but thought, What's the use? You can't tell a Kraut's already made up his mind nothin'."

Honey said, "He told you he's gonna assassinate the president?"

"In Georgia. The president don't live in Georgia."

"You tell him that?"

"Hell no, let him find out hisself."

"Poor Walter," Honey said, "nobody believes him."

Jurgen said, "Has he ever done anything?"

"Nothing I know of," Honey said, and looked at her brother. "This was yesterday and you still smell?"

"It'll wear off afterwhile."

"If you're through rustling cattle you can take off your spurs." She watched Darcy grin at her and Honey said, "You have something else on the fire, don't you? Another way to break the law?"

"It's what outlaws do, Sunshine, how they make their livin'. I'm done workin' beef. I'm lookin' at an item now hardly weighs anything a-tall, nylon stockings. I could sell all I get my hands on, twenty bucks a pair. Twenty-five even."

"I could too," Honey said, "if we had any."

"You gonna tell me you don't have nylon stockings put away for your best customers, the ones use that Hudson's credit coin?"

"We haven't had nylons in two years. Du Pont's still making parachutes. I doubt we'll have any till Japan surrenders," Honey said. "Why don't you join the navy, see if you can shorten the war."

Darcy said, "All right, but if you did have these stockings put away, where would you hide 'em?"

Honey rolled her eyes at Jurgen. Jurgen said to her, "You swear you don't have nylons?"

"Cross my heart."

Jurgen turned to Darcy. "You were telling us you became too busy with meat to call on your sister.

You said you were busier than that one-legged man we know about. Tell me, what busy one-legged man did you mean?"

"The one in the ass-kickin' contest," Darcy said. "You heard me mention that coin you use at Hudson's to buy on credit? What if you got some brass and stamped out your own coins, as many as you want, with names on 'em you make up?"

"Now he's a counterfeiter," Honey said.

"You dress up in a suit and tie, use one of the coins to charge big-ticket items, a fur coat for the wife—"

"Muriel would drop dead," Honey said.

"I don't give it to her. I return it and get cash."

"If you charged it, they take it off your bill."

She watched Darcy standing in her living room thinking, looking for loopholes. She watched him step toward her club chair done in a beige cotton tapestry she'd bought at Sears, Roebuck for $49.95, her favorite for reading. Honey told her brother if he sat down in it she'd kill him. "I hate to say it, Darcy, but you don't go with my decor. You're more the outdoorsy type, good at rustlin' cattle. Why don't you go out West and be a cowboy?"

"They's no money in cowboyin'," Darcy said. "Don't worry your head, I'll get into somethin' makes money. This mornin' I made a deal with that swishy boy, Bo?"

Darcy grinned.

"One time I'm deliverin' meat, the door opens, the back one, here's Bo wearin' a black shiny dress. He says, 'May I help you?' like we never met before. He has perfume on, earrings, rouge, lipstick.

You had to keep from kissin' him. But that wasn't this mornin'. This mornin' he had on men's clothes, pants and a coat."

"How does he get in touch with you?"

"Leaves a message with Walter's Aunt Madi. I called him this morning, he said come on over, he needed me to get hold of something for him."

"A standing rib?" Honey said.

"You get three guesses."

"A car," Honey said.

"I sold him mine on the spot. A Ford Coupe, looks like everybody else's."

"Cops are watching the house," Honey said. "If you parked in front they'll run the license number and find out you stole the car."

"You are my Sunshine," Darcy said, "my only only. No, I parked over by the cathedral, like I'm makin' a visit."

"What'd you get for it?"

"I'll show you," Darcy said. "I got it in the car."

"The same car?"

"A different one, but they're both Fords. And Jurgen's cowboy hat's in the car. You should've told me when I buzzed he was here, save me a trip."

Darcy left.

"No one changes," Honey said. "He used to blame me all the time when he did dumb things."

They were in the kitchen now, Jurgen sitting at the table in Honey's kimono sipping his coffee. He said, "I can't believe he's your brother."

"The outlaw," Honey said. "I could see growing up he'd never be smart. But I love to listen to him. He tells good stories, semitrue ones." She said, "I bet the cowboy hat's way too small for you."

The phone rang, sitting by itself on the counter. It rang three times before Honey picked it up and turned away from Jurgen at the table.

Carl's voice said, "You're home."

"I've been home, ducking Walter. He's upset 'cause he can't find Aubrey and has to get to Georgia."

"Aubrey's dead," Carl said. "Get hold of today's *Detroit News*. The front page, 'Prominent Doctor in Murder-Suicide.'"

"Dr. Taylor?"

"It looks like his wife popped him and then shot herself. Somebody else was shot in the bathroom but isn't there now."

"You think it's Aubrey?"

"Kevin says he's the only one missing. If the doctor's wife shot him he'd still be there. So Homicide thinks somebody else did all three. You know Vera's gang," Carl said, "who do you see as the shooter?"

She almost said, "Bo," seeing him in the sweater and skirt, but without a good reason for naming him said, "I don't know."

"Who were you gonna say?"

"Couldn't it be somebody who broke in?"

"It could, but who were you thinking of?"

"Bohdan."

Carl said, "We all like Bo."

"You have a reason?"

"He was in a death camp," Carl said, "and got away with killing three of the guards. Cut their throat while they're asleep. I mentioned the Bureau has a file on him? It goes back to Odessa."

There was a silence on the line.

Honey said, "Carl?"

He said, "How do you know how to cut a man's throat?"

He was quiet again before saying, "Listen, I'm at the scene with Kevin. I'll call you later. I want to hear about last night."

She hesitated. "I may not be here."

"You don't want to help me out?"

"All right, I'll be here," Honey said and hung up the phone.

She turned to Jurgen saying to her, "That was Carl?"

"He's at Dr. Taylor's," Honey said and told Jurgen about the murder scene and what Carl had to say.

"If it must be someone from Vera's group," Jurgen said, "I would say Bo. He eliminates the spy ring and there's no one left to point a finger at Vera."

"She calls him her guardian angel," Honey said.

"They're lovers," Jurgen said. "They've lived with death so close to them, they have intense sex together because they're still alive."

Honey said, "But he's a homosexual."

"Or plays the part or does it both ways. I was beginning to like Bohdan, the restrained transvestite in soft cashmere."

"But he does flaunt it, if you can believe Darcy."

"I suppose, but last night everyone at Vera's thought Bo looked quite nice."

"He did," Honey said. "I have a skirt and sweater set like that only it's black, and isn't cashmere."

"You wear black, of course," Jurgen said, "you don't need color, it's in your eyes, your lips . . . " He said, "Why didn't you tell Carl I was here? You're having second thoughts? You're not sure he'll simply come to visit?"

"I think about it now," Honey said, "I'm not at all sure what he'll do. I'm holding off, if you're wondering what I'm up to. But I'm in it now. I've given comfort to the enemy in a big way, and I may as well tell you, I loved it. I think if you and I had time, or there wasn't a war . . ."

"We would be keeping company," Jurgen said.

"I should tell you though," Honey said, "I'm older than you are. You might think I don't look it, but I'm twenty-eight."

"I wouldn't care if you were thirty-one," Jurgen said. "You know I'm madly in love with you."

She did, she knew it, but said, "Really?"

He was coming at her in his quiet way, not as quiet as Carl's, but coming with love now and the next thing on the program they'd be back in bed. She did love making love to this boy who blew up British tanks and was tender and knew how to hold her. Still, she'd need time to quit thinking about Carl.

She touched Jurgen's face looking up at her.

"I love you in my kimono, but you'd better get dressed." She kissed him, nibbling his mouth and Jurgen gave signs of wanting a lot more.

"Darcy's coming back," Honey said.

"Don't let him in."

The boy full of love.

"Let's save it for later," Honey said and got him to go get dressed. She poured herself a rye, just a nip to settle her down.

If Carl wasn't in the picture she could speed it up with Jurgen. She was already calling him Hun, Jurgen hearing it as *hon*. Hun and Honey. What a cute couple.

Carl. Not available but interested. Told her he did *not* want to fool around, have fun with a girl if she wasn't his wife. *If he could help it.* He did say that. But was he leaving it open or being funny? She had to believe that once he saw her bare breasts he'd be getting pictures of them flashing in his mind and he'd be thinking about her, trying not to become involved but keeping a foot in the door. The poor guy. She should quit tempting him. Jurgen was younger, better-looking. She loved his tan lines, midthigh and around his hips. Jurgen was thoughtful and had tender feelings for her. Carl, he could be tender, he was patient. Jurgen was ready for sex at a moment's notice. Carl, he had to be at least horny. She could walk off into the sunset with Jurgen. Except if he got caught and she was with him, she could be charged with treason. Carl was married to a marine who had killed two men, shot them on different occasions, once to save Carl's life.

Was that how you won his heart, shoot somebody?

* * *

Darcy came in holding a light beige western hat in both hands and presented it to Jurgen, still in the kimono, saying, "I got this Stetson specially for my pard."

Honey watched Jurgen take the hat into the hall by the bedroom and try it on in front of the mirror. She was surprised the hat was new. He put it on to rest straight on his head, then pulled it down a little more in front and stared at himself in the mirror.

"It's the businessman's range hat," Darcy said, "the choice of Dallas executives. You understand I'm startin' you out in less hat. You become a cowboy you can get one with a big scoop brim. You don't, you got a hat you can wear anywheres and get nods of approval."

"It fits him," Honey said. "How did you know his size?"

"I told the colored guy at Henry-the-Hatter's, 'This boy is tough, has a mop of hair and he's smart. I know he's got a bigger brain'n me.' I put this'n on, it come down to my eyes and I said, 'Wrap her up.'"

But it wasn't wrapped or in a bag or a hatbox.

"I like it very much," Jurgen said, "thank you, amigo."

"You could pass for American," Darcy said. "She loosens up on you, stuff some toilet paper in there behind the sweatband."

Honey was dying to ask Darcy how he'd swiped the hat, but was more interested in what Bo had paid him for the stolen car.

"You said you'd show us what Bo gave you?"

"For my car," Darcy said. "I got another just like it over at the Sears, Roebuck parkin' lot."

Honey said, "You already told us you have another car."

Darcy said, "Here," zipped open his jacket and brought a pistol out of the waist of his pants and held it up, "a German Luger, what officers have in the war."

"They used to," Jurgen said. "Now it's the Walther, but you see Lugers. I had one since 1939 until the MPs took it from me."

Darcy said, "You shoot anybody with it?"

"Not with a pistol, no."

"This baby's ready to fire," Darcy said. "I told Bo to load her up and gimme a box of nines." He said to Jurgen, "What would you say she's worth?"

"I have no idea. There must be hundreds of thousands of them. They go back to 1908."

"Bo says it's worth five hunnert easy."

Honey said, "What were you asking for the car?"

"Five hunnert."

"If you got a dollar, you'd still be ahead."

"I know I could get a good price for this gun," Darcy said. "I ain't about to pack it. My record, I get pulled over for a broke taillight I'm back inside." He said to Honey, "Sunshine, how about if you hold on to my German Luger for me, till I get situated?"

Twenty-five

Carl came in the afternoon to visit the murder scene, police cars filling the circular drive. Kevin said the Homicide people were calling it a triple now. "I told them the guy they wanted to talk to was Bohdan Kravchenko. He likes jewelry, doesn't he? There's a mess of Miz Taylor's jewelry missing, according to the maid, Nadia—she's from over in Central Europe someplace. And the doctor's medicine cabinet's been cleaned out." He told Carl in the living room, "Here's where the doctor was lying on his back, with his wife lying over him facedown, still holding the Walther."

He told Carl the bodies had been removed to the Wayne County morgue downtown, a few blocks from 1300 Beaubien, Detroit Police headquarters. "They all refer to it as just Thirteen-hundred. They're busy down there," Kevin said, "homicide, major crimes, bomb disposal, firearms examiners." Kevin grinned. "You ever hear of the Big Four? Four good-size guys, detectives, in a Buick sedan, two in front, two in back. They prowl the streets looking for trouble."

Carl said if there was time he wouldn't mind meeting these boys. "Sounds like they get right to the point with offenders."

He phoned Honey while he had the chance and told her about the murder scene, they talked and he said he'd call her later. She said, "I may not be here." Serious, not sounding like Honey the fun-lover or Honey on the make. He almost said, "Are you working for me or not?" But couldn't tell what was wrong from her tone. Why get tough? He said, "You don't want to help me out?" It moved her enough to say she'd be there.

He could go see her right now, ten minutes away. Seven Mile down to a block this side of McNichols, that everyone called Six Mile. Or cut through Palmer Park. He hung around the scene thinking about her, and his mind would wander to street names in Detroit; they had some good ones like Beaubien and St. Antoine, Chene, an old French town now full of war plants. Finally he told himself to quit fuckin' the dog. Go on. Show you can be alone with the girl in her apartment and not tear her clothes off. It wouldn't happen anyway, she'd have 'em off already. He thought, What if you went to bed with her . . . No, really, what if you went to bed and made love, but it was only to find out something or prove a point of some kind . . . Or, he thought, what if you just fucked her socks off and got it over with?

He followed Wellesley to Lowell to Balmoral in the Pontiac, winding through Palmer Woods

with the big English-style homes and polite maids
who told the homicide dicks going door-to-door,
"No, sir, Missus says we never heard nothin' last
night."

Carl came to Seven Mile and stopped. He could
turn left to Woodward, take it south to Honey's, or
turn right and take Pontchartrain through the park.
A car was in his rearview mirror. Stopped, the first
car he'd seen in Palmer Woods, parked or moving,
outside of cop cars today. Like it was waiting for
him to make up his mind, a '41 Ford Coupe.

Carl turned left onto Seven, not many cars on
the road, held it at thirty and pretty soon the car
was behind him, hanging back. He remembered
the police precinct on the right, came to it and
turned into the parking lot. The car following him
stopped on Seven Mile. Carl came out of the precinct lot and turned left. Now he was heading toward the Ford, staying in his lane, wanting to see
who was in the car, still a couple of hundred feet
away when the car took off and flew past him going the other way.

One guy in the car.

Carl tried to concentrate on how much of the
guy he saw, the way the guy was hunched behind
the wheel. He wanted the guy to have slick black
hair like the kid gangster Vito Tessa had and he'd
know, okay, the guy's here, the Avenger with the
big nickel-plate automatic, and he'd know who to
look for. But the guy in the Ford didn't have slick
black hair, it was a lot lighter.

He turned left on Pontchartrain Drive, the way
through Palmer Park, fairways of the public golf

course on the left, grass and picnic tables and trees on the right. He saw the Ford way back—but coming, gaining on him. Carl pulled his .38 and laid it on the seat close to his thigh. Looked up at the mirror and the Ford was coming fast, closing on him and, Christ, *shooting* at him. The only thing to do—Carl braked hard, covering the sound of gunfire with screaming tires. The .38 flew off the seat. It didn't matter, Carl was going down anyway, flat against the seat cushion, down there getting his hand on the .38 as the Ford came around to pass him and hammered away at the Pontiac, rounds shattering the side windows above him, through one and out the other, making frosted-looking circles on the windshield, with a machine gun. It *was*. It was a goddamn machine gun, but didn't sound like a Thompson. He thought of Louly saying she'd have to fire a Browning for him, "rip off a few rounds."

The Ford was making a U-turn a hundred yards ahead, getting in behind an Olds that went past, staying close, using the Olds for cover. Carl opened his door, stood up and laid the .38 on the top part of the doorframe, aimed at the front end of the Olds coming toward him, let it pass and opened up on the Ford, fired five rounds double-action at the hood and the car windows, certain he either hit the driver or changed his mind from shooting it out.

Carl got his car turned around and went after the Ford, got close when it had to slow down before turning onto Seven Mile. Now it was flying toward Woodward. Carl made the turn and gunned it, gained on the Ford going past the police precinct, coming to the golf clubhouse now, the first tee, and the Pontiac engine blew with the sound of gears grinding, steam pouring from the hood vents, Carl watching the Ford approaching a red light at Woodward. Carl, his dead car rolling to a stop, had to watch through spiderweb gunshots in the windshield and steam rising to see the speed demon run the light, weaving past cars braking and swerving to miss the nut in the Ford Coupe and somehow he made it. The Avenger gone, out of sight on a gloomy April afternoon.

The Tulsa Police lieutenant said, "I'm surprised, Carl, there must be somebody else don't like you."

"Vito Tessa from Kansas City," Carl said, using the phone on the table behind the staircase that came down in a curve toward the murder-scene living room. "Vito told Virgil he was coming up to see me."

"I love Virgil," the Tulsa lieutenant said. "The first thing he ever said to me—we're in that bar in the basement of the Mayo. He says, 'You ever been in a pissing contest?' I said no, what do you go for, height or distance? He says, 'No, we piss on the ice in urinals and bet on whose pile of cubes gets melted down the most.' But the thing about your dad, he didn't piss on any kind of regular basis. He could hold it."

"That's why he's still one of the great pissers," Carl said, "he can hold it as long as he wants, which you don't find at all in men his age. I've been in that bar with my dad, but I can't say I ever pissed next to him. Go in the woods with him hunting, I don't think I ever saw him piss, not wanting to leave his sign."

"That's your dad," the Tulsa lieutenant said. "Who'd you say, Tessa? He's out on bond. No, wait a minute, I got the latest here. He was out on a five-hundred-dollar bond till his hearing. He *was* out. Tessa and some other punk held up the wrong poker game. Both of 'em got shot in the ass going out the door, with the pot they scooped into a hat. So I was right, it's somebody else wants to shoot you."

"Was he packing that big nickel-plate?"

"Yeah, but didn't get off a shot. Had a full magazine."

"It didn't seem to me he was gonna make it in his trade," Carl said and thanked the lieutenant.

Now Kevin Dean was coming across the living room.

"You back already?"

"I haven't gone yet where I'm going. I just spoke to Tulsa Police asking about Vito the Avenger. Remember the kid gangster I told you about, with a brother? It wasn't him shooting a machine gun at me in Palmer Park, he's laid up, handcuffed to a hospital bed. So the one shooting at me was a local guy. He knew who I was, driving away from here. He had light-colored hair, like Bohdan's."

"As long as his?"

"I couldn't tell. The guy fired at me with a machine gun that wasn't a Thompson. I can hear a Thompson in my head. This one had a different sound."

"Upstairs in the doctor's bedroom," Kevin said, "a cabinet was pried open. Nothing in it but a box of nines. But now Nadia the maid says with her accent the guns are missing. A Walther, two Luger pistols and a *Maschinenpistole* 40, like the ones she saw at the War Souvenir Show at Hudson's. You recall we missed that show?"

"Having lunch with Honey." He could see her working on her salad, then wiping a roll over the empty plate, picking up any dressing that was left.

"You know what Walter calls her, Honig, the German word for *honey*, Honig Schoen." Kevin said, "Tell me what happened in the park."

Carl took him through it to where the Pontiac engine blew and he watched the Ford make it through the Woodward intersection.

"And you left your car?"

Carl said he stopped at the Palmer Park Precinct, the Twelfth, and sent them after a shot-up Ford, a black one, and told them where Bo lived. "They towed my car out of the street and said they'd have their mechanic look under the hood." Carl said, "I hate to lose that car," and said, "You wouldn't happen to have one I can borrow, do you? Or maybe the Bureau'll let me have one?"

Maybe. But what Kevin wanted to know, "If Bo's shooting people who can testify against him and Vera, why's he want to shoot you?"

"I don't know, I only met him this morning," Carl said. "I did speak loud to him. I might've hurt his feelings."

"You going to Honey's?"

"I'm thinking about it."

"You don't have wheels, I can take you, tag along."

Carl didn't need Kevin with him. He said, "You're on this case—don't you want to get hold of Bohdan quick as you can?"

"You sent the cops after him."

"When your superior asks you what you were doing, you tell him you were visiting a young lady?"

"Don't you want Bo?"

"I'd rather have Jurgen," Carl said. "Homicide wants Bo. You could drive down to Vera's with one of those boys and let me have your car. How's that sound?"

What Bo did, he ditched the Ford on a street of workingmen's homes, walked a block to Woodward Avenue and around the corner to the 4-Mile Bar, a block and a half from the cathedral. He had a shot of whiskey before he called Vera.

"Are you sober?"

"I'm glowing," Bo said. "I can't come home. I think the police are looking for me. When they come, tell them I've gone up north. It's what people around here do, they go up north. Two women at the market. 'What're you doing this weekend?' 'We're going up north.' Northern Michigan. I don't have an idea what's up there."

Vera said, "Bo . . . ?"

"I saw Carl, driving around in his Pontiac like he had no idea where he was going. He turned to go through Palmer Park, the road's wide open there, hardly any traffic, and I got excited and went after him, fired almost thirty-two rounds, an entire clip. I don't know if I got him or not."

"Did he shoot at you?"

"When I turned around, yeah, he was ready for me."

"Then you didn't get him. But why do you want him, because he insulted you? That's settled with a duel, not shooting at him with a machine pistol. What about your car?"

"It's full of bullet holes. But listen, Vera? He could've been going to Honey's."

Vera said, "Yes?"

"And I could've followed him. Honey's there, Jurgen's there, and Carl."

Vera said, "You want to shoot Carl because he called you a Bohunk?"

"He knows as much about you as they do. I could've gotten the three of them in her apartment."

Vera said, "If that's where he was going."

"I'm so fucking glad you listen. You always listen and remember. Vera, if we could get them to all be there tomorrow I could do it then. Set it up. Carl, Honey and Jurgen's Lotion. Zap."

Vera said, "Bo, I don't want to be in this house anymore. Please get me out of here before I become an alcoholic."

"You already are."

"I count my drinks," Vera said. "I never have more than twenty-five in a day."

"We're going away tomorrow," Bo said. "If we can think of a way to get all three of them at Honey's apartment again. You want to say good-bye. Or you want to leave each one of them something."

Vera said, "You have to do this, don't you."

"If I don't," Bo said, "the FBI will wring you out and hang you up to dry. You like that saying? We'll make it sometime in the evening, but not too late. We arrive last. The ones I want are there." He turned from the pay phone on the wall and looked down the bar at the patrons, a few men and one woman, blitzed, talking loud, a guy at a table reading a dream book. "I'll slip in the house tonight. Leave the back door unlocked."

"What are you drinking?"

"Whiskey, they don't have vodka."

"They ran out of it?"

"They don't have it, Vera, ever."

"I'm glad we're leaving."

"We'll each take a bag. Any treasures you can't leave behind, as long as they're small. The umbrella, that big black one like Neville Chamberlain's."

"What are you going to wear?"

"I haven't thought about it yet."

Honey jumped hearing the buzzer. She answered, pressed the button to open the door downstairs and said to Jurgen, "It's Carl."

Jurgen waited, standing in the living room, dressed now.

"I think you'd better stay in the bedroom," Honey said.

"He doesn't know I'm here?"

"I don't see how he could."

"But you don't trust him now," Jurgen said, showing his grin. "Because we're lovers? Talk to him, see what he's thinking about."

"He'll ask about you, I know."

"Lie to him, it's okay. Or tell him I'm here and I'll come out and talk to him. It's up to you."

"He'll wonder why I'm nervous," Honey said.

"You don't seem nervous to me. Listen," Jurgen said, "I know what you're going through. You have a feeling for me, but I'm the enemy. My being here could be enough to put you in a federal prison. If you want to tell Carl I'm here, do it, I'll understand."

She wished he didn't smile at her—not a big smile, almost a sad smile, but still a smile—saying things like that to her. He went in the bedroom and closed the door. Honey put "Gee, Baby, Ain't I Good to You" on the Victrola, Honey letting Billie Holiday's baby-doll voice set a mood for her, and Jurgen appeared in the hallway, smiling at her.

"You're not going to tell him, are you?"

Carl came in wearing the dark suit she liked and stood looking at Honey looking at his dark tie on a white shirt, the white against his weathered look that she liked. He paused to listen and said, "Billie Holiday. I should've known you like blues."

"How could you tell?"

"You're hip."

"I don't jitterbug," Honey said.

"I didn't think you did."

"I like slow dancing, get in there close."

Now he showed a smile, the same way Jurgen did.

"I believe that," Carl said. "Did you see Jurgen last night?"

Sneaking it in, the smile gone.

"Yeah, I did."

"You talk to him?"

"I asked him if he wanted to see you. Since you can't grab him till the FBI says it's okay."

"Who told you that?"

"You did."

"I did, didn't I? Will he see me?"

"He didn't say."

"You know where he is?"

Honey shook her head.

"Are we still friends?"

"I'll make you a drink if you want."

"But you won't tell me where he is."

"Uh-unh."

"You like Jurgen and don't want to be a snitch."

"I like you too," Honey said. "I still don't want to talk about it."

He paused, looking at her, before saying, "You don't want to tell me what you know about an escaped German prisoner of war?"

Honey smiled. "You're serious?"

Carl had to smile.

"Let's have a drink," Honey said.

She saw him glance at the hallway to the bedroom as they went in the kitchen. She said, "You drink beer? You never ask if I have any."

"Do you?"

"No, you're lucky I have rye."

She made a couple of drinks and handed him one. Honey was about to sit down. Instead, she picked up her cigarettes from the table saying, "Let's be comfortable," and took Carl back to the living room to sit in the cushy sofa and light cigarettes, not more than a foot of space between them.

Carl said, "Honey, I'm gonna tell you something. Right now I don't give a rat's ass where Jurgen is or what he's doing. All I can think about is going to bed with you."

The man quiet in there behind his eyes, Honey seeing him always as a *man*, before adding on *famous* and usually *married*, but not today.

"You want to take me to bed."

"I don't think about much else," Carl said.

"In the bedroom?"

"If that's where the bed is."

"Or we can do it right here."

Honey stood up. She pulled her blouse out of her skirt and unbuttoned it.

"You want to do it on your sofa?"

She took off her blouse.

"I'll put a sheet over it."

"When you have a big bed in there?"

Honey put both hands behind her back to unhook the bra.

She said, "Carl, do you want to fuck me on the sofa or see if Jurgen's in the bedroom? One or the other."

She unhooked the bra and let it drop.

Twenty-six

Honey opened her apartment door and picked up the morning *Free Press*, Thursday, April 12, and brought it to Jurgen at the kitchen table having his coffee. She said, "A hundred and forty-two thousand of you surrendered to the Reds in East Prussia," handing the paper to him. She went to the stove to pour herself a cup. It was 8:20. They were both dressed, Honey in her black sweater and skirt that Jurgen liked.

"Your marines are engaged in savage fighting in Okinawa. Tell me, where is Okinawa?"

"I think it's the last stop before Japan," Honey said.

"Kamikazes attacked Task Force Fifty-eight, seriously damaging the *Enterprise*, the *Essex*, and six destroyers. Meanwhile," Jurgen said, opening the paper and looking at story headlines, "a German communiqué announces the garrison commander at Konigsberg has been sentenced to death. You know why? He allowed the Russians to take the city. And that, my dear girl, is why we're losing the fucking war. We don't hesitate to kill our own people."

"When you're not killing other people," Honey said, coming to the table with her coffee.

"We have to remind ourselves that we aren't enemies, you and I," Jurgen said. "Though last night, I must tell you, I wasn't sure."

The phone rang.

"We're all right," Honey said.

The phone rang.

"But you weren't the same," Jurgen said.

Honey went to the counter and picked up the phone. It was Madi, Walter's aunt, calling from the farm and looking for Jurgen.

"Can you tell me where he is?"

Honey said she didn't know. "If I happen to run into him I'll tell him you called. Okay?"

"Don't act smart with me," Madi said. "I have a telephone number for Jurgen. From his comrade the Nazi. Are you ready?" She recited the long-distance number and Honey wrote it on the pad by the phone.

"I've got it, thanks."

"Try to be civil when you speak to people," Madi said and hung up.

Honey turned to Jurgen. "Did I sound uncivil to you?"

"Who was it?"

"Walter's aunt. Your comrade, the Nazi, wants you to call him. In Cleveland, the number's over there."

Jurgen was up from the table, dialing the operator before Honey sat down.

"Who's the Nazi?"

"Otto."

"Otto?"

"Hi, Jurgen? This is Aviva. Let me get Otto for you." Chopin playing in the background, *Andante Spianato* and *Grande Polonaise*, Jurgen wondering who the pianist was.

Otto came on saying, "Jurgen?"

"Otto, what are you doing in Cleveland?"

"I met someone. Aviva."

"Aviva?"

"Aviva Friedman."

Jurgen paused. "She's helping you?"

"We haven't been apart since we met at Hudson's and immediately got on her boat, a forty-foot pleasure craft."

Jurgen said, "Aviva Friedman?"

"I have her in my power. If she doesn't obey me I turn her over to the Gestapo. Jurgen, are you all right? What are you doing? Aviva deals in fine art. Wait a minute . . . What? Yes, I'll tell him. Aviva wants you to come to Cleveland. You have to absolutely come when we get married. Aviva says I'm the smoothest guy she ever met, especially for a Kraut."

"Aviva?"

"She has a bookstore that sells the wrong books, very old ones she wants to be rid of, sell the store if she can. I think I know about books. I intend to take over the store and try something new. Offer only mystery novels. Uh? What do you think?"

"I don't read mysteries."

"Then I won't sell you any. Tell me what you're doing."

"He's planning to marry a woman named Aviva Friedman."

Honey said, "Yeah . . . ?"

"Otto's SS and she's Jewish."

"You'll get over it," Honey said. She knew he wanted to talk about last night. All right, she thought, do it . . . and said, "Jurgen, I had way too much to drink last night."

"I did too—"

"We hardly had anything to eat."

"You were different, Honey, than if you were only drunk, believe me."

"I was nervous. Being with Carl while you're hiding in the bedroom. I was exhausted, I think from the tension. I just didn't feel like doing anything last night."

"I'm not talking about doing it or not doing it," Jurgen said. "If you don't feel like becoming intimate in bed in the dark of night, all right, I understand. I don't feel like perpetually doing it either. Certainly not more than several times a day since I first saw you." He waited for her to smile and she did. "No, what I'm referring to," Jurgen said, "you were a different person after Carl left, and I wonder why."

"I don't know why," Honey said. "But we're all right, aren't we, you and I?"

Not wanting to make love—wasn't that different enough? Otherwise, she wasn't aware of how different she must have seemed to Jurgen last night and this morning, Honey thinking about Carl, Carlos Huntington Webster, whoever he was, watching her take her clothes off.

At first Carl couldn't think of anyone he could tell.

Not Kevin. Not his dad, Jesus, no, not even on the porch having shots and beers. They were drinking tequila when he told his dad about seeing Crystal Davidson from time to time before he married Louly. His dad saying, "Crystal Davidson, you don't mean to tell me. Emmett Long's gun moll? Where do you see her?" He told his dad, when she came to Tulsa to shop at the department store. His dad said, "Does she act ladylike?" Wanting to know his boy got laid with some propriety.

Carl was in the hotel coffee shop having breakfast, his eggs scrambled with onions, fried potatoes and pork sausage, all of it doused with Lea & Perrins, a few small sweet rolls and black coffee. The waitress said, "I can tell you like that Wootsashy, huh?"

She was colored but sounded like Narcissa Raincrow, his dad's common-law wife, bless her heart. He could tell Narcissa what happened. He'd been telling her things all his life and she'd listen without any attitudes or beliefs interfering. The way he heard their conversation:

"Here's Honey, the best-looking girl I ever met, or the second best."

"She look like a movie star?"

"Lauren Bacall. 'You know how to whistle, Steve?' Honey even sounds like her, her voice."

"They call her Betty, her friends."

"She takes off her blouse."

"She's wearing a brassiere?"

"It's white. She puts her hands behind her back to unhook it and says . . ." Carl paused. "She uses an obscene word."

The fifty-four-year-old Creek woman who looked somewhat like a heavy Dolores Del Rio said, "Which one, *fuck*?"

"Yeah."

"It's all right, you can say it."

"She says, 'Carl, do you want to fuck me on the sofa—'"

"Oh my," Narcissa said.

"'Or see if Jurgen's in the bedroom? One or the other.' And lets the bra slip off. Drops it on the floor."

"Oh, she's smart. All right, big boy, what would you rather do, have sexual intercourse with me or take the German swine prisoner?"

"He's not a swine, he's a good guy. But say I did choose Honey. And he hears us."

"You make a lot of noise?"

"He's in the next room. The apartment's quiet."

"You want to give it to her, but not in the living room? Take her to a hotel."

"This was yesterday. I didn't take her anywhere. What do you think I did?"

"You been waiting a long time to catch the German. But there's Honey pointing her ninnies at you. She take off all her clothes?"

"She lets her skirt drop."

"She have on undies, a girdle?"

"A pair of white panties. Her thumbs hooked in the waist."

"Ready to step out of them."

"She waited."

"For you to make up your mind?"

"You understand I had forced her to where we were."

"'Cause you wanted to get laid."

"'Cause I knew Jurgen was in the bedroom."

"If he wasn't you'd be in there with Honey."

"I don't know."

"Listen, don't tell me this story if you don't tell the truth. Did you say you wanted to go to bed with her to fuck her, or to see if the German was in there?"

"I didn't know he was, or I wasn't sure of it till she said we do it on the sofa or we don't do it."

"So when you started out telling her of your passion, it was to get laid."

"I guess it was," Carl said. "But I didn't get laid, did I?"

"Didn't break your vow. You were lucky, uh?"

"I walked past the bedroom door and out of the apartment."

"You didn't say anything to the lovely naked girl?"

"I said, 'It doesn't look like it's gonna work out, does it?' She was smiling a little, her eyes were. She's the type, she's comfortable not having any clothes on. No, at this point she's having a good time."

"Did she say anything to you?"

"She said, 'You give up too easily.'"

"Wait. How did she know you wouldn't look in the bedroom?"

"She gave me a choice, one or the other."

"But you didn't jump on her."

"I wanted to. I would've if Jurgen wasn't there. I didn't tell Honey but he saved me from breaking my word, something I've never done in my life, 'less I'm kidding when I give it and everybody, or most everybody knows I'm kidding. No, I took a vow when I got married and I haven't broken it yet. So I feel I owe Jurgen one. He wants to run and hide, stay low till the war's over, it's okay with me. He saved me from breaking my word. I'll tell my boss, W. R. Bill Hutchinson, I couldn't find the two escapees and that'll be that."

Narcissa's voice said, "Oh, is that right? But what if you run into Honey again and no one like Jurgen is around to save your pitiful ass?"

He tried to get hold of Kevin to return his car, phoning from his room. The FBI voice said he was out of the office, on assignment. Carl asked if Bohdan Kravchenko had been apprehended. The voice said that information was not available for release. Carl left word for Kevin to call him at the hotel.

He phoned Louly at the marine air station in North Carolina, proud of his semiclear conscience, ready to say "I've been too busy" when she asked if he was staying out of trouble. But Louly wasn't available either. What he should do, get ready to take the train back to Tulsa.

The phone rang. He expected it to be Kevin or Louly.

It was Honey Deal.

"You want to see Jurgen?"

"Let me talk to him on the phone."

"Carl, Vera called. She wants to stop by this evening and visit."

"With Bohunk?"

"She doesn't know where he is. He didn't come back last night. She's worried about him."

"I can see her wringing her hands," Carl said. "What time she coming?"

"About eight. Stop in and say good-bye to Jurgen."

"Where's he going?"

"He won't tell me."

"Show him your hooters."

"They're on ice for you, Carl. You know what happens when ice touches just the tips?"

Carl said, "You sneeze?" and said right away, "You know you're hanging out with the wrong crowd."

"I know it," Honey said. "But I don't feel the least bit subversive. Do you? Or you can get away with it but I can't?"

"Something like that," Carl said.

"Listen, stop by for a drink tonight. I promise I won't show you my boobs."

"But I'll understand," Carl said, "if you can't help taking your clothes off."

She said, "Wait a minute."

He heard her lay the phone down on a hard surface and after that faint voices. Now she was back.

"Carl, turn on your radio. Roosevelt's dead."

It was the way she said it. Not, he died; he was dead.

Carl said, "You don't think Walter . . ."

Walter heard the news in the Greyhound bus station in downtown Detroit over the public-address system. He missed the first part of the announcement, the bus-schedule voice saying, "It is our sad duty to inform you that at three thirty-five this afternoon"—Walter waiting to hear where the bus was going, thought, Three thirty-five? Knowing it was almost six, looked up at the clock and saw he was right. Now he listened and heard the public-address voice say:

"Death gave the sixty-three-year-old president of the United States short notice. At about one o'clock this afternoon, in the Little White House in Warm Springs, Georgia, the president felt a sudden pain in the back of his head. At the time he was having his portrait sketched in preparation for a painting. At one-fifteen the president fainted, never to regain consciousness. At three thirty-five P.M. Franklin Roosevelt died without pain of what his doctor called a massive cerebral hemorrhage. Funeral service for the president will be held in the East Room of the White House . . ."

That was enough for Walter. He got up and

walked over to the ticket window, the PA system sounding as though it was starting over again.

"Today, April twelfth in Warm Springs, Georgia, death took Franklin Delano Roosevelt, president of the United States, and left millions of Americans shocked and stunned."

Walter turned in his ticket to Griffin by way of Atlanta and was given his refund. He began to wonder if any of the people at Vera's the other night, when they heard of Roosevelt's death would immediately say, "My God, was it Walter?" Or would they say, "My God, it was Walter." Remembering his determination. Vera comes up to him. No, first Honig. She touches his face and asks in her soft voice, "Walter, how in the world did you do it?"

"My dear," he would say, "you don't believe his brain hemorrhaged?"

"Yes, but what caused it to do so?"

They'll consider he used some type of poison and he'll tell them, "Believe what you want."

"He must have used poison."

"But how was it administered?"

"He couldn't have done it. Walter is still in Detroit."

"Walter's clever. He sent it."

"What?"

"Let's say a cake. Delivered to the Little White House bearing the name of the president's lady friend, according to Joe Aubrey, Miss Lucy Mercer. Oh, that Walter is clever. Even if the president has a food taster like kings of old, a cake said to be from Miss Lucy Mercer would arouse no suspicion. The president has a piece while having his portrait sketched, takes several bites and slumps in his chair in a coma. The time, one-fifteen, as he finishes his lunch."

It was the kind of cloak-and-dagger plot Vera would think of. Or something like it. He could hear Vera say, "By whatever means the president met his end, you can be sure our Walter made it happen. We are not surprised at the cover-up, the White House saying his death was of natural causes. I doubt that Walter will ever reveal how he brought it off. For as long as he lives people who know this cunning fellow will offer their own theories and each will ask, 'Is that how you did it, Walter?'"

His reply would remain, "Believe what you want."

Twenty-seven

Honey had an apron on over the bra and panties she wore straightening the living room, picking up newspapers, emptying ashtrays, dusting here and there with a feather duster, showing off in front of Jurgen on the sofa with *Life,* his favorite magazine. He could *not* believe she had saved every issue since Pearl Harbor, 163 copies of *Life* in the storage room, seven missing consecutively from the winter of 1942.

She astonished Jurgen. She was always her own person, a jewel, a diamond in the rough that was her own style of rough, listening to Sinatra's "Ill Wind" and saying "Fucking effortless" in her quiet way. He wondered what happened to her in the winter of 1942, when he was in Libya. He loved her. He would be in wonder of her for as long as he lived, Honey dusting in her underwear, arching her back to aim her pert rear end at him. He had told Honey he would become a bull rider on the rodeo circuit. "You know from the radio how they announce the contestants? 'Now here's a young cowboy name of Flea Casanova from Big Spring, Texas.' Soon you're going to hear, 'We have a young cowpoke now name of Jurgen Schrenk from Cologne, Germany. Jurgen'll be atop a one-eyed bull full of meanness name of Killer-Diller. Ride him, Jurgen.'" He told Honey, "The first-place bull rider at the Dallas Rodeo—it's in *Life* magazine—made seventy-five hundred dollars for staying on three bulls for eight seconds each. I rode a Tiger in North Africa. I can ride a bull."

Honey looked over her shoulder so her butt was still aimed at him. "I knew a boy on the circuit was injured one time," Honey said. "He'd write on a notepad to tell me how hungry he was, his jaw wired shut till it healed." Now she was dusting the bookcase, dabbing the feathers at the shelves.

"I forgot to tell you Eleanor wasn't there when he died. She was in Washington. Roosevelt had a full schedule today, planning to attend a barbecue where country fiddlers were going to play for him. So he wasn't thinking about dying, was he? You like hillbilly fiddles? I don't. At all. Did you know Roosevelt was president longer'n any of the others? Since 1933. He was sixty-three years old."

Now she was taking a book from the shelf, holding it toward him so he could see it was *Mein Kampf*. "Never read and no longer a conversation piece," Honey said, and tossed it in the cabinet she opened, beneath the shelves.

Jurgen said, "Isn't that where you put Darcy's pistol?"

She stooped to bring out the Luger. "Right here, I want to ask you about it." She laid it on a bookshelf and moved to her record collection in another part of the cabinet. She said, "One of the radio reports said Roosevelt was sitting in an armchair and seemed comfortable when, the guy said, 'A piercing pain stabbed at the back of Roosevelt's proud, leonine head.' You think Roosevelt had a head like a lion? I thought he was suave with his cigarette holder, but never thought of him as leonine. Now Truman's president."

She stood up with a record and put it on the Victrola. "He's a Kansas City politician they say plays the piano. We'll have to see what we have here, Harry S. Truman. I doubt he'll make much noise."

The record came on and Jurgen said, "What *is* that?"

"Bob Crosby."

"I mean that instrument."

"Bob Haggart whistling through his teeth while he strums his bass." Now she was singing, "'Big noise blew in from Winnetka, big noise blew right out again.'"

"What's the name of it?"

"'Big Noise from Winnetka.' What else can you call it? The drummer's Ray Bauduc, with his wood blocks and cowbells. Ray's fun."

"You know him?"

"I mean the way he plays is fun. I did meet him one time I was in New Orleans. Had a drink with him." Honey picked up the Luger from the shelf and brought it to Jurgen on the sofa. "I think Darcy said it's loaded, if I'm not mistaken."

"He did," Jurgen said as Honey let herself fall

into the sofa close to him. He was fooling with the Luger now, pulled up on the toggle that exposed the breech and a nine-millimeter cartridge ejected. He added the cartridge to the magazine, popped it back inside the grip and handed the pistol to Honey. "Loaded, ready to fire," Jurgen said. "Is there someone you'd like to shoot?"

"Are you kidding?" Honey said, raising the pistol and closing one eye as she aimed at the mirror in the hallway to her bedroom. "I wouldn't hesitate to plug Hitler, I ever had the Führer in my sights."

"You don't want to see him tried for war crimes?"

"What if he gets off?"

"You're not serious. He'll hang, if he doesn't kill himself, which is a distinct possibility."

Honey lowered the pistol and raised it again saying, "What about Walter's look-alike, Heinrich Himmler?"

"The world will celebrate for days when he's hanged."

"If I had a choice," Honey said, "Hitler or Himmler? I'd pick Himmler. Kick him in the nuts as hard as I can before I shoot him."

Honey lowered the pistol again. This time she jammed it straight down between the sofa cushion she was sitting on and Jurgen's.

"Boy, am I tired."

"Why don't you take a nap?"

"I have to go get booze. I think Vera likes to get smashed. Especially the way things are going."

"I think she handles it well."

"I hope so. I'd hate to see her fall apart."

"You mean get drunk?"

"No, the way she's worried about Bo."

"You believe he's missing?"

"Why would she lie about it?"

"What did you tell me Carl said? He can see her wringing her hands?"

"He's a smart-ass."

"He has different poses," Jurgen said. "One time he looks like a farmhand with a jaw full of Beech-Nut chewing tobacco."

"Scrap," Honey said.

"The next time—this one's my favorite—he's looking at something miles away that no one else can see, and you believe he actually can. I think he's himself, though, when you're talking to him. He's straight with you."

"He can stop you in your tracks," Honey said. "You have to think fast to come back at him. He's more fun than he looks."

"You like him," Jurgen said.

"I like him as a man, but he's taken. If he wasn't, you'd have competition breathing down your neck. He told his wife, Louly, on the altar, he'd stay pure as the driven snow, and he believes he means to keep his word. But then if he happens to get horny, as we all do at times, and he wants some action right now? Something happens. Dumb luck sets in and saves Carl, gnashing his teeth, from going back on his word. I might've told him it was his guardian angel fucking with his life."

"You know him well."

"I learned that about him in less'n two minutes.

You know what he is, he's lucky. And there is nothing in the world like going with a guy you know is lucky."

"I think several times in his shooting situations," Jurgen said, "Carl, yes, has been lucky. The bank robber coming out to the street, the sidewalk, with a woman in front of him, and tells Carl and the few police in this small town, 'Lay down your guns.' Carl told me he could see part of the bank robber's face over the woman's left shoulder. Carl's in the street, thirty feet away. The policemen drop their guns, Carl raises his and shoots the bank robber in the middle of his forehead. I said to Carl, 'You were risking the woman's life.' Carl said, 'I hit him where I aimed.'"

"He knows what he's doing," Honey said. "Did he tell you the woman fainted? Carl said something like, 'Yeah, she slumped over, I was afraid I'd hit her.' Then shows just a speck of a grin."

"He told you that?"

"No, it was in the 'Hot Kid' book about him. Kevin loaned me his copy. I haven't told Carl I read it. I've been comparing him to the one in the book."

"Are they the same person?"

"Identical. He's the only guy I know who can brag about something he did without sounding like he's bragging. You accuse him of risking the woman's life and he tells you he hit where he'd aimed. In the book he says, 'Dead center.' He's still lucky."

"I was in tanks almost four years," Jurgen said, "and I'm still alive."

Honey said, "I know you are, Hun. I spotted

you as Mr. Lucky in Vera's kitchen, the first time I laid eyes on my Kraut," patting his thigh.

"Yes, but if you had to choose between us right now, at this moment—"

"I'd pick you," Honey said, "because you love me. I'm getting there with you, Hun, all I have are tender feelings. I don't see why we won't make it. Right now I gotta go get the booze."

"I'll get it," Jurgen said. "Go to bed and I'll come looking for you."

Twenty-eight

Walter arrived downstairs at twenty to eight, surprising Honey. She buzzed him in and opened the door to the apartment. In the kitchen, Jurgen sipped his martini and raised the glass to Honey coming in with an empty one.

"To the love of my life. Who was that?"

"Walter—"

"I thought he was in Georgia."

"Hun, you may have to protect me from him. Walter gets horny at strange times, okay? Shoot him if you have to."

"With the Luger, it would be poetic melodrama."

She said, "Talk to him while I cut the cheese," and grinned. "As you learn more of our slang, don't ever say, 'Who cut the cheese?' in polite company."

He didn't know what she was talking about, but paused as he was walking out. "How many of those have you had?"

"This is my second," Honey said, pouring herself one.

Jurgen came in the living room looking at the sofa, the last place he saw the Luger, Honey holding it, aiming at Himmler after kicking him in the nuts, and turns as Walter said, "May I come in?"

Walter standing in the doorway.

Jurgen gestured. "Yes, please."

Now Honey was in the room with her martini.

"Walter, you didn't go to Georgia."

"No, this time I didn't have to. But he is dead, isn't he?"

Honey glanced at Jurgen.

"The president of the United States," Walter said. "You didn't hear he's dead?"

"Oh, right, the president. We were shocked," Honey said. "Where were you, Walter, when you heard?"

He said, "I was at home," and after a moment, "awaiting the news."

"Have a martini," Honey said, handing him her glass. She started for the kitchen saying, "You were waiting for the news to come on?" and kept going.

Walter turned to Jurgen. "She's like an impulsive child. As I said, I was awaiting the news of his death."

Jurgen waited a moment for Honey, back again with a martini. "His radio must have been on. Walter says he was waiting for the report of the president's death."

Honey said, "You knew he was gonna die? What'd you have, a vision?"

"You wouldn't understand," Walter said.

"Why not?"

"I prefer not to talk about it."

"He wants us to believe," Jurgen said, "he had something to do with the president's death."

"Did I say that?"

"It sounds to me that's what you're saying."

"Believe what you want," Walter said, raised the stemware and downed his martini.

Carl sat in Kevin's Chevy parked in front of the building, Honey's apartment up on four, looking at Woodward Avenue from the top floor. Carl was thinking it would be all right once you got used to the streetcars. It was twenty past eight. He was thinking of Jurgen and he was thinking of Honey, back and forth. Thinking he shouldn't act like Jurgen was an old buddy and get bombed with him telling stories to each other. You don't ignore your sworn duty, 'less you see nothing wrong in the light of eternity with giving the Kraut a break. Then thinking, If you believe Honey is an occasion of lustful ideas, show that vamping him will get her nowhere. He thought about Vera, too, anxious to see her again. He had figured out what her game was. Honey said she was coming to visit, sounding like they'd have coffee and cookies. But if Bo was missing would she step a foot out of the house? To Carl it meant Bo would be with her. *Look who showed up, my darling Bohunk.* Something like that. Once he comes in and curtseys, Carl thought, watch him like a fuckin' hawk. This is the boy who did Joe Aubrey and the other two at the same time, the doctor and his wife, stood there and shot all three of them, and knows how to cut a man's throat. Vera's game was to set her dog on anybody who could tell on her, her puppy dog, but a vicious little son of a bitch, wasn't he?

Carl had been parked here almost an hour.

He saw Walter arrive and hadn't seen him leave.

He was going to wait for Vera and Bo and ride up in the elevator with them. This late, though, they might've changed their mind. Unless they were holding off, making sure everybody they wanted was here. Carl wasn't sure if Bo wanted him or not. But if you're here, Carl thought, he'll have to deal with you. So quit thinking and go on upstairs.

He saw Jurgen standing there in his sport coat and saw him smile. He looked at Honey and she smiled at him. Everybody happy this evening. There was Walter holding what looked like a martini in a water glass, judging from the olives in it, and Jurgen and Honey both holding martinis, the killer drink meant to put you out. Carl could take 'em or leave 'em. He said to Honey, "I bet a dollar you still haven't got a bottle of bourbon."

"You win," Honey said. "Go talk to your friend, I'll get you a drink."

He walked up to Jurgen and Jurgen put out his hand and Carl took it and couldn't help grinning at him. "The escape artist," Carl said. "You ought to write a book about how you did it, slipped out anytime you wanted."

"You know who's writing a book, Shemane. I'll be in there with the whores and crooked politicians."

"I'm not taking you in," Carl said, "not now. I mean it's too late, and I don't have my heart in it."

"I appreciate it," Jurgen said. "What I'm going to do is become a star of the rodeo circuit riding bulls."

"Talk to Gary Marion," Carl said. "Remember that kid marshal, couldn't wait to shoot somebody? You know he left the marshals to ride bulls."

"Yes, I'm going to look him up, get him to show me how to stay on the eight seconds."

Carl said, "Here's a boy name of Tex Schrenk from Cologne, way out in the panhandle."

"I keep wondering if I'll ever go back."

"Why wouldn't you? Pay a visit, see your old dad."

"He was killed in a bombing."

Carl said, "I'm sorry to hear it. You can use mine if you ever need a dad. You know Virgil, you shook his pecan trees."

"I loved Virgil, with his opinions."

Honey handed Carl a highball. "He loved you too, he told me. Go ahead and pat each other's asses."

Now Walter came over with his water-glass martini.

"I don't see you people mourning your Führer, Franklin Roosevelt." Walter sounding more robust.

"I'm wearing black, aren't I?" Honey said. "You

want another martini? You've only had four."

"I want to know," Walter said, "what you think about your president and his unusually sudden death."

"I think Stalin wore him out," Honey said. "Dealing with that maniac. Vera said he was a pygmy, wore lifts in his shoes."

"I might say," Walter said, "the sudden and mysterious death of your president—"

Carl said, "What's the mystery about it?"

"The circumstances. You believe it or you don't. It doesn't matter to me."

Carl said, "Walter, quit messin' with us and say what you're dying to tell."

Jurgen said, "Tell us, Valter," sounding German, having fun drinking martinis, "or I have you tortured."

Carl said, "Honey told me on the phone. She said, 'Roosevelt's dead,' and I thought of you, Walter."

Honey was nodding. "He did. He said, 'You don't think it was Walter, do you?' I said something smart like, 'Not unless he has the paranormal ability to cause our president's brain to hemorrhage.'"

Carl was shaking his head. "You said, 'Not unless Walter got the president on the phone and bored him to death.'"

Honey said, "I did, didn't I?" and turned to Walter. "But I didn't mean it, Hun. The point I was making, no, you didn't have anything to do with the president's death, how could you?"

"Believe what you want," Walter said.

The buzzer buzzed.

Twenty-nine

Vera came in talking about the weather, how she thought this morning, good, they were going to have a spring shower for her perennials, but no, the dreadful gloomy sky remained a bore, refusing to open up and rain, for God's sake. Now she waved to Jurgen, Carl and Walter at the opposite end of the living room. She gave Honey a kiss on one cheek and then the other, close to her as she said, "What are you looking for, chills and thrills? You're too smart to be involved with these people. You sell dresses."

"Better dresses," Honey said. "I have a cocktail dress, black, spaghetti straps, that would look stunning on you."

"Really? What size?"

"Ten," Honey said. "You haven't heard from Bo?"

"Not yet," Vera said and brightened, as if starting over. "I'm sure he's with friends. He stays out all night, I say, 'You can't call, let me know where you are?'"

"They have no idea," Honey said, "how mothers worry."

"I'm not his mother."

"You know what I mean," Honey said. "Come on, I'll get you a drink. Let me have your coat and your bag."

Vera slipped off her black Persian lamb and handed the coat to Honey. "I'll hold on to the bag, with my cigarettes." Now she was looking down the length of the room. "What are the gentlemen having? Is that an ice-cold martini Jurgen has? Bless your heart—make mine very dry, please. Only a drop of vermouth."

Honey turned to the front closet and Vera raised her hand to Jurgen and Carl by the bookcase. Then to Walter seated by himself now, forlorn, frowning, and called to him, "Walter, hold your head up. Your intention will be remembered by all of us. Think of it as God's intercession, Walter, stepping in front of you to have His own way with the president." She turned to Honey waiting for her. "You people must think I'm insane talking like that. Especially Carl."

"He knows what's going on," Honey said. "Everyone seems to know what's going on, but no one makes a move to do anything."

"The end is near," Vera said, holding her Persian lamb bag that matched the coat, and followed Honey to the kitchen. "Have you heard that expression?"

Honey stood by her bar set up on the counter. She watched Vera open her big envelope bag on the table to get at her cigarettes.

"With an olive?"

"Several, please, I'm famished."

"I can make you a baloney sandwich," Honey said. "Or an egg and baloney, with a slice of onion?"

"That's what you eat? I saw cheese and crackers in the other room, I'll gorge on that."

Honey offered a martini, several anchovy olives crowding the bottom of the stemware glass. Vera came over for it and held up the martini, staring at it as she said something to herself—Honey watching her painted lips move—and finished the martini in one motion, then paused and poured the olives into her mouth, catching each one to chew and swallow, and now she was lighting a cigarette.

"Another?" Honey said.

"Please," Vera said. "I'll sip this one. Tell me how Walter's behaving."

"He's drinking doubles," Honey said. "He's louder than I've ever heard him and being very cagey. Only he doesn't know how to do it. He wants us to think he took some part in the president's death."

Vera nodded. "Because he wanted so much to be his assassin. Poor Walter. What he knows how to do is cut meat."

Honey poured Vera's second martini and watched her pick it up and finish the drink in two swallows.

"You didn't get olives that time."

"It's all right. I'll have one more," Vera said. "You can tell me how you're doing with the Hot Kid."

"We came close, but now it's cooling off."

"You're losing interest? I see Carl as a prize, if you can subdue him."

"I'm pretty sure I could get him to fall in love with me," Honey said, "if he isn't already. But I don't want to break up his marriage, be the other woman nobody likes. That's a drag."

"You don't lack confidence," Vera said.

"And I want to stay alive," Honey said. "His wife's already shot two guys trying to mess up her life."

Vera said, "What about Jurgen? You could go for him?"

"He's at the top of my list," Honey said. "He's the best-looking guy I've ever met, he's kind, he's thoughtful for a Kraut. He takes his clothes off— now there's a picture you want to keep."

"I can imagine. I actually can," Vera said. "Oh, you could have done so well in a job like mine. I can see them telling you whatever you want to know."

"I've got a question for you," Honey said. "Aren't the police looking for Bo?"

She watched Vera deciding how to answer, her makeup overdone but it was Vera and it worked for her. Now she was starting to smile. "Who told you that?"

"Carl said Bo took after him with a machine gun."

"Bo? No, it must be someone else has it in for Carl."

"What's Bo got against him?"

"I didn't mean it that way. Bo has only met him I believe once."

"Carl sent the Detroit police after him."

"That's who it was," Vera said. "The police came to the house, I told them Bohdan was up north with his friends. They go in the forest, usually at the time of the equinox. They dance—Bo calls it a rites of spring celebration."

"You're putting me on," Honey said.

"Really. Bo asked me to come along. I told him I'm not much on pagan rituals."

"You're changing your story," Honey said.

"Am I?"

"You said you haven't heard from Bo and wish he'd call."

"Only to keep it simple," Vera said. "Otherwise you'd want to know if the police believed me, what they said. One of them asked me, 'Oh, they do the dance of the fairies up in the woods?'"

"Do they?" Honey said.

Earlier that evening Bo had thought of taking one of Dr. Taylor's pills, but wasn't sure which way to go, up or down, wide wide awake or loose as a goose. He had a few belts of ice-cold vodka before they left the house, Vera saying in the car, "Can't you wait?"

"For what?"

"Until we get there."

"You want to socialize first? Have a couple of drinks and say, 'Would you all form a line here, please, against the wall?' Darling, I'm going to walk in and hose the fucking room. Whoever's there will be lying in a pool of blood as we amscray."

"Please, not Jurgen," Vera said.

"Yes, Jurgen. We agreed, anyone who knows what you've been doing. Unless you want to clean the prison shithouse for twenty years. Anyone with style, that's the job you get. You have to realize, Vera, Jurgen is not fundamental to our future. He could fuck up our ability to stay out of prison. So I told the feds where to find him."

Vera said, "You didn't—"

"Thinking they'd scoop him up and Jurgen would be out of the way. But nothing happened and now he's at Honey's. I can't help that. I prayed to the Black Madonna asking that only certain ones would be present. The Hotshot Kid I'm hoping for. Walter, we don't know what's become of him. Perhaps he'll make up for not getting to Roosevelt in time and assassinate Harry Truman."

The car was packed for their getaway: suitcases in the trunk, personal items and Vera's shoes in cardboard boxes on the backseat. She had deposited Joe Aubrey's check for fifty thousand in a new account; later on they'd see about making withdrawals.

Bo pulled into the no-parking space in front of Honey's apartment building. He said to Vera, "If you don't have the stomach for this, don't watch. But once they're down we strip them of money, anything we see of value, and we're off to Old Méjico humming 'La Cucaracha,' unless you know the words. Oh, once she buzzes you in, use something to jam the door open."

"What do you suggest?"

"Anything, a box of matches. How I get in,

Vera, is crucial. You take the elevator to the apartment. Honey's waiting at the door. You greet her,
give her a kiss. And push the button to unlock the
door. Can you do that?"

"All you have to do is knock. Don't you think
she'll see who it is?"

"Vera, will you please unlock the fucking
door? I want my entrance to be a complete surprise. 'Good God, where did he come from?'" For
several moments he was quiet, thinking. He said,
"You brought the umbrella."

"In the trunk."

"I place the Schmeisser in the umbrella—"

"You like calling it that, don't you? I wonder
why?"

"With the stock removed," Bo said, "and come
up the stairway, so I don't run into anyone. I enter
the apartment—"

"With the burp gun still in the umbrella?"

"What did I tell you?" Bo impatient now, his
nerves irritating him. "I insert the magazine while
I'm in the hall, before I make my entrance."

"You come in shooting."

"Yes, and it's done, all she wrote."

"I wonder," Vera said, "if one ever says it's all
he wrote?"

"I've only heard it's all *she* wrote," Bo said. "But
I don't think the *she* refers to a particular person.
But you know what? I should say something as I
come in."

Vera said, "You are pointing der Schmeisser at
them. What's there to say?"

"I want to get them all looking at me."

"How about *Achtung*?" Vera said.

"Or I say, 'You know what this is for?'"

"Let them each take a guess?"

This time Bo grinned. "Yes, each one has a turn. Come on, what do I say to get them looking at me?"

"'It was nice knowing you'?"

"I'll think of something."

She opened the car door. "I ask only one favor," Vera said. "Make sure, please, I'm not in the fucking line of fire."

"You have the Luger, just in case?"

"In my bag."

Thirty

It was in Vera's mind she'd forgot to do something, one item on Bo's list of instructions.

She had her handbag, holding it under her arm, martini in her other hand. She had come out of the kitchen to stand by the dining table at this end of the sitting room, Honey still in the kitchen making drinks.

Honey had put on a record, American Negro music, a little-girl voice asking wasn't she good to some guy.

Vera could sing it to Bo. *Baby, ain't I good to you?*

Letting him do this, and Bo saying what was three more after Odessa? Now four.

Coming in she saw Carl immediately and thought, Ah, Bo will be happy; though the sight of Carl, unexpected, caused her stomach to turn and gave her an uneasy feeling and she wanted Bo to come in and see Carl and shoot him before saying a word. Get rid of the Hot Kid quick or he'll put a notch on his gun to represent Bo—Carl in a

Spitfire with German crosses on the fuselage, Bo flying an ME-109 or a Focke-Wulf and if Bo didn't shoot him please right away before Carl says what he said each time, *If I have to pull my gun . . .* Once Bo shoots him he can say what he wants if he can keep it short. Get the other three together in front of the bookcase. It would be in newspapers tomorrow, late, in the newspaper wherever they were and in all the newspapers in America because one of the "Four Murdered in Detroit Apartment" was a German prisoner of war. What was he doing there? Were these people spies? Who killed them? Or were they executed? By then she and Bo could be in Texas. She was counting on Carl having gas stamps and expense money. *Sorry, Carl, it's the war.* The fucking war. Honey might have a few stamps. They'd look in her desk—there against the wall opposite the sofa and the bookcase. Bo would stand by the desk. Come in and take his position.

Wait. What did Bo say was crucial?

And thought of what she'd forgot to do because she didn't write it down and look at the words.

Unlock the door.

Carl and Jurgen were talking about rodeo-ing.

Carl thought Jurgen was the right size to ride bulls, though on the high end, as most big-money bull riders tended to be small guys, five six, a hundred and a quarter. You'd think a long-legged rider'd fit the bull better. Carl said he never stayed the eight seconds on a bull any time he tried the amateur circuit on weekends when he was eighteen. He switched over to saddle broncs, couldn't stay on 'em either and went to college two and a half years and joined the marshals.

Jurgen said he knew he could ride bulls and be good at it. Know why? Because when his family returned to Germany after living here, it was 1935, they stopped in Spain and went to bull-fights, good ones in Madrid and different towns and he wanted to be a *matador de toros*. He said he would cape bulls in a way that was both cold and serene, feet planted in the sand, taking the bull's charge and then killing the bull in the manner of Joselito, the stylist, perhaps a show-off, dead at twenty-five, but one of the great matadors of Spain. You would have worshipped him, Jurgen said to Carl.

But Jurgen didn't become a matador and kill bulls. He said now, he becomes a bull rider and the bulls will know, the way they know bull love, he never tormented bulls with a cape or ever killed one of them. He said the ones he rides will be grateful and take it easy on him.

Carl said he thought it sounded more like bull shit than bull lore. He told Jurgen if the bulls don't twist hard you don't make points riding 'em.

Honey brought them each a martini, Carl switching over because Jurgen's silver bullet looked so good in the delicate glass. Honey stayed with them. Jurgen was saying how he devoured Hemingway's book, talking about the one on the shelf here, because he loved the idea of Spain at that time, not because Germany was behind Franco. Jurgen was for the Loyalists, like Robert Jordan whose job in the book was to blow up a bridge. Carl said he read most of *For Whom the Bell Tolls* at his dad's house and thought of it as a western, up in the mountains riding horses. They could be in Mexico. Jurgen said he started reading Zane Grey at the camp, speaking of westerns.

Carl said, "'When you call me that, smile'? I didn't care much for Zane Grey."

Walter stepped over to them. He said, "You don't think Roosevelt's death was, well, curious, coming as it did?"

Carl said, "Jesus Christ, Walter, go sit down, will you?"

Honey said, "We don't accept your theory, Walter, whatever it is," and said, "I tried Zane Grey once, I thought he was awfully old-timey the way he wrote."

Carl said, "His books don't sound like he had any fun writing them. But you see ads, you can buy every book Zane Grey wrote and fill up a whole shelf. For people who don't know any better."

Honey said, "What's Vera doing?"

Carl and Jurgen looked over to watch her open the apartment door, look out in the hall and close it again.

Honey called to her, "Vera . . . ?"

She came over to them with her Persian lamb handbag and held up her martini to Honey. "Notice I'm sipping now, having quenched my thirst."

Honey said, "What were you doing just now?"

"I must be hearing things. I would swear someone was at the door."

Carl said, "We expecting somebody else?"

"Not that I know of," Honey said.

"No, no, I was mistaken," Vera said, "there's no one else."

It was the way she kept looking toward the door, fidgety now, taking quick little sips of her drink, Carl would bet all the expense money he had in his billfold, $124, Bohunk was about to walk in.

Vera would look toward the door.

So would Carl, over his shoulder.

Honey saying, "Why're we standing when we can sit down? I'll put on another record. How about Sinatra?"

Vera finished her martini, placed the glass on a bookshelf and glanced toward the door.

Carl did too, turning his head.

He watched the door come open a little at a time until there was Bo in a gray sweater and skirt holding his machine gun, Carl turning to Vera as she said to him, "Do you like Frank Sinatra?"

"I like the one playing. You know what it is?"

"'Oh Look at Me Now,'" Vera said. "How do you see what's about to happen?"

"That's a skirt Bo's wearing?"

"I said to him please, not tonight."

"He might've left off the makeup. What I'm wondering," Carl said, "if that's a war souvenir he wants to show us. It isn't, will you tell him to lay it on the floor?"

Honey said, "She isn't his mother."

"Thank you," Vera said. "I'm a guest here. You can tell him if you want."

Bo, coming toward this end of the room along the opposite wall, stopped at the bedroom hallway to glance in.

"They're all here," Vera said to him.

Bo was facing them now with the machine gun, one hand on the trigger, the other on the magazine that held thirty-two rounds.

Jurgen said, "Bo, what are you doing?"

Honey said, "Bo, would you like a drink?"

Walter, in Honey's favorite chair, didn't speak.

Bo did. He said to Vera, "I told you to unlock the door and you forgot."

Vera said, "How did you get in, darling?"

"I told you, as soon as you get here, unlock the door. I told you to write everything down. You forgot and I'm standing in the hall holding a fucking machine gun?"

Jurgen said to him, "You have a Schmeisser, uh? I like that name even though it's not accurate. But I'll tell you something," Jurgen said, "you should never hold a *Maschinenpistole* by the magazine. You put stress on it, it jams very easily."

Carl liked that—remind the boy he didn't know what he was doing, holding a loaded weapon while he argued with Vera. Now he was facing them.

"I want you three, Jurgen, Honey and Carl, to go sit on the sofa. Walter, you're all right, old boy, but move your chair closer to where your comrades will be sitting, we'll get this done. Go on, you three, please take your seats. Right *there*," Bo said, raised his machine gun and fired a short burst, loud, quick, that left bullet holes across the back cushions of the sofa.

Honey stared at Bo, not saying a word.

Maybe he did know what he was doing, Carl watching the way he handled the weapon, familiar with it, telling Jurgen, "As often as I've fired a machine pistol I've never had a problem. I was out of practice when I went after the Hot Kid." He said to Carl, "Did you know it was I?"

"It had to be you," Carl said.

"No other asshole would do," Honey said, holding her hard look on Bo.

It seemed to stop him for a moment, his eyes on Honey, but let it go and said, "Now I would like the four of you to strip. Take off all your clothes. You, too, Walter, stand up. And I'd like the Hotdog Kid to remove the revolver from his person and place it on the cocktail table."

"If you try to use it," Vera said, "Bo won't hesitate to shoot you."

She brought the Luger out of her Persian lamb handbag and put it in Carl's face.

"Or I will."

Carl said, "You want to reach in my coat and get it?"

"I want you to take the coat off," Vera said, moving away from them.

Honey saw the Luger in Vera's hand and nudged Jurgen, the Luger exactly like the one Darcy got from Bo for the Ford and gave to her for safekeeping. The one Jurgen checked and said was loaded, ready to fire and she'd shoved down between the seat cushions of the sofa. Where Bo wanted them to sit.

She watched Carl take off his coat and now his holstered .38 was in plain sight.

Bo said, "Will you people, *please*, get undressed? We don't have all night."

Honey pulled her sweater over her head, stepped out of her skirt and moved to the sofa.

"You have a cute figure," Bo said.

"The bra too?" Honey said.

"Of course the bra, the panties, everything. I want to make sure you're not concealing a weapon. I hid a razor-sharp butter knife up my butt and used it to cut the throats of three death-squad SS guards, each one in turn lying drunk on *horilka*, Ukrainian vodka. I put my hand over each one's mouth, stuck the knife into the throat and cut. I did it naked knowing there would be a torrent of blood. It bathed me. It was a stimulating experience. You can understand why it's the most memorable event of my life. Though shooting Mr. Aubrey and Dr. Taylor wasn't bad. One shot for each. Rosemary was different. I shot her, yes, but it was more like drowning a kitten. My mother made me do that when I was a boy, hold the kitten under water. Every time I thought of Puss and saw his little face looking up at me, I cried." Now he said, "Mr. Hotsy-Totsy, are you going to lay down your gun or not?"

Honey watched Carl step over to the sofa before pulling his revolver—Bo with the machine gun raised, aimed at him—and lay it on the cocktail table, the grip toward the sofa. Now he stood there pulling off his tie, starting to unbutton his shirt.

Bo said, "As gingerly as you can, Carl, would you shake all the bullets out of that gun, please? It makes me nervous to see it sitting there, the front sight filed off. You are a ferocious man, aren't you, Mr. Hotsy-Totsy?"

Honey watched Vera, holding the Luger down at her side now, walk over to Bo and say something to him.

"You're talking too much."

"Darling, I'm doing this for you."

"You're performing. 'How could a cute boy like me cut throats?' Trying to be funny and ghastly at the same time."

"You want me to do it or you want to leave? A moment will come and I'll kill them, left to right starting with the modest Nazi, Walter, and pop pop pop the rest. I started with twenty-eight in the magazine and have twenty-four left. I fucked up showing them where to sit and fired one round too many. You may have to do a coup de grâce or two." The next moment he was grinning. "Vera, look. Nudes on parade."

What astonished Vera—well, it did surprise her to see how casually they stood about naked, not at all self-conscious, quite different tan lines on the two men: Jurgen, a slender god, had kept much of his tan through the winter and was white around his loins; Carl's face and arms were weathered while the rest of him would be called white, but wasn't; his skin toned with shades from Cuba and the Northern Cheyenne.

No, what astonished Vera was how neat they were about the clothes they took off and folded on the coffee table in three piles, while Walter was holding his clothes in his lap.

Bo said, "Go take Walter's clothes away from him. He refuses to give them up, shoot him in the head, please." He said, "Notice, the two boys are hung about average. Ah, but they're both straight as gunshots. They were raised to be men who use women, love women, even adore them and dream of pussies. I see the way they look at you. Vera, you could take Carl anytime you want. But when I swish around them like I'm on the make, they don't mind, they think I'm funny. The ones who don't think I'm funny I look out for. You think I'm funny, don't you?"

"Yes, you are," Vera said. "But sometimes you aren't. This is taking too long. You understand? Bo, look at me. Do it, please, when I'm out of the way."

"Nuts, she's walking off to the side."

Honey said it looking down past her bare breasts to her bare thighs she kept slender swimming once a week at Webster Hall, a midtown hotel.

This was great, get to sit between two naked boys, both of them with neat packages, nice slender bodies with scars all over them: Carl's she thought from gunshots, Jurgen's skin tight and shiny in places where he'd been burned. These guys were all-guy. Jurgen turned his head and smiled at her and she smiled back at him. Then she smiled at Carl and Carl said, "What?"

While Vera was over there talking to Bo, Honey was able to take Carl's hand, next to hers on the sofa, and place it on the butt of the Luger stuck down between the cushions. When she put it there she was sitting where Carl was now, so it was his right hand that worked down to get his fingers around the grip. Honey told him it was ready to fire but on safety. Carl said he felt it and snicked it off.

Honey said, "Are you sure?"

"Am I *sure*?" Carl said. "Why wouldn't I be sure?"

He was pretty sure he'd never fired a Luger. A Walther P38, yeah, but not a Luger. He imagined pulling this one out of the sofa and putting it on Bohunk to shoot where he was looking, squeeze the trigger and make an adjustment if he had to and shoot him down. The Luger was a good-looking gun, he liked the way it fit his hand but knew he'd stay with his Colt after this.

All right, when?

When you're positive he's gonna shoot.

You're serious? This guy puts on his best dress and makeup and brings along a machine gun and you aren't sure he wants to kill you?

He wished Honey would quit rubbing against him. He'd told her, "Knock it off, okay?" She was probably doing the same thing to Jurgen.

She put her head down and said, "You boys aren't getting boners, are you?"

How'd she maintain acting natural when she could be dead the next minute? Always sure of herself. As soon as he took care of Bo he'd ask her how she stayed so cool.

Bo said, "Please don't take what I'm about to do personally. I have no more ill feelings than if I were to come face-to-face with you in combat, the way it was in Odessa fighting the Romanians house to house." He said, "Let me revise that. I did have ill feelings about the fucking Romanians, so hot to kill Jews and Romas and boys like myself. The SS made us wear little pink badges and threw us in death camps to kill at their leisure. It was on this occasion I decided to turn beastly myself and cut a few *Einsatzgruppen* throats."

Now, Carl thought.

Call him. Tell him to put the machine gun on the floor and step away from it. You'll have a moment. Tell him if you pull a gun—there's your moment, while he's thinking, What gun?—you'll shoot to kill.

Do it.

Carl had a grip on the Luger to yank it free in the same moment the hard blunt *bam* of a gunshot went off in the room, made him blink and turn to see Vera holding her Luger out in front of her. *Bam*, she shot Bo again, took a step toward him and shot him again. Now she stared at Bo lying on the floor by the desk and shot him in the head; making sure.

Carl watched her slip the pistol inside the Persian lamb handbag she held open and watched her place the bag on the side table, where Walter sat turned to stone. Now she was lighting a cigarette. Vera drew on it and blew out a stream of smoke, looking at Carl.

Thirty-one

S he blew smoke at you, huh? Doesn't care you're a federal marshal."

Carl told his dad she wasn't blowing it *at* him.

"You say she was looking at you."

"I think it was like she's saying, 'You got a better way?' She seemed to have it pretty much worked out."

"Saved you from certain death."

"I didn't see it that way exactly. Jurgen did, he's telling her she saved their lives. Honey's already over there hugging her."

"Bare naked?"

"Yes, she was."

"She put together okay?"

"Miss America walking around in high heels, naked."

Virgil said, "Jesus Christ."

Narcissa came from the stove with coffee to go with their Cuban brandy after the steak supper, saying to Carl, "Virgil's gonna have a heart attack before you finish the story." She sat down with them at the round table in the back part of the kitchen, raining outside on Hitler's birthday, April 20, 1945.

"What about Jurgen," Virgil said, "he ever get dressed?"

"Yeah, but he left before I called Kevin."

His dad was shaking his head. "You let him go?"

Carl said, "He left, disappeared on me. He was a felon I'd of locked him up. What he is, he's an unemployed German soldier, a friend of mine. I wouldn't be surprised he went to Cleveland."

"Cleveland? I thought he wanted to ride bulls."

"One of these days I believe he will. I think he'd want to check on his SS buddy Otto. Jurgen mentioned he's living with a beautiful Jewish girl named Aviva. Something Jurgen has to see for himself."

"I imagine you took over the crime scene," Virgil said. "Had everybody sit down?"

"Nobody was going anywhere except Jurgen. We all talked awhile," Carl said. "I called Kevin and he got hold of Homicide. We all made sworn statements to the fact Vera Mezwa acted in our behalf or we'd all be dead. Vera said she had no idea Bo was gonna get us bare-ass and then shoot us."

"You believe her?"

"Homicide does. They talked to her over three days and let her go. I told you she had it worked out. I think Vera wore herself out worrying about Bo going crazy on her from the war. She saw what he meant to do, so she popped him and became our hero. It doesn't have anything to do with her being a spy. The Justice Department'll bring her up or they won't, I don't know. I think the first thing Vera will do is get out of town and become somebody else. She already had her car packed."

"You think they'll get her?"

"If they want her."

Narcissa said, "What about Honey and Jurgen? You said they like each other. They gonna meet up down the line?"

"Maybe," Carl said. "I think Jurgen's luck'll finally run out on him. He'll be picked up and deported, once the war's over. Then have to find a way to come back, Honey waiting, looking at her watch. That's how I see her. But with Honey you never know. She might decide to go to Germany to be with him. It's the kind of thing she'd do," Carl said, but couldn't see her doing it.

Virgil said, "You had the hots for her, didn't you?"

"Why're you asking me that?"

"He's nosy," Narcissa said. "Did you?"

Virgil said, "She ever put her drawers on?"

He did watch her step in the skirt and pull it over her hips, then hike the skirt to slip her panties up her legs, and a picture of Crystal Davidson doing it appeared in his mind, in color. Honey's head came out of the sweater, her eyebrows moving up and down at him, her bra still on the table.

"Yeah, Honey got dressed, Jurgen got dressed, and Walter went in the bathroom to get dressed."

Virgil said, "What's gonna happen to him?"

"I don't know," Carl said. "I think he's stuck with being Walter the meat cutter and looking like Himmler, the most hated man in the world. His only friend was that rascal Joe Aubrey and they haven't found him yet. I should've asked Bo what he did with him. You know it? He would've told us. He was bragging about shooting people . . . cutting their throats."

"You say Vera got off," his dad said. "Did you say anything to her?"

"Honey was hugging her. I walked over and told Vera I admired her style. She said thank you, and gave me a kiss on the mouth."

"She's kissing you, you're buck naked?"

"I'd pulled my pants on."

"You'll be telling Louly all this pretty soon, won't you? She's coming in?"

"Saturday."

"That's tomorrow."

"Yeah, she's flying into Tulsa on a seventy-two-hour pass. She gets to fly just about everywhere she goes, as long as there's a military airfield."

"Let's see," Narcissa said, "you gonna tell Louly about Vera kissing you?"

"Louly doesn't have to worry about Vera."

"You gonna tell her about Honey walking around in her high heels, naked?"

BANDITS	Available in Paperback and eBook
GLITZ	Available in Paperback and eBook
STICK	Available in Paperback and eBook
CAT CHASER	Available in Paperback and eBook
SPLIT IMAGES	Available in Paperback and eBook
CITY PRIMEVAL	Available in Paperback and eBook
THE MOONSHINE WAR	Available in Paperback and eBook
HOMBRE	Available in Paperback and eBook
THE SWITCH	Available in Paperback and eBook
OUT OF SIGHT	Available in Paperback and eBook
SWAG	Available in Paperback and eBook
LaBRAVA	Available in Paperback and eBook
VALDEZ IS COMING	Available in Paperback and eBook

NOW AVAILABLE

52 PICKUP	Available in Paperback and eBook
BE COOL	Available in Paperback and eBook
GUNSIGHTS	Available in Paperback and eBook
THE HOT KID	Available in Paperback and eBook
LAST STAND AT SABER RIVER	Available in Paperback and eBook
PAGAN BABIES	Available in Paperback and eBook
TOUCH	Available in Paperback and eBook
UNKNOWN MAN #89	Available in Paperback and eBook
UP IN HONEY'S ROOM	Available in Paperback and eBook

Available wherever books are sold.